RUBICONS

IMBRIFEX
BOOKS

RUBICONS

A FREAKS NOVEL

BRETT RILEY

IMBRIFEX BOOKS
8275 S. Eastern Avenue, Suite 200
Las Vegas, NV 89123
Imbrifex.com

RUBICONS: A Freaks Novel

Library of Congress Cataloging-in-Publication Data

Names: Riley, Brett, 1970- author.
Title: Rubicons : a Freaks novel / Brett Riley.
Description: First edition. | Las Vegas, NV : Imbrifex Books, 2023. |
    Series: Freaks ; book 3 | Summary: As junior year commences, the Freaks
    must combat multiple foes--adulthood, The Team, a shadowy government
    agency bent on saving the world from supernatural menaces, and their
    most dangerous adversary yet, a dragon threatening every life in town.
Identifiers: LCCN 2022044852 (print) | LCCN 2022044853 (ebook) | ISBN
    9781945501944 (hardcover) | ISBN 9781945501968 (paperback) | ISBN
    9781945501951 (epub) | ISBN 9781945501975
Subjects: CYAC: Superheroes--Fiction. | Supernatural--Fiction. |
    Dragons--Fiction. | Friendship--Fiction. | LCGFT: Superhero fiction. |
    Novels.
Classification: LCC PZ7.1.R5475 Ru 2023 (print) | LCC PZ7.1.R5475 (ebook)
    | DDC [Fic]--dc23
LC record available at https://lccn.loc.gov/2022044852
LC ebook record available at https://lccn.loc.gov/2022044853

Jacket design: Jason Heuer
Book design: John Hall Design Group
Author Photo: Benjamin Hager
Typeset in ITC Berkeley Oldstyle

Printed in the United States of America
Distributed by Publishers Group West
First Edition: August 2023

DEDICATION

This book is for the Rolling Acres Crew: Steven, Angie, Mike, Leigh Anne, Rosie, Shawn, Wes, Sheryl, Stacy, Chris, Tonya, Ame, Donald, and all y'all that snuck out, hung out, and acted out. Our bonds will never break. God bless you all. To Jeff and Paul, we miss you, brothers. One day we'll see you again.

And to Cookie—my God, how we miss you. Wait for us. We'll be along someday.

CHAPTER ONE

Not much shocked Kenneth Del Ray anymore, but his junior year of high school had brought two surprises he would never forget.

The first one happened in September. Kenneth was less than two years away from kissing Quapaw City High goodbye forever. *Thank God*, he'd think, until he remembered he would soon have to figure out the rest of his life. His old plans had been derailed during freshman year, when the interdimensional vampire Na'ul murdered Gavin Cloverleaf. Despite the hard feelings that had separated them in Gavin's last days, Kenneth still sometimes caught himself trying to text his old buddy. Then the fact of the loss would strike him again, and he'd have to fight off tears. As early as fourth grade, he and Gavin and Brayden Sears had planned to find a place together once they graduated, or quit school, and get the best jobs they could find. But was that still the best plan? Or should Kenneth be thinking about college? Maybe he could commute to the University of Arkansas-Monticello or the University of Southeast Arkansas over in Parkview.

The thought of spending four more years in classrooms, listening to boring lectures and taking tests and writing papers, made his head hurt. Until the last year or so, college had never even looked like a possibility. Kenneth had always believed he was dumb, and school had seemed to confirm it. Now, though, other outcomes had presented themselves, and—God help him—he probably had the Freaks to thank for it. Since he had started hanging out with Jamie Entmann, his grades had improved, like being around smart and dedicated people could rub off. Or maybe he had moved from a C- GPA to a solid B because he had given up sports. If you asked the Freaks or Brayden, though, they probably would have said it was mostly because of Tyqueria Webb.

Ty had moved to Quapaw City in the first week of September. Mr. Hoon, the principal, had brought her to Mrs. Murray's study hall, where Kenneth sat in the back row working an Algebra I problem. He barely glanced up when Hoon introduced Ty to the class, and what he saw didn't impress him much—another Black girl among dozens, another kid he would probably never get to know well, another weird name he had no idea how to spell. Ty sat in the empty desk next to his, but he paid her no mind.

After class, Mrs. Murray stopped the two of them at the door. "Kenneth, please show Tyqueria to Mr. Singh's classroom," she said. Kenneth rolled his eyes. It proved how little some teachers knew their students. Kenneth should have been the last person recruited to chaperone a new kid, but he had learned that protesting when a teacher asked you to do something like this just drew everything out. Easier and quicker to get it over with. So he walked beside Ty in silence. When they reached Singh's room, Kenneth gestured to the open door.

"Thanks," said Ty.

Kenneth shrugged. As he walked away, she reached out and touched his arm. Eyebrows raised, he flinched. Then he looked her straight in the eye, really seeing her for the first time, and something about her knocked every conscious thought out of his head. Her smooth skin, her deep brown eyes, her full lips glistening with some kind of colorless gloss, the way her natural hair perfectly framed her face—he actually felt his mouth fall open, his words dry up. His legs weakened; his stomach seemed to rise into his throat. It didn't feel like lust. Was this how love started, with a punch right to the heart? If so, why weren't people falling in the streets, too stunned to stand or speak?

For the past few years, Kenneth had become increasingly, achingly aware of girls' bodies, the shapes of their asses and the way their shirts hugged their breasts, but in that moment, he couldn't stop looking into

Ty's perfect, gorgeous face and thinking of a word he had never spoken aloud: *gentle*. Nothing like this had ever happened to him before.

"Thanks," she said, bringing him back to the waking world. "I really appreciate it."

Words still stuck in his throat, he nodded. She smiled like she understood. When she turned and stepped into Singh's room, he watched her until she found a seat. Then, before she could catch him staring, he spun and hurried down the hall, his face burning.

The second surprise occurred in February, on a Friday at approximately 8:38 p.m. central standard time, when thick clouds dumped an inch of snow onto Southeast Arkansas. Neither the meteorologists on the local news nor the weather app on Kenneth's phone had even hinted that snow might be possible, but as he pushed the dust mop up and down the aisles of Larry's Grocery, he glanced out the front window, and there it was: snowfall on Quapaw City's Main Street, most of the flakes small enough to look like misting rain, some nearly as big as potato chips. Would it stick? In his sixteen-plus years, Kenneth could remember playing in snow only twice. The last time had been in, what, fifth grade? He stood in the aisle and remembered, the dust mop forgotten in his right hand, until Roy the night manager spotted him and moved him along.

But Kenneth couldn't concentrate on work. Instead, he kept thinking about the hunt he and Dad had planned for the next day. Muzzleloader and modern-gun seasons were over, but you could still bow hunt. Tomorrow was the earliest day Dad could get to the deer woods. An inch shouldn't affect anything, but if any more stuck, Dad probably wouldn't chance the drive. Southern folks don't tend to go anywhere in winter conditions. Not that Kenneth didn't like snow. Didn't people usually long for what they had never had?

Del Ray men had hunted together for generations. Kenneth loved riding into the woods before sunrise, breathing the fresh air, climbing his stand, sitting with his back against the tree, and waiting for a deer to slip into his field of fire or to hear his father's shot. Dad never missed. After he bagged an eight-point in early December, they had eaten venison steaks and chili at least once a week. If they could get another buck, they could fill their freezer.

As it happened, the snow didn't really stick. When Kenneth and his dad woke up at four thirty the next morning, the precipitation had stopped. A thin layer clung to roofs and hoods of neighborhood cars, and there were small patches on the ground here and there, but it was melting even before sunrise. The Del Rays drove to their lease, unloaded their four-wheeler, and rode out to their stands, Dad with a thermos of coffee, Kenneth carrying a plastic-wrapped bacon-and-egg sandwich in his pocket.

Three hours later, though, Kenneth had seen nothing. No signal from Dad, either. Apparently, all the deer in Southeast Arkansas had decided to spend the day somewhere else. After another half hour, a steady, low crackling suggested Dad had given up. Kenneth climbed down and waited at the foot of the ladder, his bow slung over one shoulder, quiver strapped to his back. Dad walked along the game trail that wound in front of the stand, not trying to move quietly.

"Ready to call it?" he asked.

"Yeah," said Kenneth. "Nothing happening around here. I—"

From deeper in the woods—a bit northeast of their position, Kenneth thought—something was crashing through the brush. Kenneth and Dad both started, turned toward the sound, and glanced at each other. Once, during deer season a few years back, an armadillo had stomped its way past this stand. In all the quiet, it had sounded like a tank. This racket was even louder, like something knocking down small trees.

"What in the world?" asked Dad.

"Maybe it's deer," said Kenneth. "Like, a whole herd. Or two."

Dad's eyes narrowed. His graying hair fluffed out from under his insulated orange cap. "If somebody's tearing up the woods in our lease, I want to know about it. Come on."

They moved deeper into the woods, not hunting now, just walking as fast and as safely as they could, following sounds that faded as they closed in. A few hundred yards farther, they came to a clearing. Near the far edge, at least two dozen deer lay in groups of three or four with their noses tucked under their hind legs. The groups were spread in a rough semicircle, only a few feet apart. At least four of the deer looked like dominant bucks. A couple of smaller males, several does, and a handful of fawns had gathered around them. Kenneth had never bothered to learn all that much about animal sleep patterns, but he felt pretty sure that big bucks didn't usually share space with other alphas. That wasn't even the weirdest part, though. Groups of other animals were also snoozing in proximity: a passel of feral hogs, enough squirrels for six or eight nests, a herd of rabbits, even . . . was that a *bobcat*?

"Dad," whispered Kenneth. "What the . . . ?"

"I don't know," said Dad. "This shouldn't happen. And why are they just laying there in the open? You know they've heard us, especially them deer. They ought to be running like hell."

Kenneth and Dad had both nocked arrows, but neither had drawn. Now Dad raised his bow.

"What's up?" asked Kenneth.

"Gonna take one of them big'uns. That twelve-pointer on the right. If they're stupid enough to sit still, might as well make 'em wish they hadn't."

As far as Kenneth knew, this clearing wasn't close to any water or food source. None of the deer were facing the wind. And inside that semicircle of sleeping critters, all the grass and weeds had been tamped down. No big sticks or downed limbs lay anywhere in that crushed foliage. Like something had made its bed there. But what? And if all those deer and such were going to sleep in a big group, why had they avoided that area?

Something was wrong here. Not just weird, *wrong*.

Dad, preparing to shoot, exhaled.

"Dad, wait—"

But the arrow flew. The head buried itself just behind the twelve-point's shoulder.

The deer's eyes opened. He snorted several times in rapid succession and stood on unsteady legs and staggered away from the herd. He grunted, grunted, grunted again. All the other animals awakened. The bobcat turned to the Del Rays and hissed, showing teeth long and sharp enough to rip out someone's throat. The rabbits and squirrels scampered away as the other deer jumped up and ran into the trees.

Not a single animal stepped on the trampled flora.

The buck staggered several steps. Then his front legs collapsed. The arrow's fletching bobbed as he breathed and shifted. He fell on his uninjured side, the arrow sticking straight up like an exclamation point.

Dad grinned. "Perfect shot, if I do say so myself."

But Kenneth was barely listening. He was watching that grass, because now it was shifting, even though the wind hadn't changed. A few smaller patches rose a little and then tamped back down.

They looked like footprints, each with five long toes.

Still focused on the deer, Dad walked into the clearing and unstrapped his knife, ready to cut the animal's throat if necessary.

The footprints *moved*.

Something seemed to snort just over the deer. The buck's fur rustled.

"Dad!" yelled Kenneth.

His father stopped, turned, and looked at Kenneth like he had gone nuts.

Whatever was hovering over the dying buck roared. Dad's hat blew off. His eyes widened, and he nearly jumped out of his boots. "What the hell?"

Another roar. Something inhaled. The sound was like when an airlock was breached in one of Jamie's sci-fi movies. Dropping the bow, Kenneth sprinted forward. The quiver bounced against his back. As he dove, he drove his shoulder into Dad's gut and tackled him.

Another roar, and a stream of ice as thick as a tree trunk passed over their heads. It struck the ground, freezing it and Kenneth's bow. Dad could have been turned into a popsicle. Instead, he lay there, wincing and groaning, holding the back of his head.

Kenneth stood, letting the energy cycle up inside him. *Time to even the odds.* Last year, Baltar Sterne had given him a second stealth charm after he lost the first one. The new charm's effects had been unpleasant, to say the least. Someday he would pull the old man aside and demand an explanation, but given that he avoided the Sternes as much as possible, he hadn't yet found a good time. Besides, he looked forward to conversations with Baltar about as much as Dad liked plunging the toilet when Kenneth clogged it.

At least the stupid charm worked. Every time he used it, he collapsed for a moment, too weak even to hold up his head, but if there was a chance he could stay safe long enough to save Dad, he had to take it.

"Evanescent," he said, concentrating on the empty air where his unseen enemy stood.

It felt as if a strong blast of wind simultaneously struck him and burst forth from his own pores. He fell to his hands and knees, every muscle aching with sheer exhaustion. His stomach turned over. He had to fight to keep from vomiting. Letting himself fall, he rolled along the forest floor, gasping for air, until he lay between his groaning father and whatever they had found.

The invisible thing had paused, the forest floor crushed under its feet. Was it looking for Kenneth?

As had happened every time he used the charm, his strength began to return after only thirty seconds or so. Every passing moment made him feel a little better. Something to do with his healing power?

The invisible thing took a couple of hesitant steps. Maybe it could still smell him—that, or it was locking onto Dad.

The energies that jumpstarted Kenneth's powers kept revving higher. He stood, feeling almost like himself again. Not sure what else to try, he threw a punch at empty air and connected with something hard enough to draw a grunt out of whatever it was. More footprints appeared as the massive, invisible something stumbled away. Kenneth scooped Dad up, draped him over one shoulder like a sack of potatoes, and ran like hell. Behind them, the roaring continued. Dad groaned and asked Kenneth what the hell he thought he was doing, but Kenneth didn't stop until they reached their ATVs. Only then did he realize the thing hadn't followed them. His heart hammered as he set Dad down. He started to say the magic word that would deactivate the charm, but he hadn't directed it to hide him from Dad, so there was no need.

After Kenneth caught his breath and Dad's head had cleared enough to drive, they rode out of the woods. Kenneth helped his father into the truck. He did not return to the clearing, nor had he heard anything more from whatever they had awakened. When Dad asked why he hadn't brought their bows, Kenneth replied that he had looked, but they were gone.

CHAPTER TWO

Jamie Entmann flew high over town, watching for signs of anything supernatural.

Flying seems easier with the new costume. Gotta remember to give Christian props.

Originally, the Freaks had worn the ancient robes they had found in Baltar's trunk, along with cheap ski masks. Those outfits had looked about as cool as a minivan and felt like wearing sandpaper. Swiping the materials from various stores—a necessary evil since none of them had much money—Christian had continued to refine the costumes to the point that they actually looked pretty dope now. She'd converted the original robes to closer-fitting tops, which they wore with black jeans, motorcycle boots, and leather gloves. The rudimentary ski masks had been replaced with personalized originals Christian had crafted from nylon.

Each Freak got a unique costume design. Jamie's featured a sunburst in the center of the chest, simply because the sun had been the most prominent image on his original robe. Likewise, Christian had created a sunburst pattern on his mask, the face bright yellow with flames licking backward across the head. Gabby's had a starburst across the chest, and her mask had thick white lines flowing from the face to the back of the head to represent her power beams. Micah's outfit sported a horned demon like you might see on the back of a tatted-up MMA fighter, all fangs and bulging eyes, with blue and red lines on his mask for ice and fire. Kenneth's chest piece also showed a demon, but this one was full-bodied and bulging with humanoid muscles. Hands on his mask appeared to be gripping Kenneth's face from either side. When he had asked Christian what the hell that was supposed to mean, she had just shrugged and said, "I thought it looked strong. That's you, right? The strong dude?" Kenneth had turned away, muttering about how stupid he'd look in that getup. For her own costume, Christian had chosen the classic symbol of the speedster, the lightning bolt. The vertical lines on her mask were supposed to look like comic-book speed lines.

"Maybe by next year I can find some Kevlar or something and build costumes that make sense," she had said during one of the game nights when neither Ty Webb nor Bec Villalobos was there. Thank God Gabby was a Freak like Jamie. Unlike Kenneth and Christian, he hadn't had to keep secrets from the person he loved. So far, the Freaks had agreed to go by the old superhero rule that anyone who knew your identity would automatically be in danger. It made sense, but man, what a pain in the ass.

More than a year had passed since the end of the Rabbit affair, and a lot had happened, but none of it had involved monsters like Na'ul. As the Freaks had been gearing up for their final battle with Rabbit, Baltar Sterne—Micah's great-uncle and guardian, a powerful wizard, the group's would-be Rupert Giles—had hexed each Freak's house and car so that the Team's surveillance equipment now showed only typical teenage behavior and conversations, no matter what the Freaks actually did. A few months ago, Baltar had cast a spell that disguised their texts—no more talking in code—and disrupted the GPS on the Freaks' phones, though it also meant they couldn't use any map apps. Try to follow directions to Crossett, say, and you might wind up in Mississippi. Baltar had also camouflaged their favorite meeting place, the abandoned pavilion on the far side of the park. No one but Micah seemed to trust the old man—he looked at you like he was starving and you were an all-you-can-eat buffet, and Jamie suspected he knew more about how his spells worked than he let on—but at least Baltar had proven useful in some ways.

As for the Team, they had grown into a much more annoying, even direr threat than before, even as they had spent less time in town. Three months after the trickster left, the Team had come after Gabby. In costume, she had snuck onto the Gilchrist farm from the rear, trying to find a different vantage point for countersurveillance. Chip Mossman spotted her on camera and sounded the alarm. Gabby shot her way off the property, blowing a hole in the farmhouse and destroying some of the Team's computers. Then she crossed the street and lost the feds in the woods. Their sonic rifle concussed her and nearly shattered her eardrums, but she was able to double back to her car and drive home while they were still thrashing around in the forest.

Another time, Christian had literally run into Jeffcoat and Kragthorpe on a routine patrol. She had been crossing an intersection when, by pure chance, the feds' SUV had smacked into her and sent her careening through somebody's yard, their chain-link fence, and two more yards beyond. At least none of those people had a pool for her to fall into. Christian lay on the street, staring at the sky and willing her hip to stop throbbing, until Kragthorpe followed her trail of destruction and blasted her with the Team's sonic cannon. She zipped toward the nearest corner, with Jeffcoat and the damaged Chevy Tahoe bearing down on her. She dodged him easily, but her aching hip slowed her down just enough for Jeffcoat to spin the car around and fire a laser pistol at her. Moments later, Christian's healing factor had finished repairing the damage to her hip, and she left the feds far behind. If she hadn't been wearing her costume—these days, at Jamie's insistence, the Freaks wore them anytime they were using their powers—the Team might have finally gotten solid proof of her identity.

Maybe missing those chances had pissed McCreedy off, because after that, the feds had shifted focus to the Freaks' parents. Counterintelligence missions had revealed that McCreedy wanted to anger the kids so they would do something stupid. He had used his influence to get Jamie's father fired from the light-fixture factory over in

Lake Village where he'd worked as a spinner for fifteen years. Dad had since taken a job as a security guard at First National Bank in Pinedale. Drew Greenwalt had offered to get Dad reinstated if Jamie would give up Micah Sterne. When Jamie refused, McCreedy turned to Christian's mother. Ms. Frey had been a hospital nurse all her adult life. Now she worked the night shift at a retirement home in Crossett. The job paid a lot less, and the Allens had never been rich to begin with.

The most important development regarding the feds, though, had come when McCreedy reassigned them all. The whole Team had lived and worked in Quapaw City since Na'ul's arrival. As it turned out, supernatural beings had appeared in half a dozen other places around the country, too, so over the past year, various Team members had been shunted around to eliminate the so-called threats on missions that lasted anywhere from days to a few months. As a result, the Gilchrist farmhouse had occasionally been almost empty, with maybe one Team member monitoring their cameras and bugs. No SUVs following the Freaks around, no attacks, no clandestine meetings with Drew Greenwalt.

Still, given the Team's various direct attacks on individual Freaks, Jamie had insisted on maintaining their countersurveillance. Each member of the group spent at least one afternoon or evening a week out here, watching the dooryard and listening to whatever members of the Team happened to be home.

Despite his attempts to keep up routines, though, Jamie felt like everything was in flux. In the fall, they'd be seniors, so the Freaks were looking at colleges and weighing their options. On top of that, now a new supernatural threat had revealed itself. Kenneth had sent the group a 911 text that morning. Mr. Del Ray had apparently been knocked silly and wasn't sure what he had seen or heard. Jamie had driven over to talk to Kenneth that afternoon and had learned this much about their enemy:

1. Animals were drawn to it. Even species that would normally eat each other had looked chill.
2. The bogey could breathe ice, like Micah on steroids.
3. The damn thing was invisible.

And so here Jamie was, flying over miles of thick, darkened woodlands, his senses enhanced, looking for any movement or unusual noises. So far, he had seen only smaller animals scampering around in search of food, plus the occasional deer. Maybe this was stupid, trying to get a visual on an invisible enemy. Still, it felt better than just waiting around. So far, the Freaks had let the monsters bring the fight to them, and look what had happened. When they were freshmen, Na'ul had murdered Gavin, Micah's mother, and several others. Last year, Rabbit had kidnapped Bec, killed Agent Parker, and wiped the forest floor with the Freaks. From now on, Jamie and the others needed to take a cue from the Team and strike first.

It ain't happening tonight, though. All I see is a whole lotta nothing.

Something struck him in the chest hard enough to knock him off course.

"What the hell?" he cried as he fought to regain control.

On the ground, two black SUVs sat on either end of a street. Some kind of satellite dishes had been affixed to their roofs. A Team member stood beside each truck, one of their special rifles shouldered. One of them shot at him again, a laser beam as thick as his wrist. He evaded as the other fed fired. Jamie's teeth chattered as the sonic blast missed him by inches. Jesus, why weren't people pouring out of their houses to see what was making all that racket? Maybe the townspeople had finally learned to mind their own business when the weirdness started. The laser fired again, then both weapons. Jamie flew faster and dropped altitude as he circled. On his next pass, the sonic cannon hit him again, the noise screaming deep into his brain. Jamie fought to keep his eyes open, to keep going forward, to drop altitude just enough to get out of that beam's path. When he got low enough, the feds—Mossman and Kragthorpe—set down their rifles and took out their service weapons, probably to make sure they didn't blow off anybody's roof with pure noise or set the landscaping on fire. But their pistols could do nothing against Jamie's aura, so he flew at 70 percent speed and smashed into the first SUV, driving himself through the engine block and pushing it through the seats, the trunk, and out the other side. Letting what was left of the engine fall to the ground, he swung around and cannonballed straight through the other truck.

Now people were looking out their windows. Some had come outside. Another case when curiosity trumped common sense.

Jesus, how'd the Team even spot me? Those satellite dishes. Some kind of radar? Sensors tuned to our energy signatures?

He would have to tell the others to watch out. The Team had found a new way to locate the Freaks, at least when their powers were engaged.

Jamie headed back to town, specifically toward Gabby's place on Mississippi Street. When he got there, everything was dark. The Davisons must have crashed for the night. No sense in waking Gabby just to tell her he had nothing to tell. He headed home.

Mom and Dad had insisted he go with them to Pine Bluff tomorrow. They wanted to visit Jamie's aunt, who had recently gotten out of the hospital after back surgery. By the time they got back, it would be close to his school-night curfew, so, back in his room, he sent the others a flurry of texts detailing the attack. He finished up with a suggestion, which was really an order, since he was supposed to be the leader:

let's meet at lunch on Monday

In the small hours of the night, he awoke and checked his phone. Everyone but Micah had replied. Jamie frowned. The kid had gotten quieter, less interested in . . . well, everything. Even on game nights, he never really seemed present. He might eat a slice of pizza or two, drink a Coke, take a turn here and there, but he grunted more than he talked and stared at his phone in a corner when he wasn't playing. What could Jamie do about that?

Nothing tonight, that was for sure.

His phone illuminated the papers on his side table—recruiting mailers from something like five dozen universities, everywhere from the University of Southeast Arkansas to Harvard. College was still a good way in the future, but a lot of these places had already started the full-court press. Yes, it was time to find the best place to follow his dreams. But what even *were* his dreams? Once he had wanted to be a filmmaker or a comic-book writer. When he was in seventh grade, his mother began mentioning how much a good engineer could accomplish, plus all the money he could make. Dad had suggested an HBCU, maybe Howard, and some sort of career in politics or activism, like Jamie could be the next Barack Obama or Ta-Nehisi Coates. But what did *Jamie* want? Maybe this side career as a superhero meant he should do something with criminal justice.

Of course, for all he knew, he would die tomorrow, torn apart in the mouth of something from another part of the universe. And none of this was getting solved tonight. He set his phone on the side table. Troubled but tired, he rolled over and fell back to sleep.

CHAPTER THREE

Gabby and Jamie zipped up their jackets as they exited the school building and walked to their favorite table, where they took their seats on the same bench and opened their lunches. Mom had packed Gabby's that morning: a bottle of water and a Tupperware container of Spanish rice and chorizo, one of Mom's dishes that Gabby liked to eat cold. She popped the top and dug in. Jamie sipped water and ate his sandwich. Soon, Christian joined them, pulling her own coat closed. A cold wind kept driving the longer parts of her hair over her face. She wore her backpack and carried three paperbacks by Indigenous writers: Tommy Orange, Louise Erdrich, and Stephen Graham Jones. A bookmark stuck up from the top of each one. Starting a couple of months after Rabbit left, she had begun posting videos on social media, sharing little-known facts about the histories of the LGBTQ+ community and Indigenous tribes like the Quapaw. She and Bec and Gabby had even started a diversity club at school. So far they hadn't done much beyond talking strategies for increasing their membership, but still. They had come to the attention of Quapaw City's more reactionary and prejudiced parents, who had already raised a stink with the school board, but so far, no one had shut them down or sent Christian home to change clothes. Her activism efforts du jour included a pair of rainbow earrings and a T-shirt that read *Every Road in America Is a Trail of Tears*.

Next, Kenneth appeared with a lunch bag almost as big as a backpack. What did he have in there, a whole pizza? He was lucky his teenage metabolism and his powers took care of the calories he shoveled in each day. The kid ate enough for three people. He wore a fleece-lined coat and kept wincing whenever the wind kicked up a notch.

23

"Where's Ty?" Jamie asked Kenneth, looking back toward the door.

"Make-up test," said Kenneth.

Micah came out carrying nothing and dressed like it was July. At least in the fall, he had usually remembered to keep up appearances. Now, though, if he even thought about consequences, he just didn't care. Jamie had spoken to him several times, and Micah had always said yes, he'd be more careful, sure, sorry about that. But then a day or two later he would show up to school or game night in some old, thin T-shirt faded from a thousand washings. At least he had worn jeans today, not shorts or his damn swimsuit or something.

He walked like he was moving through tar, hands in his pockets, head bowed. Several times he almost bumped into someone who then invited him to open his stupid eyes. His hair had grown well past his shoulders, but not because he had gotten into the rock-and-roll aesthetic. He just hadn't thought about it. If Mr. Sterne had been around more, he probably would have made Micah cut it, but he pretty much lived on the road these days, and Baltar apparently didn't care about Micah's look. The kid's fingernails had grown long and sharp. When it occurred to him, he polished them a screaming red, like he was daring people to say something.

As he got closer, Jamie scooted over, and Gabby moved to the end of the bench. Micah sat next to Jamie and lay his head on his folded arms. At least his eyes were open, though he said nothing. Was he even curious about the meeting, or had he drifted so far into outer space that he couldn't be bothered to notice events here on Earth?

More than Micah's image had changed over the last months. The Freaks no longer needed to eat constantly when using their powers, as if their bodies had adapted to their new conditions. Gabby had learned to create force bubbles of varying sizes that would float along and explode on contact, or whenever she wanted. In addition to feeling other people's emotions, Jamie was learning to project his own. At their last game night, he had gotten pissed at *Jungle Raider 2* and tossed his controller backward over his head. It landed on the bed as he clenched both fists and cursed. Gabby had gotten up and started massaging his shoulders when she realized Kenneth was moving forward with Jamie's rage in his eyes. He might have smashed the console, but Jamie had grabbed him and said *Calm down, calm down.* Kenneth looked around like he was just waking up. Since then, Jamie had spent a lot of time sitting still and quiet, learning to keep that part of his powers turned off. He could also fly faster and make tighter turns.

Christian had learned to vibrate objects until they basically disintegrated. Micah burned both hotter and colder than ever. And Kenneth had grown much stronger. They had no real way of testing just *how* strong, but he could easily perform tasks that used to strain him.

Baltar Sterne was just as creepy as he'd always been, like a vampire who packed school lunches and sometimes vacuumed. He had continued to prove his worth, though. Just last weekend, he'd cast a spell that made the Freaks' voices change whenever they wore their costumes.

School had changed a little too. Across the way, the new Spanish teacher, Ms. Herrera, patrolled the grounds, making sure no one was smoking behind the trees near the edge of campus, that no one littered, that no fights broke out, and that no public displays of affection offended the allegedly tender and innocent eyeballs of teenagers who could see far worse on Netflix. When would adults realize that treating teenagers the same way you treat little kids never works? As for Ms. Herrera, several students had marveled at her flawless skin, her loose and shiny ringlets, her voice. She spoke English with an accent; apparently, she was Dominican. Some kids had described her as kind and patient, as a teacher who really loved her job.

Maybe I ought to take one of her classes. Mom's always after me to learn more Spanish, maybe get fluent. Mrs. Figueroa always intimidated me, but Ms. Herrera sounds more—what's the word?—approachable? Besides, I already know more than most of the kids around here. Could be an easy A.

Jamie wadded up his lunch bag and interrupted her thoughts. "Kenneth, tell everybody what you told me."

Kenneth finished his lunch and drank a long swig of water before he began. "I don't know how much I *can* tell you. It happened fast, and there wasn't much to see." He explained the hunting trip, the weird phenomenon with the animals, what had happened after his dad took the shot. Everybody leaned in closer, eyes wide. Enough time had passed that Gabby had allowed herself to hope there were no more monsters to fight. So much for that. And this one was invisible? Great. Just great.

Kenneth kept wiping his mouth with the back of his hand. One leg bounced like it was playing a bass drum. Gabby understood. The Freaks had more or less gotten used to government agents and monsters trying to kill them, but she could imagine few events scarier than watching a parent nearly die. Kenneth was probably thinking about Micah's mom, about Jake Hoeper, about Gavin. No one was safe.

"That everything?" asked Jamie.

"Yeah," said Kenneth, his voice steady again. Good for him. "Look, whatever this thing is, we need to kill it. That new hunting lease— there's probably forty people in our club."

Gabby got his point. Still, what had happened to Kenneth sounded accidental, like those old comics stories where two superheroes met for the first time, and one assumed the other was a villain, and they threw down over the streets of New York just because of a misunderstanding. Maybe—

"I'm down," said Jamie.

Gabby did a double take.

"Wait, what?" said Christian.

Jamie shrugged. "There's something nasty and dangerous in them woods. It's our job to stop it."

"Damn right," Kenneth said, glaring at Christian like she had personally attacked Mr. Del Ray.

"Oh, quit it," said Christian. "I ain't scared of you." She turned to Jamie. "Look, I get it. The monsters we set loose belong to us. But we don't know that this *is* a monster."

"What else would it be?" Kenneth's expression suggested he believed the girls had gone crazy. "You think it's, what, a freaking teddy bear? Maybe you should go out yonder and try to hug it. See what happens."

"I don't know what it is," said Christian, "and neither do you. That's my point. It might be something that got dragged to Earth, and now it's lost and scared. I mean, if you were chilling and some dude came along and shot one of your friends, what would you do?"

"Excuse me for caring more about my dad than some piece of shit from another world," said Kenneth. "It would have killed him if I hadn't been there."

"Yeah, we already know what happens when we sit back and wait," said Jamie. "It's long past time we got aggressive."

Gabby could barely believe what she was hearing. Jamie had always been the most level-headed one in the group. Now he sounded like . . . well, like Kenneth. Or Micah.

Christian laughed bitterly and threw up her hands. "I can't believe this shit. You *do* remember Rabbit wasn't some vicious monster who killed anybody he came across, right? He was a *god*. He wanted to protect Indigenous people and their culture. Protect 'em from *us*. To him, *we* were the bad guys. And in the end, he still let us live."

"Rabbit didn't come after our families," Jamie said.

"Neither did whatever's in the woods," said Christian. "It didn't stomp into town looking for Kenneth's house. It just defended itself and ran."

They all fell silent for a minute. Then, staring at the tabletop, Jamie said, "Maybe we should vote."

Kenneth hardly let Jamie finish before answering. "Kill it."

Jamie nodded. "I vote yes too. Micah, you ain't said shit all day. Get your head in the game."

Micah cut his eyes at Jamie. He looked exhausted and resigned, like he had gotten so used to being tired that he couldn't even remember feeling any other way. His voice was barely audible. "If it's supernatural, it's dead. That's my motto."

Christian sighed. "Dude, *we're* supernatural."

"Well, your haircut is, anyway."

"Bite my ass."

"I guess we know how you're voting," Jamie said to Christian.

Christian and Gabby had talked many times about last year's incident with Rabbit and how it had shaken Christian, caused her to reexamine her assumptions and her identity, forced her to see that surface appearances often masked a deeper and more complex truth. But instead of examining the intricacies of the situation, now even Jamie seemed to be arguing for simple solutions, and none of them even knew what the *problem* was yet.

Christian looked from Kenneth to Jamie and back again. "I'll help find it and figure out what's up. But not everything's Na'ul. Not everything that's different deserves to die."

Now Jamie turned to Gabby. "And you?"

"I'm with Christian. I think we should check it out. We shouldn't go in hot to kill something we haven't even tried to understand, though. Not when it's stayed clear of people for nearly three years. If Kenneth hadn't accidentally found it, we wouldn't even know about it."

Jamie frowned. "How much human blood are you willing to shed to protect some monster?"

"None," Gabby snapped. "Don't act like I am. I fought Na'ul and Rabbit just like the rest of you. But lumping everything we don't understand into one category—Jesus Christ, Jamie, don't you remember that's exactly how everybody in this town has always treated us?"

"That's what I'm getting at," said Christian.

"The difference is we didn't kill anybody," said Jamie.

"Neither did this thing!" Gabby felt flushed. Were she and Jamie . . . fighting? That had never happened before.

"What are you so mad about?" Christian asked Jamie. "You won the vote. We're going out there. Since when do you need everybody to agree on every single point?"

Jamie turned on her, scowling. He started to speak. Then he seemed to think better of it. He took several deep breaths, hands flat on the table, eyes downcast. When he looked up again, his expression had softened. "Okay. For now, just checking things out will be enough. But if me and Kenneth and Micah have to keep our minds open, so do y'all. If this thing needs killing, we kill it. Okay?"

Christian looked away, but she nodded.

"Okay," said Gabby.

Now Jamie grinned. He reached across the table and nudged Christian's hand. "You say Rabbit made you think different, but maybe it's Bec. All that love. You going soft on us?"

"Eat me," said Christian, not without affection. Some of the tension drained out of the atmosphere.

We never used to argue, unless it was about something like who would win in a fight, Batman or Wolverine. If this is just part of getting older, I wish we could skip it.

As if they had heard the Freaks talking about Christian's love life, Bec and Ty walked through the doors and headed for the table. The two of them were talking, smiling. According to Christian, Bec had been conferencing with a teacher, another reason Jamie had called the meeting during school hours.

"To be continued," Jamie said. He turned toward Bec and Ty and waved.

A moment later, Bec sat on the tabletop and said, "'Sup?" They put one hand on top of Christian's, squeezed it, and let it go before Ms. Herrera noticed. Most teachers wouldn't say much about such a small gesture, but you never knew. Bec still wore their caramel hair in an undercut, though the longer parts had been dyed pink. The lowest of their three piercings were rainbows, the same kind Christian wore. Today they had chosen a vintage *Asteroids* T-shirt and a pair of faded black jeans, plus their favorite black boots.

"Just lunch," said Christian. "What are y'all up to?"

Ty nudged Bec. "Just talking shit."

"About what?" asked Jamie.

Bec and Ty looked at each other and laughed. Then Bec winked. "About how y'all are so close, it's hard for us to wedge ourselves into the group."

"Yeah," said Ty. "We were thinking about forming our own group. The Double Outsiders—not really part of the crowd, but not full members of your little club, either."

Gabby laughed. "Nah. Y'all can hang anytime."

Ty stood behind Kenneth and rested her hands on his shoulders. He looked up at her and smiled. Gabby had never thought about it before, but when he smiled, he looked handsome and kind, the polar opposite of how she had seen him back in his bully days.

"Love your shirt, Bec," said Gabby. "Hey, Ty."

Kenneth raised his chin in Bec's direction, but Micah didn't even look up. When had he last interacted with Bec or Ty? Gabby couldn't remember. She also didn't have much time to worry about it because the bell soon rang. Everyone stood and threw away their trash.

On the way in, Christian walked with Bec. Kenneth and Ty followed a couple of feet behind them, with Micah shuffling along in the rear. Jamie and Gabby strolled together, but they didn't speak. When they reached her locker, she broke off and fiddled with her combination lock while he continued down the hall. It was the first time since they had gotten together that they had parted without a word.

CHAPTER FOUR

After school, having made their excuses to Bec and Ty—essentially proving Ty right about them being outsiders—Christian sped through the Del Rays' hunting lease, looking for any sign of whatever Kenneth and his dad had encountered. Jamie was scouting from the sky, too high for anyone to spot him with the naked eye. The other Freaks stayed in reserve near Kenneth's truck and Gabby's car. So far, Christian had seen and heard nothing unusual, just the same animals you would have expected to find in the woods. She zipped by them so fast that she was long gone before most of them could react, though a couple of deer hopped away.

She kept thinking back to the conversation at lunch. Kenneth's attitude hadn't surprised her; his dad had nearly bought it, after all. She had even expected Micah to say what he'd said; a hatred of the supernatural seemed to be about the only thing he and Kenneth ever agreed on. But Jamie? Everybody knew he had been feeling the pressure of leadership, that every injury and death landed directly on his shoulders, but his worry hadn't manifested like this before. He wanted to turn their group of Original X-Men into X-Force. That made Christian nervous. When you decided to take out someone or something before they actually did anything wrong, you risked becoming the villain yourself.

Maybe I can talk him down, she thought as she leaped a small meadow in the proverbial single bound. *Jamie can't want to be like the feds. After the Team tortured me last year, I would have lost the use of at least two fingers on my left hand if I hadn't had my healing power. Who knows what would have happened if Rabbit hadn't busted in and turned me loose?*

Rabbit. So much of her life these days came back to the Indigenous trickster god. He had saved her that day and nearly killed her on a couple of others. He had also set her on the path leading to the Indigenous parts of her heritage and a deeper understanding of contemporary issues facing the Nations. Ever since, she had been researching the Quapaw, bugging Mom about using a genealogy service to learn more about their relatives, scouring Goodwills in search of shirts with slogans supporting Indigenous rights. Added to all her Pride accessories—three flags in her room, rainbow stickers on her notebooks and her laptop, a history of Stonewall in her backpack—the new stuff helped her make a political statement every day. It wasn't much, but it was a start. She had also started posting about being Indigenous-descended and queer in the small-town South, status updates and videos that were getting more likes every day. It was kind of funny when she thought about it. Most kids started to find themselves in high school, but how many of them owed their discoveries to a giant killer bunny?

Speaking of which, when Rabbit had gone west to observe the descendants of the tribes he had once tricked, he'd promised to return if the Freaks' still-evolving powers threatened this world. What if this whole aggressive trip of Jamie's brought Rabbit back? How could they survive a fight with whatever Kenneth had stumbled on *and* a furious god? They—

Christian tripped on something, her momentum causing her to hit the ground and somersault. The world spun as her body smashed through downed limbs and upright saplings until she struck a tall, thick tree several hundred yards from where she had stumbled. Even with her protective aura, the impact knocked her silly. The tree quaked; leaves and branches and hickory nuts rained everywhere. Then, with a loud cracking sound, the trunk broke and fell. When it landed, it sent splinters and wood dust in the air. "Ouch," Christian said. She lay there in the wreckage for several moments, taking careful inventory of her body. Her back ached where she had struck the tree roughly three feet off the ground. Her head spun, but that felt more like dizziness than injury. Her aura had taken care of the rest. Without it, she would have been torn in half. Still, now she knew how a car felt after a head-on collision.

I hope I didn't flatten any animals.

Sitting up and groaning, she checked her costume and found no tears or cuts or bloodstains. Her head already felt better. To speed up her healing, she vibrated one hand to engage her speed powers. By the time Jamie landed, she was standing up and brushing herself off.

"Jesus," said Jamie. "What happened?"

Christian felt more embarrassed than hurt. "I tripped. Over what, I don't know. Maybe I just stepped in a hole."

"Let's go see," said Jamie. "I don't think we'll have trouble finding the place."

A line of destruction led directly to this newly fallen tree: shallow depressions where Christian had landed, all those broken saplings. It looked like a really small tornado had touched down.

"Damn," she muttered.

"You want to run or walk?"

"Let's walk. I could use a little more time to get my head on straight."

Though daylight was leaking out of the sky, they could still see without enhancing their vision. It took them only ten minutes to find where she had tripped. They stared at the ground for quite a while before either of them found words.

The dried footprint was at least ten feet long from heel to toe. Whatever had made it possessed five long and comparatively skinny toes, each ending in a claw. Jamie moved in the direction the print was pointing. Christian followed. They kicked the fallen leaves around and found more prints. Five hundred yards to the north, the tracks stopped. Next, Christian and Jamie walked back to the tripping point and searched the backtrail. The prints went for maybe two hundred yards in that direction, as if something had landed and walked a while before taking to the air again.

Jamie put his hands on his hips and surveyed the woods like he expected a monster to step out from behind a tree and wave. "You don't reckon Rabbit made these last year? When he turned into a T. rex?"

Christian thought about it. "No. This ain't where we fought him. I mean, I guess he could have turned into one some other time."

"Yeah, but I don't think tyrannosaurus had this kind of foot, did they?"

"Well, not in any of the stuff I've read. And here's something else. I ain't no tracker, but Rabbit's been gone well over a year now. This looks fresher than that."

Jamie squatted and ran his fingers along the print's edges. "Hmm."

"How do you know what you're looking for?"

"I don't."

Okay, then. Christian left him to it and walked along the trail. A parallel path could easily be traced in the trees. Fresh piles of snapped-off branches lay to either side of the prints. At least, she *thought* they were fresh. Kenneth would probably know. They should have brought him, too. Jagged stumps where branches had been broken studded the trunks for the entire length of the print trail. Whatever had walked through here had damaged the trees, all the way from the ground to dozens of feet up.

Something off to the right caught the sunlight, rendering a patch of soil a little brighter than the rest. Christian veered off and found it, teardrop-shaped and roughly a foot long. She picked it up and brushed the dirt from its surface. Only a few millimeters thick, it was almost weightless. She ran her fingers over it and held it up to the light filtering through the canopy. The object's surface was completely smooth and purplish. She tried to bend it, and while it gave just a little, she couldn't fold it or break it. Maybe Kenneth could have done it using his super-strength, but she wasn't sure about that.

Christian tucked it under her arm and walked back while searching both sides of the path. By the time she reached Jamie, who met her halfway, she had found another teardrop. "Check these out," she said, handing him one.

He tested it much like she had done. "What do you think they are?"

"I know I'm sticking with the maybe-it's-a-giant-reptile theory, but to me, they look like scales."

Jamie considered this for a moment. "That's exactly what I was thinking. But what *kind* of reptile?"

They stood there a while as the shadows grew longer. Whatever it was could have been watching them, waiting. Maybe even planning. Christian shivered.

CHAPTER FIVE

Micah sat on his sofa in the dark living room and stared at the blank TV screen. When had he last watched anything on it? These days, he stayed in his room as much as possible, scanning online videos or listening to music, sleeping more hours than he spent awake. He used his TV mostly for video games, but unless his friends came over, he didn't play much anymore. Instead, he would just sit still for an hour, two, even three before he realized how much time had passed. He'd read an article on heroin addiction once, and this junkie had said you could shoot up and spend all day looking at the lines on your palm. Micah had never done heroin, or any other drug for that matter, unless you counted caffeine or the occasional beer swiped from the fridge. Now, though, he wondered if he had somehow gotten addicted to something without realizing it. But where would it have come from? With Dad gone all the time, there wasn't even any alcohol in the house. Micah would have needed to drive to a bootlegger, since Quapaw County was dry and no liquor store across the county lines would sell to him for another few years. Besides, if he had taken such a trip, surely he would have remembered. Right?

For that matter, how long had he been sitting here now?

The curtains in the front windows were parted just enough to show that night had fallen. Not all that long ago, Micah's stomach might have hinted at the time, but he didn't eat much anymore. Breakfast usually consisted of a granola bar or a single Pop-Tart. He never felt like packing a lunch, and Baltar had stopped offering at some point, so he generally did without.

Because Dad had gone back to long-haul trucking and pretty much lived on the road, Great-Uncle Baltar was now Micah's unofficial guardian. Baltar had apparently decided to crash here forever, or until he got so old he turned to dust. Micah barely even talked to Dad these days; when he called and Micah asked to speak with him, Baltar used that soothing bass voice of his and told Micah that Dad had to go. Thirty seconds later Micah would fall asleep or just sit, like he was doing now, brain activity barely above zombie level. What was up with that? Maybe the old man was trying to protect Micah from Dad's ambivalence about coming home. Or maybe something else was going on. What reasons might that creepy dude have for wanting to keep a son from his father?

The old man cooked dinner most nights and talked about maintaining his various spells, but Micah had little interest in the magical equivalent of changing your oil, and the food didn't really taste like anything. Micah still drank Cokes and cups of coffee with milk and sugar, but mostly out of habit; when he did do his homework, he often couldn't remember the point. Worse, he wasn't retaining information like he used to. His grades had slipped, first into the B range, and this semester, deep into the Cs. If he kept forgetting to do his work or turn it in, they would fall even further. But who really cared? Mabel Jansen, his old social worker, had mostly vanished from his life, and soon he would reach the age where nobody could say shit if he decided to bail on his English test.

Now that Micah thought about it, when *had* he last done any homework? Had Baltar even asked about school?

Not that Micah wanted to ditch. His plan had always been to go to the University of Arkansas and major in something related to game design. If Jamie decided to stay local, they would room together. If not, Micah would live in the dorms and get some kind of work-study or a loan so he could find an apartment by junior year. Now, though, college was starting to seem like a planet in a different universe, accessible only via a light-speed craft that hadn't been invented yet.

Life in general had grown gray. Nothing seemed to matter. Sometimes Micah wondered whether he had lived the last two years in shock. Maybe he had suffered a breakdown. He wished he could talk to Dad about it, but they didn't have that kind of relationship. Dad had never gotten too deep in his own feelings, much less anyone else's.

Earlier, Jamie had sent the group a handful of texts. The gist: he and Christian had found something in the woods and wanted to talk about it in person. This seemed like a tough week to schedule a meeting, though. Gabby had a dentist appointment one afternoon. Del Ray had planned another stupid hunting trip with his stupid dad, like he had forgotten they were the ones who had started this shit. Jamie was supposed to attend some super-brain crap like Model UN or debate team or whatever. It was a good thing no monster had decided to rampage down Main Street, because the Freaks would have been too busy to stop it. *Hey, look, I'm Christian. I can't fight today because I'll be picketing Mr. Hoon's office, trying to make him rename the gym after some Quapaw chief nobody's ever heard of. Tell the new monster to hang out, and maybe I'll get to it tomorrow. And me? I'm Jamie. I gotta stay home and study or my GPA might fall to only a 4.0. My mom's gonna flip her wig!* Micah's friends had some screwed-up priorities.

His friends. Picturing them—thinking about their conversations and their game nights and even all the ways they had disappointed him—drove back the fog in his head, at least for a little while. They still mattered to him that much. Very little else did. When he looked at the world, when he heard people talking and birds chirping, when he smelled some of the food people constantly shoveled in their faces, Micah had to stop himself from setting everything on fire. Most things either offended him or didn't merit his attention. Plus, the only two people he had ever liked romantically had rejected him in favor of another Freak. Not for a pretty-boy jock airhead asshole like Steve Whitehead—for Jamie and Christian. Even Del Ray had gotten a girlfriend—would wonders never cease? Happiness had walked through everyone's front doors and made itself at home, everybody's but Micah's. Sometimes he wanted to make them all pay. Sometimes he even hated them. And during those times when he gave in to the old affections and the old ways of relating to each other, the momentary happiness he experienced made him feel even worse when it went away again.

Maybe he should just pack up and leave. Get away from Baltar, from all the lovey-dovey rom-com sickly sweet cuddling or self-righteous political posturing his friends were into these days. Carjack something badass and drive until he found an abandoned cabin on some nameless lake. He could learn to hunt and skin animals. If Del Ray could do it, anybody could. Grow a few vegetables and clean fish. Maybe, if enough time passed, he could clear his head. *Feel* again.

But no. Dad didn't deserve that. He had already lost Mom. Micah needed to be here when Dad got back. Maybe he would have made enough bank to stay home for a long time. They could kick Baltar out and get their lives back on track. Something to look forward to.

Still, sitting on this piece-of-shit couch in this piece-of-shit house on this piece-of-shit street, Micah could barely keep his eyes open. Sleep chased him down and tackled him even more often than the Brainless Bastard Brothers used to. Not that he got much rest. Maybe you couldn't even call it sleep. More like a shallow doze, just deep enough to dream those same dreams.

Even now he was drifting down, eyes closed, breathing deeply. And, as usual, the voice came to him—deep like the loudest thunder, insistent, and now, after all these months, familiar. Had Micah accepted it the way he had accepted his own inner monologue or Baltar's constant suggestions, which, even when they irritated him, made perfect sense to his exhausted brain? And if he had accepted the voice, what did that mean?

Images formed in the air. There sat the TV, there the easy chairs, there the walls and the ceiling and the shitty carpet Mom and Dad had always wanted to replace. They had probably never imagined it would outlive Mom. Baltar preferred his own room or one end of this couch, like the chair held Dad's shape so well that no one else could find it comfortable. Micah shook his head. This train of thought had distracted him from what was appearing between the couch and the TV, standing on that same carpet without actually touching it: the hooded figure he had seen so often in his daydreams and nightmares. It looked wavery, transparent, like a bad hologram. Deep in its hooded cloak, shadows played over its bloodless white skin. Its face was featureless, as smooth as still water.

Huh. That's weird.

Micah blinked. Time seemed to have passed. The figure now hovered over him, even as some other presence stood *behind* him. Thin, strong hands touched his shoulders, then gripped them hard. Baltar. The old dude was chanting, though Micah couldn't catch the words. They probably weren't in English anyway.

Micah let his head fall back against the couch. "What are you doing?"

Baltar kept chanting.

Micah opened his eyes again, though he didn't remember closing them. More time had slipped away. It felt later, but more than that, the specter had vanished, as had his great-uncle's voice. Some other sound cut through the brain fog . . . knocking? Yes, knocking, steady and loud. Now something else, muted footsteps on the hall carpet. Baltar heading for the door.

The old man spoke softly. Someone replied. Micah didn't bother enhancing his hearing or looking up to see who it was. Better just to stay here, comfortable and warm, and let all the world's bullshit carry on without him. That abandoned cabin sounded better and better, though it probably wouldn't have running water. Meh. Since temperature didn't affect him anymore, he could bathe in the lake or river or whatever. He could pee anywhere. Taking a dump would be harder, though. He would have to look up how to build an outhouse or dig a latrine. He—

"Micah," said Baltar. "Micah, wake up."

Huh. He must have drifted off again. Baltar stood over him, those creepy eyes wide open and unblinking, his dark eyebrows knitted

together. Moonlight from the window shone off the old man's shaved
head. In his black clothes, he looked like a floating head and a pair of
hands. Weird how those features never changed. In all the time since
Baltar had come to Quapaw City, Micah had never seen a new wrinkle
form, had never noticed any stubble on his face or head, had never even
witnessed the old man clipping or painting his nails. Like the weeks
and months passed by without touching him.

"What is it?" asked Micah. Both his own voice and Baltar's sounded
far away.

"That was Chief O'Brien." Baltar sounded . . . what, sad?
Sympathetic?

God, what *now*? Had Gabby fallen down a manhole? Maybe Jamie
had walked outside and a safe dropped on his head. What could make
this old weirdo sound morose?

"Somebody cancel your subscription to *Spooky Old Dude Monthly*?"

"It's your father. Something has happened."

Micah felt his consciousness slipping away. He shook his head.
Speaking was like lifting weights. "What's going on?"

"The South Carolina state police called the chief and asked him to
pass along the news. There was an accident near the Georgia border.
Something about an icy road and a blowout. A terrible wreck. Micah,
I'm afraid Malcolm is dead."

Micah understood the words, but they seemed empty, like they had
no relation to him or his life. "What?"

"I have to go and claim the body. I'm leaving tomorrow. You can
come with me if you like. Or I can arrange for you to stay with Jamie
or Gabby."

"Uh."

Baltar nodded as if Micah had said something profound. "I understand. This is a lot to process, especially after what happened to your
mother. I will make some calls."

"Uh-huh."

The old guy headed back down the hall. Micah hadn't moved. His hands still lay in his lap. The words echoed in his mind like they had been shouted into a canyon: *Dad is dead.* And deep, deep down within him, something curled up like a kicked dog and howled.

This miserable world had taken something else from him. Someday, if he could get off this couch, he would pay it back. With interest. But for now, he closed his eyes and let himself drift through the darkness, where he didn't have to care about anything.

In that darkness, he was not alone.

CHAPTER SIX

She slept deep in the forest, surrounded by this world's small and graceful inhabitants. They had sought her out, finding her by scent and hearing and, when she allowed it, sight. Now they had bedded down against her in lounges of their own, like keeping to like. It had been much the same in her own forest, though the creatures that came to her there had differed from these. Those woods had been different too: the trees so much taller and thicker and older, their branches and the ground full to bursting with fruits and greens, the tasty ten-pointed leaves. In the cold, she had slept except when she needed to hunt. In warmer weather, she frolicked and flew and ate, and though she took flesh from the forest, no creature begrudged her. In this world, where she had lived for some time, the land gave far less, and so she had been forced to consume too many of those who came to her for shelter and peace. Though they, too, seemed to understand, she dreamed of the land she had left behind, and she wept.

The little ones who followed her lacked the language to give her a name, but the two-legged hunters who had invaded her original forest and struck down the helpless friends she'd made there had called her the Stoic. She knew why: Despite what those beings had done, she'd never responded with anger or sadness, so they had assumed she felt none, even when she killed. In truth, her feelings belonged only to herself. She would not allow such a brutal breed to know them, not even when she was tearing the hunters to pieces.

Among her own kind, she had earned another name: Arsiss, which in their tongue meant "gentle."

Arsiss often dreamed of the day she had come to this new world.

She had been flying above her favorite forest, enjoying the day's heat on her back even as the cold wind in the skies fluttered through the fringes around her head. Then a deep ripping sound had scattered the little ones on the forest floor, had sent whole flocks of birds flapping from the trees. The day turned dark, though the sky-orb still shone. A greater wind had blown in, seemingly from the woods themselves, and when it gripped her, it dragged her down. Arsiss flapped her wings as hard as she could and stretched her neck as far as it would go as if that alone would help her regain the sky, but that reverse wind pulled her ever downward. When she saw the hole torn in the air, she shrank, knowing that if she hit it at full size, it would tear her apart. Even as she fell through, she tried to grab the sides of the aperture with all four feet, but how could you hold air? There was nothing to fight. And so she had fallen through. The gale winds between worlds threatened to rip off her wings. She roared. And then she was through. Beings like those who had hunted in her forests lay scattered on a ground made of trees, while other creatures who, like her, did not belong here came through the rift in the universe.

Those others had nothing to do with her. Arsiss flew out and took to the skies, growing as she soared. When she reached a size that seemed likely to frighten away whatever beings she encountered, she held steady and looked for a good place to land. Soon spotting a tract not so dissimilar to the grounds she had always roamed, she set down, found food, and hid. If she concealed herself well enough, perhaps she could live in peace or even find a way home.

This cold weather chilled her blood. Each wing, each leg seemed to weigh tons. If the two-leggers had kept their distance, she could have slept for months, waking only when hunger cried louder than dreams. That seemed unlikely, though, especially since she had already encountered some and left them alive. They would probably tell others of their kind, and sooner or later, someone would come, bearing weapons and ambition. And so, as Arsiss the Gentle slumbered in the forest she had unintentionally claimed simply by living in it, she trembled. Who knew when more two-leggers would come slinking along, bearing their strange weapons? She had warned the first two away with her roars and her ice, but would they know she had never intended to harm them? Would they care? And what would happen to her if they returned in greater numbers, with more powerful armaments?

Arsiss only wanted to be left alone. Surely that wasn't too much to ask.

CHAPTER SEVEN

When Kenneth got to Ty's house, he texted her. He wasn't going inside if he could help it. He and Ty had mostly avoided discussing their parents' disapproval of their relationship, but they had both adopted the same strategy: spend as little time as possible in each other's house. Easy enough on Kenneth's end; he didn't dare bring Ty over. No telling what Dad would say, even if it horrified Mom and her whole Southern-hospitality fake-ass niceness. As for Ty's place, every time Kenneth saw Mr. or Mrs. Webb, they looked about as friendly as Micah Sterne. Maybe someone had told them about how Kenneth used to act.

Used to? What, you think you're woke now? He scoffed at himself.

Ty came out, got in the car, and kissed him on the cheek. Kenneth spotted a hand pulling back the front curtains just enough for someone to look out. The hostility practically radiated from the house. He drove away as soon as Ty closed her door.

At Pizza of Mind, they ordered the buffet, as usual. While they filled their plates, the Villaloboses came in. Christian was with them. The four of them took a table on the far side of the restaurant, away from most of the other diners. Bec's dad looked like somebody had captured a sasquatch, shaved it, and put it in a flannel shirt. Their mom was hotter than shit, though— flawless brown skin without so much as a pimple or wrinkle, deep brown eyes, tight body. You'd have to fight your own homies over a mom like that, at least if you were a guy. Kenneth had never really thought about his own mother's looks before, but he doubted he would ever have to worry about it. She was pretty, as far as moms went, but Mrs. Villalobos could have been a model.

Ty leaned in close and smiled. "You got a little drool hanging off your lip."

Kenneth laughed. "Sorry."

"You wanna go over there? Say hi?"

"You kidding? *Hell* no."

Ty's eyebrows rose. "But they're our friends."

"Yeah, but this is our date night. Can it just be you and me?"

"Okay."

The more time Kenneth spent with Ty, the more he wanted to spend *all* his time with her. And yet, he'd been reluctant to bring her to lunches and game nights with the Freaks. Putting her in proximity with people he used to bully had always made him feel like he was one stupid mistake away from being exposed. He wanted to keep those parts of his life separate. But what was he supposed to do when she wanted to come? Tell her no? Let her think he was ashamed of her? He could only make up so many bullshit excuses before she'd start to smell them. The discomfort had been his alone; Ty fit right in with the Freaks' shit-talking and jokes. Still, on the nights she hadn't been able to join them, Kenneth had felt relieved, which kept him up at night sometimes. He was going to have to let that shit go. If Christian could manage to get close with Bec and still do her Freaks business, so could he.

As Ty ate, Kenneth kept an eye on Bec's family. Bec and Christian had moved their chairs close to each other. Mr. Villalobos mostly kept his eyes on his plate, but when he did look up, he talked with them and even smiled a time or two. Mrs. Villalobos kept putting one hand on Christian's forearm and laughing. She looked interested in whatever Christian was saying. Bec seemed to have a solid family with parents who had accepted their kid's weird-ass identity and relationship with public displays of affection and everything.

Nothing in Kenneth's immediate experience had suggested such a situation might be possible. Maybe the world in general had gotten more accepting, but in *his* world, a kid who wouldn't call themselves male or female risked getting smacked around, physically or verbally or virtually, sometimes all three. The alphabet crew, LGBT-whatever? Same thing. Outside of school and sports, kids tended to hang with their own kind. Yeah, you could find so-called "diverse" groups in books and movies, but in real life? Not from what he'd seen. Now, though, as Kenneth watched Bec, who had inherited their mother's skin and eyes, snuggle with Christian, who looked lily white no matter how much she wanted to be an Indian; as he sat here across from Ty, his Black girlfriend; as he thought about how, if he concentrated a little, he could actually remember a bunch of times when kids from different backgrounds *had* hung out and seemed to get along just fine, Kenneth wondered how much life he had already missed. Funny how you remembered stuff the way you wanted to instead of the way it really happened, how something as simple as seeing your friends fall in love could bring back the truth. If his environment had taught him to dislike, distrust, or even hate Black people or gay people or whatever, he had just accepted those lessons, and that was on him. Was that one reason people thought he was dumb? Because he had *chosen* not to think?

If I was gay, he wondered, *would Mom and Dad love me? If me and Ty ever got married, would they love our kids?*

Kenneth had always been told—and believed—that being gay or transgender or whatever was a choice. He had never understood Christian, why she *chose* to like girls. But what had happened with Ty, the way a bomb seemed to go off in his chest when her fingertips brushed his bare arm that day and he looked her in the eye, had made him reconsider. Given how he had grown up, surrounded by white people who liberally used the N-word, it never occurred to him that he might like a Black girl. And since he had fallen for Ty despite a lifetime of racist conditioning, since he had no control over who he fell for, then maybe nobody did. And what was wrong with it, anyway? This world needed a hell of lot more love.

Ty was watching him. "Looks like you got a lot on your mind."

He wiped his hands and then reached over and took one of hers. "Just how I'm glad you didn't think I was an asshole that day we met."

She looked mischievous. "Well, I thought you *acted* like an asshole."

He laughed. "I'm glad it didn't drive you off. And I'm glad to be here, with you."

Her eyes narrowed. "What's up? For real?"

He sighed and shook his head. "I don't know how to put it. I guess being with you, watching Allen and Bec over there, hanging out with Entmann and everybody—I'm realizing there's a lot of shit people were wrong about."

"What people?"

"Everybody I've ever known."

"Okay. What shit?"

He pulled his hand back and turned away. His face burned. "Just . . . everything. Like, you and me."

Those eyebrows rose again. "What *about* you and me?"

"Like, our races and stuff. I've learned more real shit about Black people since we've been going out than I ever knew in my whole life. It's like I've only seen one teeny, tiny piece of the world, and now I'm seeing . . . more."

Her eyes seemed to turn cold. She didn't let go of his hand, but something about her expression and posture suggested he'd said something wrong. "I ain't your Magical Negro, K. I'm with you because I took the time to get to know you before I decided what kind of person you are. If you hadn't already seemed like you was trying to walk a good path, I wouldn't have looked at you twice."

"Ty, come on." He leaned toward her with his other hand stretched out. "That ain't what I meant."

She just looked at him for a minute. Then she sighed and took his other hand too. "No, I guess it probably isn't. You just need to be careful with that. Black folks ain't here to teach white people how to behave."

"Okay." He leaned back and put his hands in his lap. His face still burned. Even when he tried to say or do something good, he made a mess.

Ty went back to her pizza. After a moment, Kenneth did the same. Across the restaurant, Allen and Bec talked and laughed and leaned against each other like nothing was wrong in the world. How did they manage to get their relationship right? How could they be so *happy*? Why was it so easy for them?

Or maybe it hadn't been easy at all. Maybe he just hadn't paid attention to how hard it had been.

"You wanna go see a movie next weekend?" asked Ty, breaking up his thoughts. Her plate was nearly empty.

"Okay," he said. He could have added *if I'm still alive*, but he didn't. She still knew nothing about the Freaks, or vampires, or tricksters, or things that could turn invisible and freeze you with a breath. This whole secret identity thing was bullshit. Sometimes Kenneth wished he had read more comic books, so he would know how Batman and Spider-Man pulled it off.

I should tell her. Who knows if I'll get another chance? I could walk out of here tonight and get sniped.

But he said nothing. Entmann was right. If Ty knew about the Freaks, she and her family would get caught up in all this. People had already died. No, Kenneth would keep it all to himself.

Kenneth followed his parents into the Quapaw City First Baptist Church. On most Sundays, Kenneth and his dad watched sports or hunted or fished, while Mom worked in her little backyard garden or, in cold months like this, curled up with a book and a cup of coffee. Sometimes they collaborated on some housekeeping or landscape project. As a general rule, they only stepped inside a church for somebody's wedding or when Mom felt guilty about backsliding. Kenneth had also attended three funerals: Jake Hoeper's, Doreen Sterne's, and Gavin Cloverleaf's, all victims of the vampire Na'ul, all closed-casket affairs. Now, back here in the same church where he had attended two of those services—Jake Hoeper had been a Presbyterian—the Del Rays were paying their respects to Malcolm Sterne. Kenneth wasn't sure why his parents had wanted to come. They probably thought he and Micah were real friends. If they had bothered to ask him, he would have told them he no longer hated Micah, but he didn't like the kid, either. He and Sterne had learned to coexist, even fight for each other, but friends? Nah. Probably never.

Ty walked with him. She wore a blue dress and a gold necklace she had gotten for Christmas last year. Kenneth hadn't wanted her to come, given it would put her in proximity to his parents. She had insisted, though. *It's our friend's daddy, K. Everybody needs support at a time like this. Even you.* He hadn't been able to think of a good argument against that. Only full disclosure would show Ty the true nature of his current relationship with Micah, or the fact that he had spoken maybe two words to Malcolm Sterne in his whole life.

When she had met them at the doors, Dad had clenched his jaw and looked away. Mom had said hello and smiled, though her face looked strained. And if Kenneth had noticed, so had Ty. It was pretty damn cool that Ty would put up with his parents' bullshit just to support him.

The front pews were empty so far, though Micah and Baltar would probably sit up there once the service started. So would the pallbearers, whoever they might be. The Entmanns and the Davisons had taken up the second row on the right. Opposite them, Christian and her mom sat beside Bec and their parents. The Del Rays and Ty ducked into the second pew from the back and scooted all the way to the right, as far from the aisle as they could get.

Mom leaned over. "You can go up there with your friends if you want to."

Kenneth glanced at her. "I'm good."

She made a *hmph* sound but didn't push it, thank God. Ty left it alone.

Once the service ended, Micah and his great-uncle stood beside the coffin while everyone filed by and offered condolences. Jamie hugged Micah and thumped him on the back three times. Gabby hugged him too, though Micah didn't return either embrace. Christian squeezed the kid's shoulder. Bec did the same. All of them shook Baltar's hand, though he barely acknowledged them.

When Kenneth reached the head of the line, he started to stick out his hand, but if Micah left him hanging, it would be awkward for everybody. Instead, Kenneth awkwardly patted Micah's upper arm. "I'm sorry about your dad," he said.

For a moment, Micah just stared. Had he even heard? Was anybody home in there? Then Sterne focused and looked Kenneth in the eye. "Thanks," he said.

It wasn't much, but it was better than trying to kill each other. "I'll see you," said Kenneth.

"Yeah."

As Ty hugged Micah's neck, Kenneth moved on to Mister Creepy, who towered over him and stared with those unnerving, unblinking eyeballs. *He's like a vulture that mutated into a human being but don't know how to act right.*

"Kenneth," said Baltar, as tonelessly as a robot in one of those old 1950s movies the Freaks sometimes watched.

"Hey," said Kenneth. They shook hands. The old dude wore black leather gloves, so at least Kenneth didn't have to touch him.

After that, Kenneth and Ty followed his parents toward the front doors. As they stepped outside, Kenneth excused himself and ducked into the men's room. After locking the door, he did his business in the single toilet and washed his hands. Mom had made him wear a tie with his white shirt and dark slacks. Now he unknotted it and stuffed it in his pocket. Man, ties were stupid. He unbuttoned his shirt.

Last year, before that final fight with Rabbit, Kenneth had forgotten the simple stealth charm Baltar had given him. The old man had handed him a different kind than the other Freaks wore. The new one hung on a stainless-steel chain. It was bigger than the others and made of some glasslike jewel. That fight had unfolded in such a way that Kenneth hadn't used the charm, but later, when he said the magic word, some force had knocked him to his knees. For several moments, he had gotten weak, nauseated, dizzy. The feeling had eventually passed, but when Kenneth got home, he had discovered something nasty. He hadn't told anyone about it all year, hadn't gone shirtless in last summer's heat, hadn't even walked from the bathroom to his bedroom unless he wore a robe or something. If he had, someone would have seen what he saw now in the mirror.

The charm had sunken into his chest. It rested directly against his breastbone. When he jiggled the jewels, they scraped bone. He had planned to confront Baltar about it, but whenever he started to, something clamped his jaw shut. Maybe he didn't really want to know what this charm would do to him.

Sooner or later, though, he would have to deal with it. How much longer could he keep Ty from touching his chest without seeming like a weirdo or a straight-up jerk?

Two hours later, as the day wound down, Kenneth drove to the park in the used Chevy Silverado his father had bought after Kenneth turned sixteen. Kenneth was paying him back slowly, but it was still a great deal for his parents since they no longer had to chauffeur him around. Plus, they made him run so many errands it sometimes felt like a second job. Today, though, the errand was his and his alone.

The park was deserted, probably because of the cold and the late hour. Kenneth kept his head down anyway. He followed the walk until he came to a bench perched on the back side of a rise that obscured it from the street. Special Agent Drew Greenwalt of the FBI was waiting. He wore jeans, a sweatshirt, and a gray peacoat. His red hair waved in the breeze. A box from Pizza of Mind sat on the bench beside him. Kenneth settled in so that the pie was between them.

"Pepperoni with extra cheese," Greenwalt said, still looking straight ahead even though there was nothing to see. The trees hid most of the pond.

Kenneth's stomach grumbled. He hadn't eaten anything at the reception, and he hadn't gone home yet. He was starving. Still, that pizza had come from the Team. "No thanks."

Greenwalt shrugged and opened the box. He removed a slice and took a big bite. "So how was the funeral?" he asked, his mouth full.

Kenneth shrugged. "How do you think it was? It sucked."

"Uh-huh," said Greenwalt. He chewed and swallowed. "And our mutual friend?"

"As out of it as ever. I think maybe he's taking medicine."

The Special Agent nodded, ate, wiped his mouth on his hand. "I'm less interested in his mental state than in what he might be plotting. You've got to give me something, son."

"I'm not your goddam *son*," said Kenneth. "I don't even want to freaking talk to you."

Greenwalt threw his crust into the box and closed it. Kenneth hated people who didn't eat the crust. "Talking to me is better than watching while my partner invents a charge and hauls you and your friends to federal prison. Right?"

Kenneth turned toward the fed and gripped the back of the bench with one hand. He had to be careful or he'd tear the slat right off the structure. "I'm starting to think you're bullshitting me. I can't see your buddy Mossman holding back if he's got any proof at all."

"And yet you can't take that chance, can you?" Now Greenwalt sounded sad. "We've been through this before, kid. You're on the hook. What would your friends think if they knew we were talking?"

"I ain't told you nothing you couldn't find out for yourself if you so much as looked at Sterne."

"Come on, Kenneth. Time's flying."

"I'm telling you, I got nothing. Me and Micah, we ain't hung out much, and when we have, it was just for games or movies and shit. You want me to tell you how far he's got in some first-person shooter or what kinds of toppings he likes on his pizza? Fine. But if you're wanting me to tell you I seen him knock down a daycare or whatever, well, I haven't."

They fell silent a while. Greenwalt ate half of another slice. Kenneth turned away and let his thoughts race. He acted a lot tougher and surer than he felt. He was straight-up lying about Micah, of course. He really hadn't seen him use his powers in a long time, what with the constant surveillance and the old no-powers-in-public rule, but he had seen enough in the past to justify a hundred Team strikes. He couldn't rat on a Freak, though. He just couldn't. Even if it meant Mossman came for them all.

"It's too chilly to sit here for nothing," said Greenwalt. "My pie's already cold." He stood, picked up the box, and started to walk away.

"I told you Micah's zonked out of his skull," said Kenneth, hating himself for revealing even that. "Maybe you can use that to get him away from the old man."

Greenwalt laughed. "Sure. Teenager turns surly and sleepy. What a unique story. The press will have a field day."

"Whatever."

Greenwalt looked at Kenneth for a long time. "Once we move on you, all deals are off the table. Grow up, son. Make the hard decision. It's your best chance."

Kenneth didn't answer, so Greenwalt walked away. After a while, Kenneth got up and headed for his truck. His stomach grumbled again. He should have taken some of that pizza.

CHAPTER EIGHT

The Quapaw City School District was closed on Presidents' Day, but Christian couldn't enjoy it, not after what had happened to Mr. Sterne. So, when Jamie came over and asked if she wanted to scout the woods, Christian had said what the hell, might as well. Jamie's "first strike" plan still seemed like the kind of macho-man testosterone bullshit she would have expected from Kenneth in the old days, not an Entmann strategy. If she found this new whatever-it-was first, or if she could be there when Jamie found it, maybe she could convince him to stop and think before he waded in with both fists. Who could have predicted anybody would ever need to tell Jamie to think? Maybe every guy went through a phase where they could have used a strong slap upside the head.

Kenneth's dad had told their hunting club that something weird had happened on the lease, but having gotten knocked silly, he couldn't provide many details. Kenneth had made up some story about how the thing had moved too fast among the trees for him to get a clear picture of what it might have been. Apparently, the other members hadn't found the story all that impressive; no one had stopped hunting or scouting the lease, including Mr. Del Ray. Did they really think their little bows and arrows could save them from everything they might find out here? Since they had lived their entire lives at the top of the food chain, maybe they just couldn't imagine that kind of danger in Southeast Arkansas.

Rabbit might have called that white vanity, the very concept that you could own land and everything that lived there, that animals were as disposable as trash, that weapons equaled might and trumped skill. He might have called it ironic that this sense of superiority and a nearly religious faith in weapons ultimately made the hunters vulnerable. People rightly talked a lot about the great horrors accompanying white America's march across the continent, Indigenous genocide and slavery and gross exploitation of Chinese and Irish labor and more, but far fewer people seemed to grieve the loss of ancient forests and the living things that had sheltered there. Once there had been bears here, and cats, and flocks of birds that blotted out the sky. So much had been lost. So much could never be found again.

Jamie was nowhere in sight. He might have been flying over some other part of the woods or too high for her to see without enhancing her vision. Maybe—

Christian skidded to a stop. The wind had picked up, carrying some scent she couldn't place. Rich, damp, and hot, but also spoiled, like someone was smoking rotted meat. No unusual sounds at normal hearing levels, though, and no strange sights. So, for the first time in a long time, she enhanced her sense of smell. A thousand odors sprang to life: dark soil; pine and oak and hickory; decaying wood and plant life; and there, *there*, that swampy, burned scent. She locked onto it like a bloodhound.

"Okay," she whispered. "Here I come."

She speed-jogged in the direction of the smell. After stopping for a moment and enhancing her vision, she walked around several trees and tried various angles until she found the least-obstructed view. There—a hundred yards away, several deer, squirrels, and rabbits lay together, bodies on bodies. The stench was coming from them or something near them.

This called for a little super-speed recon. Usually that meant a grid search. This time, she had a target, so, except for avoiding the trees, she could run in a straight line. If she moved fast enough, she might not even disturb the sleeping critters. They might think she was just the wind, though her own scent would probably be enough to make them scatter.

She tensed, took a deep breath, and zipped toward them.

A fraction of a second later, approaching the clusters of animals, she judged that at her present speed, she could easily clear them all and examine the area before she hit the ground. Christian jumped—and collided with thin air. She bounced up and back, the sky and earth exchanging positions over and over. She struck the ground and came to rest on her back.

"Duuuuude," she muttered, sitting up and holding her head. What the freaking hell had she hit?

Groaning, she rolled to one hip and pushed herself to her feet, brushing dirt from her costume. Back at the point of impact, the animals had awakened, but they hadn't run. They were watching her, sniffing the air. A few tucked their heads onto their paws and went back to sleep. Huh. Christian wasn't an outdoor person, but even she knew that didn't make sense. Having spent her life in hunting country, she had heard a hundred and fifty million stories about somebody scratching their nose and scaring away a deer. Now, after all that ruckus, some of them had gone back to *sleep*?

"All right," Christian said as she walked forward. "What's up?" She stomped, kicked leaves out of her path, and deliberately stepped on sticks, but still the animals only watched her. When she closed to within twenty feet, a few finally stood. Could she just mosey on up and pet them? "Look at me!" she cried, waving her arms over her head. "I'm a scary human! Run like hell!"

The ground behind the menagerie shifted, like something big was moving, and the animals parted like a curtain and trotted away. After several yards, they stopped and turned back, standing in mixed groups that still made absolutely no sense. Maybe they expected a sporting event to break out.

The air shimmered, like Christian was looking through a thin veil of water. A new shape began to form.

Aw, hell. Whatever this is, it's big.

It faded in from the ground up: four legs with five-toed feet; a thick, scaly torso; two huge wings, leathery and dense, pulled in tight beside the body; a neck so long you could probably tie it in a knot; a snout like a Komodo dragon's, triangular ears, and fringe collaring the head. The creature was lilac-colored, though its claws were stark white and its eyes bright blue, like summer skies. A long, tapered tail curled around its legs.

"Oh my God." Christian leaned backward so she could see it all. Her heart thundered like most people's did after a hundred-yard dash. She assumed a fighting stance, but what was she going to do, kick it in the shin?

The creature stared at her with those blue eyes, so bright you couldn't look at them for long, like something inside was heating them. It grumbled deep in its chest.

"Hey, girl," Christian said, easing forward, one hand reaching out. What the shit was she *doing*? This seemed like a great way to lose an arm. But still—was this thing really what she thought it was? An animal straight out of legend, direct from her own daydreams and the half-baked fantasy plots she had conceived on a hundred game nights. She had no idea whether it was even a girl, but it felt right. She could not have explained why.

Those eyes kept boring into her. The grumbling grew a little louder.

"Easy." Christian put her hand against the creature's leg.

It snorted, blowing away forest trash in two parallel streams. The smell that had drawn Christian here now overwhelmed her and constricted her throat. She staggered backward and turned down her olfactory system to prevent herself from choking on pure stink.

Then, as quickly as it had made itself visible, the giant lizard turned, shimmered into invisibility, and crept deeper into the woods, leaving Christian bent over, hacking and gagging with her hands on her knees. The various critters followed like they could see it even when it was cloaked. Maybe they could. As Christian's lungs cleared, she straightened up and watched them go.

She was still watching when Jamie landed next to her. He looked where she was staring. "'Sup?" he asked. When Christian didn't reply, he put a hand on her shoulder and shook her. "Hey. What are you looking at?"

She didn't answer for a moment. Her brain was still processing what she had seen. Holy shit. Holy *shit*.

When Jamie shook her again, she turned to him. "Dude," she said, and couldn't manage anything else.

"What? I mean, you must have seen *something*."

"Yeah."

"Well? You gonna make me guess?"

Christian glanced back at the woods. "I think it was a dragon."

Jamie's eyes bugged. "Um, what?"

"A real-life, scaly, purple freaking *dragon*."

Jamie walked forward like he intended to follow the trail, but he stopped after ten or twelve yards and just stood there, hands on his hips. Neither he nor Christian spoke for a long time. Then Jamie shrugged. "Okay, then. I guess we're gonna be dragon slayers."

Christian was too stunned to think of a good reply.

After she and Jamie left the woods and he flew back toward home, Christian ran to Johnny Cash Way and into the woods across from Bec's house. She took off her costume and wrapped it around a low-hanging oak limb. The cold wind blew right through her; by the time she reached the edge of the woods, her teeth were chattering. Brushing hair out of her eyes, she walked out of the trees, crossed the street, and knocked on Bec's door.

A dragon. She still couldn't believe it. Her nerves felt jangly, like she might jump twenty feet in the air if someone came up behind her and said *boo*. Yet she wasn't afraid. She had faced down a super-strong vampire and a god. That didn't make her immune to fear, but this felt like something else. What, though?

Maybe awe. When the dragon revealed itself, she had been . . . excited? Yes, that seemed right. Excitement, the purest kind, like little kids on their first trip to Disneyland, or when they really, truly believed they were sitting on the real Santa Claus's lap in some cruddy mall. Excitement, awe, and a kind of pleasure, because Christian loved dragons. Freaking *loved* them. If she could have turned herself into something else, she would have chosen a dragon. She had read George R. R. Martin's A Song of Ice and Fire books mainly because of the dragons. And now one had shown up near her town, in real life. Holy freaking *shit*.

Her phone buzzed. A text from Jamie, calling a team meeting for tomorrow afternoon at the pavilion. She secured her phone just as the door opened. Mr. Villalobos looked down at her, his expression blank. He was as big as an MMA heavyweight and even more intimidating. When he looked your way with his steely gaze and his strong jawline, your spine turned to ice and started to crack. Even now, he only stepped aside and gestured for her to come in. He seemed about as welcoming as a junkyard dog. Odd how he acted warmer when Bec was in the room. Did he have something against Christian? Or was he just moody?

"Thanks," Christian said as she moved past him. A moment later, she knocked on Bec's door.

Bec opened it, smiled, embraced her, and kissed her on the cheek. "Hey, babe."

"Hi," said Christian. "Can we chill for a little while? I've had a hard day."

Bec opened the door further. "Sure. Come on in."

CHAPTER NINE

In the park, Jamie followed the concrete walk around the pond until he reached the Freaks' pavilion on the far side. Scattered along the tree line like toys some kid had left out overnight, the remains of several grills lay where they had fallen when Kenneth had ripped them out of the ground and thrown them at the other Freaks. That had happened back in freshman year, and no one had even taken the grills away, much less repaired them. Jamie loved the seclusion. It wasn't remote enough to escape the Team's notice, though; by sophomore year, the feds had bugged the place and set up security cameras. But thanks to Baltar's whammy, the Freaks had gotten at least some privacy back.

The others were waiting on the picnic tables. Even Baltar had come. He and Micah sat together, Micah on the tabletop. The old man had taken a spot on the far side bench. Arms folded, he shifted his gaze from Freak to Freak and seemed to miss nothing. Christian, Kenneth, and Gabby were gathered at the next table, facing the Sternes. Everyone but Micah wore coats and stuffed their hands deep in their pockets. At least Micah had put on a long-sleeved shirt.

Jamie took a seat near Micah, making sure to leave enough room for Baltar to see and be seen between them. "So," Jamie said. "Let's hear it."

Christian told them what she had seen, what the dragon had done. Gabby's eyes widened. Kenneth either wasn't impressed or managed to keep his expression neutral. Maybe the last two years had jaded him, and now nothing short of Starro the Conqueror would surprise him. Micah looked about as interested and involved as one of the pavilion's support posts. Baltar, on the other hand, leaned forward, his pale blue eyes shining. He wore all black, as usual, including a turtleneck and a long coat, not of the trench variety. What did you call those things? As for Jamie himself, he had already heard Christian's story, but he got jittery all over again. Even after everything they had seen, he found the idea of a dragon in Quapaw City hard to believe.

When Christian finished her story, everyone sat in silence for a bit. Then Baltar rapped his knuckles on the table. "You cannot imagine a full-grown dragon's capacity for damage. If it decides that too many humans have intruded upon its territory, it will not just defend itself. It will come for all of us. We must kill it."

"You damn right." Micah's voice was toneless, his face expressionless. "Find it. Freeze it and break it into a million pieces. Rip out its heart and eat it for lunch."

"Now, wait a minute," said Christian.

"Everybody cool out," said Jamie.

Christian stood. "Screw that. Instead of talking about how to keep people away from it, we're jumping straight to killing it? Are y'all *serious*?"

"Hell yeah," said Kenneth. "Maybe it don't mean nothing to you that it almost killed my dad, but I don't plan on giving it another chance."

"I guess I gotta repeat what we already know just to get anything through your thick head," Christian said, scowling. "*You* went after *it*. *You* were the intruder."

"Whose side are you on?" asked Kenneth. He stood too. They glared at each other.

"I said everybody cool the hell *out*!" Jamie put one hand up in Kenneth's direction and one in Christian's. "Yelling at each other won't get us anywhere."

Christian sat, grumbling to herself. After a moment, Kenneth, still red-faced and grinding his teeth, took his seat as well. Half the problems with Kenneth came down to his deep investment in his own self-image as a tough-guy jock. His entire life had prepared him to be the jerk who believed his way of looking at the world was the only way, that his desires should determine everybody else's priorities. In short, Kenneth's major issues came down to privilege. *I'm a straight white male, so the rest of you better get in line behind me.*

You might have thought his relationship with Ty would have opened his eyes to that kind of garbage. From what Jamie had seen, Ty took no shit and had no problem calling out racism and white privilege, including her boyfriend's. It was like Kenneth put on one face with her and another with the rest of the world, but it couldn't be that simple. Ty would have seen through it. Maybe Kenneth wanted to change but just couldn't get out of his own way, so he tended to regress right in front of everybody, ready and willing to throw punches instead of talk. Until people got past that kind of thinking, someone would always have to step in and make them chill before they started a fight, or a war, or Kenneth dragged them all backward in space and time to those moments when he and Brayden and Gavin had made the Freaks' lives hell.

At the same time, Jamie couldn't forget how Kenneth's current attitude came from his fear of losing his father, not from hatred. Maybe that was progress, if only a little.

Jamie put a hand on Christian's shoulder. She laid her hand over his and squeezed, though she didn't look at him. "I'm good," she said.

Jamie turned to Kenneth. "And you?"

Kenneth shrugged and looked away.

"Okay," said Gabby, her voice so forceful it made Jamie start. "I think Christian's right. Just because something looks scary don't mean it's bad. We need to know more about this dragon."

Kenneth, sounding disgusted, exhaled. Christian held out her fist for Gabby to bump. Micah looked into the distance.

"What you're suggesting is highly likely to get people killed," said Baltar. "I know dragons. Even the gentlest carry within them the capacity for destruction on a scale you have not yet encountered. Imagine these woods burned to cinders, every living creature dead. Think back to images of heavily bombed cities in war zones and apply that to your town. Consider the thousands of lives you now hold in your hands and how letting this dragon roam free is like squeezing those lives to paste."

"Dude," said Gabby. "The dragon's been here for years, and it didn't do shit until somebody walked up on it and shot a bow in its direction. Even then, it didn't actually hurt anybody. And what do you mean, you *know* dragons? Know 'em from where?"

Baltar turned those cold eyes on her. "I do not answer to you, young woman. I reveal my experiences when I will."

"Listen, creepo—"

"Okay, okay," said Jamie. Everyone else fell silent, waiting on their fearless leader to proclaim something. To take all the responsibility for whatever happened next. Well, if that was what they wanted, then they'd have to live with his decision. They couldn't have it both ways. He took a deep breath and plunged ahead. "I'm not saying I agree with Baltar. I'm not saying we gotta kill this dragon. But like the girls said, we need to assess its threat level. If we have to, maybe we can drive it deeper into the woods. But we absolutely can't just leave it out yonder and hope for the best."

Gabby frowned. Christian scoffed. Kenneth nodded, looking smug. Baltar shook his head. Micah might as well have been asleep.

"So what now?" asked Kenneth.

"We find it again," said Jamie. "See what's what. Do what we have to."

Gabby and Christian still looked unhappy, but they circled up with the others. The group talked for over an hour.

CHAPTER TEN

Gabby parked her car at a little trailhead a few hundred yards from the Gilchrist farmhouse and dug her costume out of her backpack. She detested coming here alone. A town girl through and through, she loathed dirt and bugs and animals that moved around in the brush. The whole mess with Rabbit had doubled her dread of forests. Now this latest news—a real, literal, no-shit dragon in *Arkansas*?—had trebled it. Sooner or later, the Team would probably realize the Freaks were watching them, and then whoever came out here would wind up strapped to a chair, like Christian had last year. God, Gabby was so sick of being afraid—of monsters, of the Team, of what might happen to her friends.

Still, if she had learned anything over the last couple of years, it was not to let fear stop her from living her life or doing what was necessary. Not even fear of the dark and spooky woods, where anything might be hiding.

Stop it. You're here to do a job. Go do it.

Gabby followed the trail she and the other Freaks had used ever since the Team took up residence in the farmhouse. Soon she located the Surveillance Tree, as they had begun calling it, the thick trunk perfect for leaning or sitting against, only a dozen yards from the road. The ongoing countersurveillance was a pain in the ass, but Jamie had insisted on regular patrols, and now that she thought about it, the plan matched his attitude about the dragon.

Had he even stopped to think that his decision to send the Freaks into town, fully costumed and using their powers, had played right into the Team's attacks? Whenever she had tried to bring it up, he had snapped at her, claiming she had no idea how much stress he was under, how stopping more killing before it could happen weighed him down. Gabby hated to admit it, but dealing with monsters and the federal agents had changed Jamie, and maybe not for the better. How would Jamie feel if she came out here on his orders and the Team discovered her, captured her, tortured her, or worse? And what was all this spying preparing her for anyway: the CIA? A private detective's license? Jail?

Not college, that was for sure. Gabby, Christian, and Jamie had taken the ACT in the fall. Now SATs loomed. Thank God colleges had stopped caring so much about standardized tests. She would never get a score that really spoke to who she was and what she had to offer. She excelled in English and history and various science courses, but for whatever reason, math just wouldn't stick in her brain. If Jamie chose a good engineering school she couldn't get into, or one that didn't offer whatever she decided to study, well, that would probably be the end of their relationship. And even if they went to the same college, even if they got an apartment together at some point, nothing could guarantee they would last.

If they didn't make it together, was it possible that might be . . . good? Or at least not as bad as it might have seemed last year?

Did Bec and Christian think about stuff like this? Or Kenneth and Ty? Every passing day brought them one step closer to graduation. Dozens of couples faced uncertain futures, but some of them talked about their plans like even an apocalypse couldn't intervene. It had been a long time since Gabby had felt that confident about anything further ahead than the next five minutes. With the life she was living, even thinking about college might have been a waste of time. Hard to study for a test when you spent your days and nights fighting supernatural threats. *Buffy* had taught her that, and old *Spider-Man* comics. In any case, though, change was coming, as it always did, whether they were ready or not. High school would end in a little over a year. The Freaks could fight monsters, but they couldn't punch or blast their own futures.

None of which had anything to do with why she had come to these woods.

She sat against the tree. The ground was cold. She turned up her hearing and focused on the voices in the house. She no longer had to concentrate; it had become a voluntary but unconscious act, like walking. In less than a second, the voices faded in, as clear as if the Team members were standing right next to her.

"—something," said the woman with the accent.

Gabby sat up straighter, concentrating hard now. The Freaks had first heard this voice—along with a new, deep, gruff, male one—not long after Rabbit the trickster had vacated the woods around Quapaw City. None of the Freaks had seen anyone new coming or going from the farmhouse or in town. Jamie had instructed all of them to be alert for any hint as to their identities or their purposes.

"Any idea what that something might be?" McCreedy's harsh and raspy voice.

"No sir," said the woman. "I've gone over the data from the sensors we installed last year. They've detected a powerful presence moving in and out of range over the last few weeks. The energy signature isn't in our database."

"Keep monitoring. When you lock onto a position, we'll deploy."

They had to be talking about the dragon. Gabby wished she had been there to see it. She also thanked God she hadn't been.

"What about the kids?" asked a voice with Southern California inflections: Kragthorpe, the CIA asshole who had tortured Christian last year.

"My profile suggests that Davison and Entmann are heading for a breakup," said the woman. "That would be a hell of an opportunity."

Gabby scrambled to her feet. "What?" she cried. The woods didn't answer. Her hands began to glow bright white; she had to take several deep breaths before she obliterated a bunch of trees, or worse.

"Body language and voice inflection analysis suggest tension, perhaps even rancor." The woman's musical voice belied the meaning of her words. "One really odd wrinkle, though. The video and audio from inside their houses and cars profile differently from what we see and hear when they're outside. It's almost like they have two related but subtly different sets of personalities. One set gets along so well they could be in a fifties sitcom. The other doesn't."

Uh-oh. She's not just picking up on our fights. What if she guesses we've futzed around with their cameras and microphones?

"Continue to monitor the situation and adjust as necessary," said McCreedy. "In the meantime, someone needs to make a food run. And by the way, whoever's been eating my ice cream sandwiches—"

Gabby turned down her hearing and headed back to her car, her vision enhanced so she wouldn't step in a hole and break her ankle or trip over a branch. What had she learned tonight? One, that the new woman seemed to be an analyst, which might explain why she hadn't joined a surveillance team. Two, that the feds had placed energy sensors in the woods. Did that mean they had put them in everybody's houses and cars too? If so, Baltar might have to whammy the new devices. Three, that this analyst believed she had found fault lines in Gabby and Jamie's relationship.

Was she right? Of course there was arguing and infighting, and not just between her and Jamie. The Freaks were about as close as friends could get, but they were still teenagers, and the pressures of defending Quapaw City from supernatural threats would make anybody testy. And sure, she and Jamie disagreed about this whole "strike force" concept. Still, you could disagree with the people you loved. That was one of the best parts of the whole deal. You could get mad, argue, throw things, swing punches, yell, flip the bird, swear you hated each other and always had and always would, but sooner or later, you whispered apologies and got on with your lives, knowing love could save you.

Still, if this stranger convinced the other feds that the Freaks were vulnerable, the Team might step up their attacks even more. They could even break into everyone's houses, go after the kids' parents physically.

When Gabby reached the trail, she took off her costume, stuffed it in the backpack, and threw the pack in the trunk. Then she headed home, wishing she could leave all these troubles behind as easily as she did the farmhouse.

CHAPTER ELEVEN

Arsiss had reduced her size until she could lie safely on an upper limb. Below, a herd of creatures grazed. One large male with a broad rack of antlers, three females, two juveniles. They resembled the nahrs of her homelands, although nahrs were winged and three-legged. She had sometimes been forced to eat from the nahr herds, just as she had sustained herself on the flesh of other animals, especially during the cold months when grasses and fruits and plants died. On those occasions when she had spilled living blood, she had wept, and on the spots where her tears fell, dragontrees had grown, growths of sturdy wood with long, six-pointed leaves and purple fruit that the surviving denizens of her woods had consumed. In this alien place, she might have lived on what remained of the greenery if she had been able to maintain a size similar to the females below. When the two-legged intruders had stumbled upon her, though, she had instinctively and defensively grown. Changing sizes always made her hungrier. She had put off feeding for as long as she could, but hunger clawed her insides beyond the green's ability to satisfy it. She would have to eat flesh and hope the rest of the forest would forgive her.

She dropped from the limb and landed on one of the males' haunches, twisting her neck to avoid the horns. Something crunched. She darted her head forward and tore out its throat, ending its misery quickly. Swallowing the flesh as she pivoted, her claws still clamped onto the male's body, she belched ice, freezing the rest of the creatures to the spot. Would others of their kind return and seek her protection, as the nahrs had done, or would they avoid her, even to the point of starvation or running headlong into the bipeds' teeth? Arsiss hoped for the former but feared the latter. Once some being had slain members of your family, it was hard to trust them again.

She knew that all too well, having seen half a dozen of her kind hunted and bloodied and eventually slaughtered. The bipeds of her world had come in force, stomping the forest green into dirt and mud, kicking apart the beds and dens of untold innocents, and they had not come for life-sustaining meat or to defend their villages from some imagined predation. No, they had come with dreams of plunder and glory. They believed dragons hoarded shiny coins and sparkling jewels, never stopping to ask themselves why such should be true. Could you eat bright metals or drink sharp rocks that happened to glow in the light? What good would such objects be? No matter how many times the bipeds triumphed or ended their days in smoking heaps of charred bones, their surety never waned. Nor did the ways in which their world glorified the slaughter of dragons. Some of their greatest heroes attained that status through nothing more than outliving a dragon in a combat only the biped had sought. They kept the bare skulls of slain dragons—or, in most cases, of dead ones the bipeds found in the woods and claimed to have killed—and left them in the centers of their villages. They forged weapons from dragons' teeth and claws, shields from shed scales, jewelry from bones. How was this heroism? Why not monstrosity, this raging desire to kill creatures that only wished to be left alone?

Arsiss shook herself, willing these thoughts away. Better to get this distasteful moment behind her.

She backed away from the bodies, opened her mouth, and set the carcasses aflame, pouring hotter fire onto the frozen bodies, melting the ice that had killed them, and roasting their flesh. Like most of her kind, she preferred her meat cooked, when she had to eat meat at all. The thought of raw flesh gushing blood turned her stomach.

She grew bigger, and then she ate.

She had finished only half her meal when something behind her crackled. It happened again, and again. Footsteps. Something creeping through the woods, trying to be silent, failing. From the rhythm, a two-legged being. Arsiss grunted. She could never escape them. Yet she could not in good conscience abandon her kill. If she fled, leaving the carcasses to spoil and rot, these creatures' lives would have been wasted. When you took a living thing from the world, you gave up a part of yourself. Your life could never be completely your own because some portion of it belonged to the dead. You had to honor them. You had to honor yourself. Otherwise, the world devolved into waste.

And so, though her instincts urged her to flee deeper into the forest, Arsiss held her ground. She cloaked herself, hoping that would be enough, knowing it would not.

Soon—too soon—the biped blundered into sight. He must have spotted the burned creatures and the remains of those Arsiss had already consumed, because he froze in place, eyes wide, mouth open. A bright covering stretched over his chest and back. He wore a similarly colored piece on his head. Something had been slung over each of his shoulders. Arsiss did not know the precise nature of those objects, but she knew their genus—weapons.

From his pocket, he took a glass bottle filled with an amber liquid. He opened it and took a long drink. A strong smell wafted over; Arsiss recognized its like. The bipeds of her world had drunk a similar substance, which made them stagger through the forests like wounded beasts, shouting and shooting their arrows at nothing.

Still, she kept eating. Leaving her kill before she had converted it into fuel for her body and spirit would have been its own kind of death.

"I *knew* it!" cried the biped. "I knew you were real!" He must have seen her rip meat from the body, the carcass shiver and shift. But his shock was not her concern. Perhaps it would frighten him away.

Instead, he took another long drink and unslung one of his weapons. Now that she could see it all, she recognized it—a bow and arrow—though it looked different from those she had seen on her home world. This one appeared to be stronger, more lethal.

"I ain't scared of you!" he shouted. "I wasn't when I seen you last year, either, no matter what it looked like. Now I'm gonna prove it." Arsiss did not understand the language, but she recognized the action. He pulled an arrow from a container on his back, nocked it, and let it fly. It struck her in the side, crushed itself against her armored scales, and bounced away.

Arsiss tore off another hunk, chewed, and swallowed.

The intruder dropped his bow, drank again, and gripped his other weapon. This one she had never seen before—a long instrument with a piece that fit against the hollow of his shoulder, a cylindrical barrel pointing at her.

She took a bite, watching him.

The object in his hands came alive, the sound startling birds out of trees. Arsiss had never heard anything like it—several loud cracks like a tree exploding during a deep freeze. The sounds paused only when the biped took out part of his weapon and replaced it with another, similar part. He babbled as he attacked, so loud and angry that she could not differentiate his strange words from mere gibbering. This beast clearly believed in the absolute power of whatever he carried, in his own invincibility, even though he could not see what he confronted. Just like the two-leggers who had hunted her kind and everything else that breathed in the woods, as if the world had been made for them and their kind alone. As if this weapon and his use of it grew naturally from the very fact of his own existence.

But sad little beings like him had little effect on Arsiss the Gentle. She ate.

"Gonna kill you," said the biped, swaying on his feet. "Show you I ain't scared. Show everybody." Then he charged, a headlong stumble, as if he had forgotten how to run.

Arsiss turned toward him and made herself visible. He skidded to a halt, fell on his backside, skittered backward through the forest refuse. She snarled deep in her throat, a warning, if he had brains enough to understand. But now he was screaming. He threw his almost-empty bottle at her. It sailed wide.

Perhaps he had never seen her kind before. Perhaps he regretted his empty bravado.

No. He stood, stumbled backward still holding his noisemaker, and then braced himself, raising it to his shoulder again. More of those loud cracks. Whatever the weapon fired bounced off her face and chest.

Arsiss thrust her head forward and shot blood from her eyes. Some missed him as he leaped back, but much of it struck him in the face and chest, knocking him back down. Again he screamed, for her blood ran hot, and she suspected his pale and almost hairless skin provided little protection. She backed away and sat next to her kill. The sheer noise he had made would likely drive away any creatures that might have otherwise wandered into his field of fire, but she had warned him twice now. If he came at her a third time, she would stop him, for the little ones' sakes.

Sure enough, he stood, stumbled, flung her blood from his face and hands. "Get outta my woods," he sputtered. "This is America, goddammit!"

He raised his weapon.

He fired.

Arsiss inhaled, opened her mouth, and spat a tongue of flame. It struck the biped and engulfed him, set the ground afire, and sent small licks into the lower-hanging branches of nearby trees. She had used a low-intensity flame, so he was not consumed at once. He kept screaming, his voice going higher and higher until it vanished. The weapon fell. The biped stumbled about, blind, until he fell to his knees, then onto his face.

His burning body sent acrid, bitter smoke high into the air.

Arsiss iced over the flames before turning back to her kill and wolfing down the rest. Then she walked deeper into the forest. A profound sadness gripped her heart—all that death, and some of it wasteful after all.

CHAPTER TWELVE

Kenneth and Ty found seats in the theater's middle row. Ty tucked her purse between her body and the armrest. She squeezed Kenneth's hand before he went back to the lobby for popcorn and Cokes. He liked the theater in Monticello better, but this one, the Cotton Valley Cinema 8 in New Everton, sold cheaper concessions. He still couldn't believe he had gotten a whole weekend off, though it was going to be hard to enjoy it. They'd just heard about Marla Schott's father. Another funeral Kenneth would have to attend, since Brayden was still dating Marla. Those two had broken up and gotten back together half a dozen times since sophomore year, but now Brayden wouldn't leave her side except when he had to go to class or home for the night. Kenneth had never really thought much about Marla. She was hot, sure, but she had always had the personality of a rabid porcupine. Brayden must have seen something in her, though—maybe the way Ty had recognized something worthwhile in Kenneth.

There was no way Ty hadn't heard about the shit he'd pulled before the Freaks turned his world upside down and he learned how it felt to be an outcast. Growing up as a macho straight white guy in small-town Arkansas, he had accepted without question the way most Quapaw City neighborhoods were still segregated, how so many of the old white people he knew believed other races were loud and promiscuous and either too smart for their own good or way too dumb. He was ashamed to admit it now, but he honestly hadn't considered how screwed up it all was until he had been forced to spend time with Jamie and Gabby and Christian. *Real* time. Time that made him see them as people and not just targets or types.

Most folks probably still thought of him as a bigot, the asshole most likely to punch you or share an embarrassing video of you all over social media. So why in God's name was Ty with him? She could have easily done better. Even Kenneth knew that.

He carried a large buttered popcorn and two large Cokes back to theater seven. Ty had wanted to see the new rom-com *Before It's All Over*. The very thought made him want to gag, but he had smiled and nodded, had given Mom some cash and gotten her to buy their tickets online, and had picked Ty up early enough to get seated well before the commercials and the trailers started. He preferred action or horror. Gooey shit about relationships didn't excite him. But there was another weird truth: ever since meeting Ty, he had never been able to deny her anything she wanted. All his old tough-guy posturing and his disdain for girly, wimpy shit simply washed away in her presence, like he had written his old self in the sand just before high tide.

He thought back to a conversation he'd had with Christian earlier in the week. Another sign of the times—confiding in a Freak. For more than a year, Christian and Bec had stayed together, had seemed happy despite the whole Rabbit mess, despite how some people talked shit about them. Maybe Christian had a secret she could share, something that would help him accept his awesome luck and stop waiting for that other shoe to drop.

"I mean, it's not like I'm out there marching with Black Lives Matter or women in pussy hats," he had said.

"Truth," said Christian.

"So what's up? Am I, like, a project? She says I'm not, but I don't know. Does she think she can change me? Make me a better person?"

"Dude," Christian had said, laughing and shaking her head. "She ain't no manic pixie dream girl."

"A what?"

"The girl who's in the movie just to help the guy change or reach his goals. Those characters aren't people, just tools."

"I didn't say Ty was any of that shit!"

"Maybe not, but you gotta be careful, bruh. She's got her own life. Her own dreams. She's a person."

That conversation had really chapped Kenneth's ass. These days, it seemed like if you were a guy and you said anything negative about any woman, ever, *you* were the asshole. He had just wanted someone to explain what Ty could have seen in him. He hadn't needed a damn lecture on sexual politics and gender roles.

Still, Christian's words had echoed in his head ever since, and he hadn't put the question to Ty herself. Christian was right about that much: Ty wasn't some minor, one-dimensional character in a story about him. He wanted this relationship, however long it lasted, to be *their* story. Part of that meant telling her about the Freaks, sooner or later. But not tonight. He and Ty deserved a little fun, a little relaxation.

Kenneth managed to open the theater doors and edge his way in without spilling any popcorn or dropping the Cokes. The theater had filled maybe halfway up, so when he got to the row he and Ty had picked, he had to ease past half a dozen people's knees. At least there were no little kids yet. In fact, though this movie was rated PG-13, he and Ty seemed to be the only people here under the age of thirty.

Ty was scrolling on her phone, but she turned it off and put it in her pocket as he approached. She took the popcorn and a Coke so he could sit down. Kenneth wiped his buttery hands on his pants and glanced toward the back of the theater. Then he did a double take.

Kragthorpe and Vincent sat directly behind them, five rows up. When they saw Kenneth looking, Kragthorpe grinned and waved.

Kenneth glared at them. Assholes. Couldn't a man even take his lady to a damn movie without being harassed? He had half a mind to march back there and get in their faces.

Ty had balanced the popcorn in her lap. With her free hand, she took him by the wrist and gently tugged. He looked at her. Those kind brown eyes disarmed him. All his anger faded away.

She held out the tub of popcorn. He took some, ate it, drank some Coke. Ty stuck her drink in her cupholder and snaked her arm through his. How strange it still was to see her dark skin against his. But there was no question that he was changing, and not just because Ty had moved to town. It had started before that, when he had first wondered what had ever bothered him so much about comic books and smart kids and role-playing games. When it had first occurred to him that maybe he had wasted a whole lot of time being mad about stuff that had never affected him at all. No, maybe some people would see his relationship with Ty as the next step in his evolution, but to Kenneth, it felt more like he had simply stopped fighting against the most natural thing in the world—opening yourself up to good, kind people who could also see the good in you.

So let those pricks stare at the back of his head. He had come here to be with Ty. The rest of the world fell away when they touched.

Even when he had to watch a rom-com.

An hour and forty-five minutes later, Kenneth and Ty walked arm in arm out of the theater. On the way home, Ty sat against the passenger door, scrolling on her phone. The waxing crescent moon provided a little light, but the road mostly ribboned into darkness beyond the reach of the headlights. Kenneth kept a close eye on the ditches and woods to either side. Every time he saw a pair of eyes or the graceful bodies of deer, his foot crept over the brake. In this part of the world, deer were often suicidal. They'd run right in front of you.

In the rearview mirror, a pair of headlights kept a steady pace several lengths back. Probably the feds. Assholes.

Kenneth had turned on the radio and found a station playing classic rock. Not his favorite genre, but better than the country and gospel stations. Man, he couldn't wait until he could update the stereo. Get some USB connects, maybe satellite radio. Twenty-first century stuff.

"You didn't say much about the movie," said Ty.

Kenneth started. He had fallen into the rhythm of the road. "Um. It was okay."

"I'ma convert you yet."

"Ha. I doubt it."

"You been clocking all those glowing eyes between the road and the woods?"

"Yeah. Deer. Let me know if you see any real close to the shoulder. Or if one makes a run at us."

"Okay."

They fell back into silence. That was one way Kenneth had known how much he really liked Ty; they could sit quietly for a long time and never feel awkward.

Those headlights were keeping pace. A part of Kenneth wanted to slam on the brakes, just to see what would happen. Even if the feds rear-ended them, it might be funny to let the Team try to explain to the state troopers why they were following two high school kids so closely on a dark country road. But no, he would never take a risk like that with Ty in the car.

Truth is, I think I'd let the Team run me over and set this truck on fire first. Does that mean I love her? How the hell did that happen?

When Ty spoke again, she knocked those thoughts right out of his head. "You never talk much about Gavin."

It felt like she had hit Kenneth upside the head with a brick. That would never have made a list of things he had expected her to say. Gavin had been murdered two years before Ty even came to town. Kenneth couldn't remember the last time he or Brayden had mentioned their old friend. Talking about him felt about as good as dragging a cheese grater across your face. Usually at least once in every conversation, Kenneth and Brayden would realize one of them had been about to mention Gavin, and they would both shut up, shut down, verbally walk about ten miles out of the way so they could keep up the illusion that he had never existed. None of that was fair to the guy's memory, but some things just hurt too much.

Ty had said nothing else, hadn't even looked at him. She watched the road and the occasional deer, glanced at her phone when it dinged, and let him think. Something else to love about her, that she believed he could and did think. Most people would have disagreed.

"It's a sore subject," he finally said. "Me and Gavin, we kind of fell out just before he died. Thinking about it makes me feel like shit."

She put a hand on his shoulder. "I don't mean to hurt you. But if you ever wanna talk about him, I'll listen."

"He was one of my best friends. One of my *only* friends, if you wanna know the truth. We had this stupid fight and barely talked for weeks, and then something killed him."

"What was the fight about?"

I got superpowers and freaked him out. "Just some stupid crap. Like I said, I don't really talk about it."

"Okay." She pulled her hand back, checked her phone, put it in her lap.

After a while, Kenneth said, "I miss him. He wouldn't have liked you, though."

"Because I'm Black."

"Yeah."

"And you wouldn't have liked me much then either."

"Maybe. But it seems stupid to think so now."

"Racism *is* stupid."

"Yeah."

They were hitting the outskirts of Quapaw City. The houses on both sides of the road grew more numerous. They passed two or three streetlights per mile, then more. Soon Kenneth would turn off the main road and take Ty home, but still those damn headlights followed them. One of these nights he was going to find Mossman under his bed.

"You got new friends now, though."

"Yeah."

"They're cool, K. Maybe I can come to some more game nights with you? If they're important to you, they're important to me."

Kenneth scoffed. "Sure, if you wanna. But hell, *I* don't wanna go most of the time. I'm still half afraid I'll catch geek."

"Stop it."

"What? It's true. I ain't half as good as you think I am." Even after everything that had happened in the last few years, he still got irritated when the other Freaks went on and on and on about all their geek shit.

"I don't believe that. But if you think it's true, it's up to you to do something about it. You can't just keep repeating that bullshit about geeks or whatever. It's like you're determined to stay that way."

"Hmm."

He pulled onto her street, face burning. Was Ty right? Was he sabotaging himself, maybe trying to do some kind of half-assed penance? How messed up would *that* be?

Kenneth didn't open his mouth again until he walked Ty to her door and kissed her goodnight. After Ty had closed her door and Kenneth had gotten back in his truck, he sat there for a while, hands on the wheel. The Team car was gone. Thank God for that much, because he had other things on his mind.

For instance, if goodness shone out of his ass like a flashlight beam, then why did he still feel so hinky when he thought of what his family might be saying behind his back? *We taught him better than that. Next thing you know he'll be eating chitlins and collard greens.* He had seen those kinds of ideas for what they truly were, ugly and outdated and hateful, but he was also just a kid who wanted his parents to be proud of him. How long before Ty realized he was still just a piece of garbage? How long before she gave up, knowing she could do so much better? And if a sweet, smart, open-minded girl like her couldn't love him, who would?

Ty's bedroom light turned on. Her shadow moved behind the curtains. When the light went out, Kenneth drove away.

CHAPTER THIRTEEN

When Micah dragged himself out of bed around one thirty on Saturday afternoon, Baltar was sitting on the couch, a crumb-covered plate on the cushion beside him, earbuds in and snaking down to his phone. His eyes were closed. Micah had seldom seen him doing things most people did, like watching TV or checking sports scores, but maybe he liked music or podcasts about cannibal serial killers or something. Or maybe he had downloaded one of those positive affirmation apps: *You are the best little wizard in the world. The shaved-head aesthetic looks good on you. Keep filing those pearly whites.* Another night of interrupted sleep and terrible dreams had kicked Micah's ass, so he let the old dude snooze and went to the kitchen, where he put on a pot of coffee and fixed an enormous bowl of cereal. His appetite had never really returned, but he needed to keep his body fueled, and so every day he shoveled down food he barely tasted until his stomach threatened to send it all back up. Even that was getting harder, though. Yesterday, he had forgotten to eat until nearly ten p.m., and even then, one peanut butter sandwich had done the trick. No chips. A small glass of milk. Someone his age should have been practically eating his weight in junk food and red meat, but everything tasted like cardboard, and much of it ran right through him. If he had known, he would have bought shares in toilet paper companies. The other Freaks had noticed and sometimes bugged him about eating more, but what could they do, hold him down and stuff a pizza down his throat or make his stomach behave? As for Baltar, either he hadn't paid much attention, or he didn't care. A dude that skinny probably thought eating, like, four baby carrots a day counted as good nutrition.

Micah pulled his jeans away from his waist. It wasn't hard. He was still losing at least a few ounces a week, and he hadn't had much meat on his bones in the first place. Ironic—he looked more physically fit than ever, but his energy reserves had never been lower. Could Baltar find a spell to settle upset stomachs? Now *that* would be useful.

After finishing the cereal and rinsing out the bowl, Micah sat in his father's easy chair and kicked back with the remote. He turned on the TV but kept the volume low. Otherwise, his great-uncle would probably take out those earbuds and start a conversation. Man, it would have been nice if Micah could have streamed on his own TV. It wasn't big, but it would have been better than his phone. Mom and Dad had never gotten more than one streaming device, though. *If you could watch TV in your room, we'd never see you.* Well, now they were both dead, and since Baltar seemed not to care about shows or hanging out, why the hell couldn't they bring Micah's room a little further into this century? Get something good out of the shit sandwich the world had served him.

Baltar stirred and removed his earbuds. "I have been scouring the local news, from the Little Rock television affiliates to this town's AM radio station. Human remains have been discovered in the woods."

All the complaints and annoyances blasted right out of Micah's head. "Whose? Where?"

"The authorities have not released the location, other than the general descriptors 'out in the woods.' As you know, that could describe half this state."

Sitting on the couch's armrest and taking out his phone, Micah said, "I wonder if Jamie and them know."

Baltar rolled up his earbud wires and dropped them into his shirt pocket. "I would advise that Jamie or Christian use the stealth charms and investigate. This may need our attention."

"Way ahead of you," said Micah, tapping rapidly. The whole situation might turn out to be ordinary—a hunting accident or a health crisis, no phone signal, no one to hear screams. Or the dragon might have done it. That actually might be the better situation, because it could force Gabby and Christian to drop their sympathy bullshit.

Baltar got up and puttered around the kitchen. Micah slid onto the couch proper and waited for a reply. Odd how he didn't feel any real anxiety or excitement or even rage, just mild curiosity about what would happen next. A human being had died, probably someone from town. Time was, that kind of news would have put him on edge. He might have known the person, might have even liked them. Now? He felt about the same way he did when one of his friends' parents got a new car—sort of interested, but not invested. Maybe his sleep problems had affected his ability to process stuff like this. Or maybe he was losing touch with the world, unable to feel much beyond anger at the Team and supernatural, parent-killing forces. Maybe—

Someone knocked on the front door.

At the same time, Micah's phone chirped twice. He wanted to see what the others had written, but Baltar hadn't come out of the kitchen. Cursing, Micah jammed his phone in his pocket and went to door.

Five men stood on his front walk. Mossman, Kragthorpe, and Vincent had taken the center positions. They wore their usual suits and sunglasses. Mossman's left sleeve dangled from the wrist. Hadn't Micah seen him wearing a prosthetic at some point? Why not wear it now—to send some signal to the local cops? Mean Old Teenager Somehow Responsible for Homeland Security Agent's Maiming? Anyway, no guns were visible, but Micah would have bet his house that they had come strapped. Mossman and Kragthorpe, anyway. Those guys were the Team's pet Nazis. No way they'd walk up on a Freak without their artificial courage.

Chief Mark O'Brien and Officer Lyman Heck flanked the feds. Heck's arms were crossed over his chest. O'Brien's hands were in his pants pockets. His uniform hat was tucked in his right armpit. His eyes looked like chips of gray rock.

Baltar appeared behind Micah. The feds kept their faces expression-less even though their body language screamed tension. "Yes?" asked Baltar.

"We'd like to speak to Micah," said Mossman. The other two didn't move. They were staring at Micah. He couldn't feel other people's emotions like Jamie, but their dislike and anger were written on their cold faces.

"Concerning . . . ?" asked Baltar. "Surely you gentlemen have better things to do than harass children."

"Hey," said Micah. He *hated* being called a child. And, though he could barely find enough energy to care these days, he also hated it when some adult tried to speak for him. Just because he wasn't sixteen thousand years old like Baltar didn't mean he needed a mouthpiece.

"May we come in?" asked Mossman, though it didn't really sound like a request.

O'Brien opened his mouth and started to move forward, but Baltar shouldered his way next to Micah. *Dude, back the hell up.* "You don't need to come in," the old man said in that same deep, soothing preacher's voice he used when trying to talk Micah into going to bed early. "And I can assure you that Micah has done nothing wrong."

The feds' jaws slackened a little. Vincent swayed. Even O'Brien faltered, while Heck actually opened his mouth and drooled, his gaze blank and far away. Baltar was whammying them. *These aren't the droids you're looking for.*

Well, screw that. Micah wasn't afraid of anybody, especially not these petty little fascists. He hip-checked Baltar and stepped in front of the old man. "Come on in," he said. "I got nothing to hide. If we had known you were coming, we would have baked cookies." It was hard to imagine a bigger, more outlandish lie than *I got nothing to hide.* He had more to hide than most career criminals.

Mossman shook his head and seemed to snap back to reality. "We appreciate that," he said, almost certainly lying.

"No problem." Micah stepped aside and ushered everyone in. "Always nice when the federal and local authorities stop by for a little chat and some good old-fashioned crapping on private citizens." Baltar scowled. Micah ignored him.

Mossman's eyes narrowed, but he said nothing. O'Brien cleared his throat and shook his head. The locals had probably come to protect the Sternes. Hilarious, like the half-assed Quapaw City police force could do jack shit against what threatened Micah. He supposed he should have felt grateful for the effort, but like so many other emotions, he just couldn't access it.

As O'Brien and Heck followed the feds past them, Baltar squinted at Micah, who shrugged, grinned, and shut the door, brushing past the old fart and gesturing toward the couch. The feds sat, Mossman in the middle. The locals stood behind them, arms crossed. Kragthorpe and Vincent removed their glasses. Mossman didn't. Sometimes it seemed like that dude had night-vision eyeballs. Micah took Dad's chair again. Baltar stood beside him.

"Can you account for your whereabouts on the twenty-fourth?" asked Mossman, getting right to it. Good. Micah wanted this done as soon as possible.

"Why?" asked Baltar. How freaking irritating. Couldn't the old man see that Micah wanted to handle this?

"Let him answer the question, Gramps," Kragthorpe said with a smile that looked about as genuine as a three-dollar bill.

"Mr. Sterne is Micah's legal guardian," O'Brien said, still watching Micah with some combination of protective concern and suspicion.

"That is correct," the old dude said, an edge in his voice. "Tread carefully, or I will terminate this interview."

"Sure," said Mossman. "Maybe you already know about this. Sometime on that date, a local man named Elvis Schott went hunting. He never came home."

"Elvis?" said Micah. "Marla's dad?"

Vincent, who had been scribbling in a small notebook even though nothing of note had been revealed, flipped through his pages and nodded. "That's right. The girl's in your grade, correct?"

"Yeah," said Micah. Marla was a stuck-up bitch who barely acknowledged his existence, but they were the same age, in a few of the same classes. Micah offered none of that information to the Team. If they didn't already know, they could look it up their damn selves.

"Your whereabouts?" said Mossman. The dude had a good poker face. He might as well have been asking about the best temperature for heating up frozen pizza.

Micah looked from one fed to another. "I was in school all day. After that, me and Jamie Entmann went to the City Café. He bought me a grilled cheese sandwich and a Coke. Our server's name was Meg. After that, I came straight home. Watched some TV. Listened to some tunes. Did a little homework. Then I played video games until bedtime."

Vincent and Kragthorpe both cut their eyes at Mossman, but that spooky one-handed asshole still didn't react. He crossed his legs. "You know, the people we interview aren't usually this prepared. Most of them have to think about where they were and what they were doing, and even then, there are usually gaps in their day."

Micah shrugged. "Maybe they're just old. Anyway, it was only two days ago."

"Still."

"Jeez, what do you want from me? If I don't remember everywhere I went and everything I did, you suspect me of something. If I do remember it all, you suspect me anyway."

"Take it easy," said O'Brien.

"Or what?" asked Micah. "You'll arrest me for getting mad?"

"The child has a point," Baltar said before O'Brien could reply. That word again, *child*. Had he used it just to bug Micah? "I have heard you found a body burned to ash. Only a handful of bone fragments remained."

Micah started. This time, even Mossman seemed surprised. "I'd be very interested to know your source," said the fed.

"I have my ways."

"We can't confirm or deny," Kragthorpe said. "But let's pretend that's true. Who can incinerate a full-grown human body without burning down the woods around it? Maybe the same unsub who attacked the football field a couple of years back. I wonder who that guy was?"

Mossman leaned forward, elbows on his knees. Micah could see himself reflected in those stupid sunglasses.

"This bullshit again," said Micah. Whenever he truly felt something these days, it always seemed to be anger. "God, how many times do I have to tell you *I don't know anything about that*?"

"Micah," hissed O'Brien.

"Gentlemen—" Baltar began.

"No, hold on," said Mossman. "Micah, you say you're tired of the bullshit. Okay, let's cut through it. We know what you are and what you can do. Maybe you're responsible for Elvis Schott's death. Maybe Lex Luthor here is helping you cover it up."

Mossman's words, Kragthorpe's and Vincent's hungry and suspicious gazes, cleared the remaining fog from Micah's mind, reached into the deepest parts of him, and tapped his anger, his frustration, his hate. These dickheads had hunted him, accused him of being a terrorist when all he had done was save this stupid town. They'd bugged his phone and his computer and his house, harassed his friends, kidnapped and tortured Christian, nearly killed Del Ray. Every single move Micah made, every single word he spoke, had to be chosen carefully, like life had turned into a never-ending standardized test designed to trip him up. In one sense, his brain fog had been a blessing; without it, he might have developed a bleeding ulcer or panic attacks. These feds were responsible for at least half of that. Now more accusations. He wanted to show them what he could do when he wanted somebody dead. He wanted to freeze Vincent to the couch and roast

Kragthorpe like a big-ass marshmallow and give Mossman a taste of both, maybe freeze his left side and burn the other to a crisp, right here and right now—

Baltar's hand fell on his shoulder. Micah realized he was trembling, clenching his fists, letting his energy build to a point where a single wisp of steam had risen above each hand, thin and gone in a split second. Had the feds seen it? They seemed focused on his face, but what if—?

"I believe that's enough," his great-uncle was saying. "Micah has answered your question. You can check with the school and with this Meg person. And I can confirm that he did not leave this house once he came home."

"Not that you'd lie for him," Kragthorpe said, still staring at Micah.

"Not that you're a tool," said Micah.

"Listen, you little shit—"

"Leave our house this instant," Baltar said, calmly but firmly.

Micah glanced at his great-uncle, who had fixed those spooky eyes on Mossman's face. For the fed, it must have been like staring down a dangerous animal that had singled you out for dinner.

For a moment, none of the feds moved. O'Brien circled the sofa and stood in front of them. Heck joined him. "You heard the man," said the chief. "Time to go."

The feds wouldn't look at O'Brien. The moment stretched out, Micah gripping the chair's arms, willing himself not to burst into flame. Then Mossman got up, straightened his jacket, and gestured for the other two to follow. Vincent did, though Kragthorpe took a few beats, still staring a hole in Micah. When he stood too, O'Brien led them to the door. As they exited, Micah got up, and he and Baltar moved into the doorway and stood shoulder to shoulder with their arms crossed. They probably looked like they were shooting an album cover.

Mossman looked back over his shoulder. "We're not done, boy."

"Yeah, okay," said Micah. "Make sure you get a side of fries next time you eat a dick."

Kragthorpe laughed. Micah would have sworn the corners of Chief O'Brien's mouth twitched. Even if he suspected Micah, the man clearly had no love for the Team.

Baltar shut the door. Funny—that fog seemed to be descending over Micah's mind and senses again. The rage was fading like a stubborn filament in a lightbulb someone had just turned off. Only its afterimage remained.

What was happening to him?

"Those odious men," Baltar said, his brows knitted. At moments like this, he reminded Micah of Sam the Eagle from *Muppet Treasure Island*, only not funny. "If there is truly a dragon in those woods, I hope it eats them."

Micah laughed, but without much energy. God, he was tired. Baltar had just shown more personality than he had in the last two years, but with every passing second, it seemed to matter less and less. As did the Team's visit and their suspicions. Let them come after him. He would show them what a body looked like when he wanted it to burn. He would show them all.

"Perhaps our lives would be easier if something happened to those agents," said Baltar.

Whoa, the old dude was *pissed*. That should have intrigued Micah, even made him a little proud. Instead, it just felt like another boring event in a dull day, as momentous as a leaf falling off a tree or a dog scratching itself. Micah didn't even answer; he went into his room, closed the door, and fired up his console. He played games for three hours without really paying much attention to what he was doing, and when he went to bed, he realized just before he drifted off that he had not eaten supper.

In dreams, he returned to that long, flat, barren field. The mountainous creature waited in the distance. It told him to burn the men who tormented him. To burn their dwelling. To burn the woods, the town.

To burn the world.

CHAPTER FOURTEEN

The day after the Team visited Micah, Jamie stood in a ditch near the woods and gripped his stealth charm, which hung under his shirt. Two Team SUVs were bearing down on the Freaks, so it was too late to use the charm. No one had gotten into costume yet. If a bunch of teenagers just vanished in front of the feds, that would end the Freaks' shot at any kind of normal life. Besides, they had driven out here. Jamie doubted the feds would believe that a bunch of vigilantes had just happened to borrow the prime suspects' cars.

Kenneth and Brayden had brought their ATVs. Baltar had agreed to run interference if the Team got bold and knocked on the Sternes' door again, so long as the Freaks would bring him any evidence they found so he could analyze it. That had seemed reasonable. Jamie, Micah, and Christian had ridden out with Gabby. They had not expected company, but maybe they should have. At least no one was shooting at them. Yet.

"Everybody cool out," said Jamie. Kenneth and Brayden backed their four-wheelers out of the trucks on portable ramps. Then they shut off the engines and sat there, waiting.

The feds parked only feet behind the Freaks' cars. After a moment, the doors opened, and Mossman, Greenwalt, Vincent, and Jeffcoat climbed out. Jamie barely recognized them. Their usual government suits had been replaced with camo outfits and orange vests and caps, like they had gone down to Monroe and raided the Duck Commander gift shop. Mossman still wore his sunglasses.

"Howdy, y'all," Mossman said in an exaggerated Southern accent.

Jamie raised his chin. Micah grumbled something and turned away. The others barely reacted. Good. Better not to take the bait.

Now a third vehicle rounded the curve, an extended-cab pickup pulling a flatbed trailer holding two ATVs, larger and fancier than Kenneth's and Brayden's. This truck's windows hadn't been tinted. Kragthorpe was driving. He parked, killed the engine, and got out. Like his friends, he had worn hunter's orange. Unlike them, he had skipped the camo in favor of cargo pants, boat shoes, and a long-sleeved sweatshirt with a UCLA Bruins logo. Jamie shook his head. The winter wind would probably cut right through those pants, and who in the world thought it was a good idea not to wear socks in the woods?

"The hell y'all doing out here?" asked Jamie.

"It seemed like a good day for a drive," said Mossman. Jamie wanted to knock those sunglasses off his stupid face. "Fancy meeting you here, on the exact spot the locals used as a staging area when they retrieved Elvis Schott's body."

Jamie tried to look surprised. "Huh. That *is* weird. We're just here to keep Kenneth and Brayden company while they clean up their lease and lay down some fresh corn."

"Maybe we'll see you out there."

"Maybe so." Jamie turned to his friends and gestured for them to follow him. He led them a good way from the vehicles and talked in a whisper. "Change of plans. No costumes, no powers, no fighting unless we get attacked. Just recon. Since me and Christian can't use our powers, two of us will have to stay here. I ain't breaking my tailbone trying to ride on the gas tank or some shit."

"Me and Brayden gotta drive," said Kenneth.

"I know. Micah, you ride with Brayden. If shit goes down, you got a good chance of holding it off till the rest of us get there. Christian, go with Kenneth. You can get back here the fastest and let me and Gabby know if anything happens. We'll stay here and watch the road."

Christian nodded. "Text us if anything happens."

"Like we'll have a signal out there," said Micah.

"If it comes to that, I'll use my stealth charm and fly out," said Jamie.

"Y'all be careful. Turn up your senses. If you spot anything, try to find a landmark we can recognize later."

"Got it," said Kenneth. "I can't believe those dicks knew enough to wear orange."

The group split up. Kenneth and Christian climbed onto his ATV and led Brayden and Micah into the woods. A minute later, Mossman and Vincent rode double on one of those big-ass monsters they had brought. Kragthorpe and Jeffcoat followed. Jamie felt no surprise at all when the Team took the same route Kenneth had chosen.

"I hope they don't get eaten," said Gabby. "Well, maybe Mossman and Kragthorpe."

Greenwalt had stayed behind. To watch Jamie and Gabby? To guard the vehicles? Because the feds couldn't count well enough to bring three ATVs? Now he was walking their way.

"Nice day," Greenwalt said, looking at the sky. "I never get tired of the air in places like this. Little Rock isn't exactly Cleveland in the 1960s, but it's not this, either."

Jamie had no idea what he was talking about. "Probably a good idea for you to stay here. If your friends get lost, you can call for help." This was pure flex; Jamie couldn't navigate the woods, either, unless he flew above them.

Greenwalt laughed. Then he nodded at Gabby. "Miss Davison."

She raised a hand briefly. "Hi, I guess."

"You two ready to come in yet? You're not the only ones I'm talking to, and it's going to work pretty much like it does on TV. First ones to cooperate get the deal. The slowpokes ride free all the way to maximum security, plus they win three hots and a cot for the rest of their lives."

Jamie tried to keep his expression neutral and hoped Gabby would do the same. They couldn't let any of the feds sweat them. But who else might Greenwalt be talking to? Or was he bullshitting?

"Come in where and do what?" asked Gabby. "We're just teenagers chilling in the woods. Didn't know that was a crime."

Jamie tried not to smile. *Go, baby. Kick his ass.*

"Sure. The same teenagers who always show up at ground zero for bizarre occurrences and brutal violence. Just a series of coincidences, I'm sure."

"Huh," said Jamie. "I didn't know y'all could be sarcastic."

"We can also be generous. For instance, if you were to work with us, help us get the real troublemakers and baby terrorists out of your group, I could probably sell my bosses on the idea of training you to work for the government. Maybe even replace us someday. And you wouldn't have to hide anymore, not from the authorities, anyway."

Jamie felt like Greenwalt had bopped him over the head with a giant cartoon mallet. He never would have guessed that any member of the Team would conceive of such an idea, much less say it out loud. He must have looked as surprised as he felt, because Greenwalt smiled, just a little. Gabby crossed her arms and turned away, watching the woods. She leaned against her car and kept her mouth shut. Not a bad strategy, because what could they really say? Greenwalt had to know they wouldn't accept those terms. If not, he had badly misjudged them.

"Still don't know what you're talking about, bruh," said Jamie.

"We can't do this dance forever. Your little scout troop's been more careful than I ever would have believed a bunch of teenagers could be, but you'll slip up sooner or later. And then I won't be able to help you."

"I doubt you've got our best interests at heart," said Jamie. "Not when you spend half your time threatening us."

"It's not a threat. It's a practical assessment of your future. Now, if you were to provide crucial information that leads to the arrest and conviction of, say, Micah Sterne or Kenneth Del Ray or both, things might be different."

Jamie groaned. "I knew y'all was after Micah, but Kenneth? Why him and not me, or Christian?"

"He attacked your classroom when you were freshmen. Don't even bother denying it. Sterne has the fire-and-ice powers. Del Ray's your strong guy. We know it, even if we can't prove it."

"God, just leave us *alone*," Gabby said, still watching the trees. "We just wanna hang and be quiet. Take the freaking hint."

Greenwalt shrugged. "Okay. But that sound you hear is a ticking clock." He walked back to the SUVs and leaned on one.

Jamie turned and put his arm around Gabby. The wind whispered in the trees. They wondered when their friends might come back. Keeping their voices low, they talked of homework and video games and whether they should take a break from pizza and grab some burgers or barbecue for the next game night. Greenwalt kept to himself, eventually getting back in an SUV. Probably bored and cold, though he did not start the engine. Soon after that, Gabby suggested they get out of the wind, so they started her car and turned on the heater. Jamie closed his eyes and tried to listen deep into the woods, but he heard nothing unusual. Even the ATVs' motors sounded natural in a place where people practically lived in the woods. The conversations he could pick up mostly amounted to *Let's try over that hill next* and *Close the distance some, or they're gonna lose us.*

Around an hour later, the other Freaks drove out of the woods. Jamie and Gabby got out and spoke to them in whispers. According to Christian, no one had seen, heard, or smelled anything except each other. Nothing had happened. Either the dragon had moved on, or it had done an even better job of hiding than usual. After the debrief, Jamie helped load up the ATVs. The Team had come back, too, but they secured their vehicles without a word and drove away.

Well, now *what?*

CHAPTER FIFTEEN

After school, Gabby parked outside Pizza of Mind and asked Bec, who was riding shotgun, to reach into the glove compartment and get her wallet. Bec handed it to her. From the back seat, Christian swore as something went wrong on whatever game she was playing on her phone. Ty laughed and pointed at something on Christian's screen. When Christian finished, they all headed inside. The "Please Seat Yourself" sign was posted on the hostess stand, so they walked past the buffet and took a window booth in the back corner. Gabby sat with her back to the wall under an Iron Maiden poster, the cover of their *Killers* album. Their ghoulish mascot—Eddie? Ernie?—seemed to be reaching for them with one hand; the other one held a bloody hatchet. She had seen that poster a million times, but now it occurred to her that the Freaks could run across something like Eddie/Ernie in real life. They had already fought a four-armed vampire and an immortal, shapeshifting trickster. Now they were hunting a dragon. Why not a tool-using zombie?

Jamie and Christian had been patrolling the woods whenever they got a chance. No sign of the dragon. That was fine with Gabby. The boys' hunger for killing it hadn't waned. Gabby had hoped that shit was just a blip for Jamie, and the fact that he hadn't backed down disturbed her. This whole the-enemy-must-die deal wasn't like him.

A twentysomething woman with frizzy dark hair and cat-eye glasses came over to take their order. Everyone wanted the buffet. Big shock. The server nodded, wrote it on her pad, and put four red plastic glasses on the table. After Gabby and the others had piled their plates high, they tucked into their food. Christian and Bec sat close together and exchanged lovey-dovey glances. They sometimes even fed each other. The way one took a bite of the other's slice seemed almost . . . erotic. Ugh, Gabby did *not* want to picture her friends' sex lives. She wasn't even comfortable picturing her own, even though it didn't really exist yet. With those two wrapped up in each other, Gabby and Ty talked as they ate, about everything from school projects to Kenneth and Jamie to when the next game night might be.

Up front, the door opened. Someone walked inside, paused at the hostess station, and moved into the dining room. Gabby glanced up and did a double take.

Oh, you son of a bitch.

Chip Mossman took a booth on the other side of the room. As usual, he wore his dark suit, his tie, and his stupid shades. He would have looked more at home in some fancy big-city restaurant with jacked-up prices and portions the size of a candy bar. He took one of the flimsy napkins from the rectangular metal dispenser on his table, then made a show of unfolding it and tucking it into his collar. Gabby couldn't be sure because of the glasses, but he seemed to be staring at her, or maybe at the back of Christian's head.

The same server took his order and gave him his glass. He pushed it aside, put his elbows on the table, and kept watching.

Gabby ate. If he wanted to stare, fine. She wouldn't let him ruin her day. She even got up for a refill and another two slices, looking Mossman in the face as she passed, careful to keep her expression neutral. Today, he was just another guy in a restaurant. She would not give him the satisfaction of seeming rattled.

But something must have registered on her face. As she sat back down, Christian studied her a moment. "Okay, what's up?"

"Nothing," said Gabby.

Christian turned, spotted Mossman, grunted. Then she returned to her food. When she wasn't chewing, her jaw clenched.

"Okay, now what's up with *you*?" asked Bec. "You look like

somebody took all the 2 Minutes to Mushrooms." Christian shook her head and didn't answer. Bec looked at Gabby, eyebrows raised. Gabby wouldn't meet their gaze. "Really? You're both gonna pretend nothing just changed?"

Ty's brow wrinkled. "This a private situation or something? Should I give y'all some space?"

"That's a good question," said Bec. "I'd like to know the answer too."

Gabby and Christian kept eating. Bec dropped their slice and swiveled. It would have been a great time for the whole place to be packed with teenage couples and families with four or five screaming, sticky kids. Unfortunately, Mossman was the only other diner. Bec watched him for a minute before they wiped their hands and turned toward Christian.

"Don't," said Christian.

"Let me out," said Bec.

"Just chill."

"Scoot, or I'll stand up in this seat and climb into the next booth."

Christian set down her pizza, turned to Bec, and took their hands. "Baby," said Christian. "Please. Just don't. It's fine."

Ty glanced at Gabby, who shrugged and looked away. She knew the Freaks had agreed to keep Bec and Ty in the dark, and it wasn't her place to tell them anything anyway, but man, this was uncomfortable.

Bec looked into her eyes, and for a moment Gabby was sure it would happen just like Bec had said: they would yank away from Christian and stand up on the bench seat and swing one leg over the back, step into the empty booth, and stomp up to a Homeland Security agent with fists raised. Instead, Bec just sighed. Christian picked up a slice, looked at it, and set it down again. Gabby understood. If the sight of Mossman wasn't enough to spoil your appetite, watching your partner nearly step to a government agent would do the trick.

"This shit got weird real quick," Ty muttered. She picked up her slice and took a small bite, still watching the rest of them, waiting to see what would happen.

Gabby looked at Mossman. He waved. She resisted the urge to flip him off.

They spent the rest of the meal in miserable near-silence, only broken when Gabby or Ty said something to each other. Soon, the four of them left. Gabby had no desire to spend one more second in the same room as Mossman. Christian threw her arm around Bec and steered them straight to Gabby's car, probably afraid that if Mossman followed them, Bec might go off. Bec, Christian, and Ty climbed in as Gabby opened her door and turned back to the entrance. Mossman walked out, slurping something in a to-go cup. He waved at Gabby again as he got in his black Tahoe and drove away.

By the time they reached Christian's house, the mood had shifted again. Ty still looked a little anxious, but Christian and Bec were speaking to each other. As they all got out and headed inside, Christian put her arm back around Bec, who leaned into her.

"I kinda like that side of you," said Christian. "All protective and shit."

"Quit it, or no snogging for a week," Bec said, but they were smiling.

Ty snorted. "Y'all are too cute."

Jealousy tugged at Gabby's heart. She and Jamie had barely spoken over the last few days. Because he had been so busy patrolling, or because she no longer agreed with how he was running this show? She didn't know. Maybe she would call him tonight.

CHAPTER SIXTEEN

Micah was scheduled to surveil the farmhouse that night, though he had totally forgotten until noon, when Jamie sent a text reminding him. He had still slept most of the afternoon, deep in dreams of an empty plain, a giant shape on the horizon, a voice promising him power and glory and women and revenge. Around four-thirty, Gabby had beaten on the front door until the sound invaded his dreams, woke Micah up, and sent him staggering down the hall while wiping sleep from his eyes and cursing. Where the hell had Baltar gone, anyway?

Gabby hadn't wanted to come inside. She told Micah about Mossman in Pizza of Mind, emphasizing how Micah would need to stay alert for any similar visitations. She hadn't said what they both knew she was thinking: *We don't trust you to keep your head out of your ass.* Ty had been sitting in her passenger seat, Bec in the back with Christian. They waved.

When they left, Micah shut the door and went back to bed after setting an alarm on his phone. Sure, he had homework in English, Spanish II, and Geometry, plus a paper in Economics and Personal Finance that was due in a week, but he could barely keep his stupid eyes open. Besides, when monsters and government agents wanted you dead, what was the point of learning geometric proofs?

He fell back to sleep and dreamed that same dream, as if it was a movie he had paused.

The alarm woke him a few hours later. The house was dark and quiet. Micah's stomach grumbled, so he forced himself to eat a turkey sandwich and take a sip of Coke. Then he walked outside and turned up his vision. No Team vehicles on the street. Good. He got in the Escort and drove toward Grisham's Loop.

After parking on the little access trail the Freaks favored, he fought his way through the dark forest until he reached the spying tree. One downside to spy duty was that you had to sit in the woods, no matter the weather. Jamie and Christian had used their stealth charms and checked out the farmhouse's barn. The Team hadn't posted guards out there, but they had installed cameras and microphones, and Baltar claimed he couldn't whammy the place from a distance; he needed to draw the runes onto the barn somewhere. Micah wasn't sure that was true, but at least the old man had been consistent; when he had whammied the other Freaks' houses and cars, they had let the old dude in after their parents left for work or errands.

As he settled against the tree, Micah reached into his shirt and palmed his stealth charm. He shouldn't need it, but it was an insurance policy. He turned up his vision. Nothing worth seeing in the yard. He enhanced his hearing. Now that was more like it.

McCreedy: "Our forest sensors have indicated a massive otherdimensional energy surge. We've definitely got another target. And while it hasn't threatened any towns, the death of Elvis Schott proves how dangerous this being is. To humans and the natural fauna."

Vincent: "I've studied the scans all afternoon. I'd estimate we're dealing with at least a Class Four sentience. Probably more like a Three. I believe it could devastate a major city."

McCreedy: "Then we'll prepare for a Two. Manticore, Shrike—I want you in those woods tonight. See if you can track the signature. If you find the bogey, call for backup. Do not engage alone. Understood?"

Mossman and Kragthorpe left moments later, taking one of the Tahoes and two of those sci-fi rifles with all the weird attachments. The rest of the Team kept talking, so Micah kept listening. The next voices he heard caused him to straighten up and pay careful attention—that same feminine voice they had heard several times, plus a new one, deep and rough, accented like the woman's. Micah took out his phone from a pocket Christian had sewn inside his costume.

McCreedy: "What's the latest on Hannibal?"

Mysterious woman: "Still expensive. Still on schedule. Does Congress know why that money was appropriated?"

McCreedy: "Not your concern, Badger."

Badger: "Of course, sir. My apologies."

Mysterious man: "I'm concerned about the chassis. It needs more reinforcement, and I'm not sure the heat resistance is working like it should."

McCreedy: "Thank you, King. I'll make some calls. Prince, can you—"

Micah missed that next part, though, because he was typing as fast as he could.

New woman = Badger
New guy = King
Spanish? Mexican? Dominican? Puerto Rican?
What is Hannibal?

He had other questions he didn't write down. Why had none of the Freaks ever seen Badger or King? Just bad luck, or did the newcomers literally never leave the farmhouse? Plus, why did their voices seem familiar?

Before he could figure it out, Micah's head seemed to expand, as if his skull was filling with gas. His enhanced vision and hearing returned to normal levels, but he hadn't turned them down. What the hell?

Now the dark woods were growing darker, the trees losing their definition, the moonlight fading. Another voice thundered in his mind, not any of the feds' but still familiar, the one he had been hearing in his dreams for two years now, the voice of that giant standing at the far end of an empty field on the other side of the lightning.

SERVE ME, it said, and Micah shoved his hands over his ears and dropped to one knee, groaning. *COME WHEN I CALL, AND I WILL SET YOU ON HIGH. THE AFFAIRS OF THOSE LITTLE MEN IN THAT HOUSE WILL BE AS THOSE OF ANTS.*

"Shut up," said Micah, his teeth clenched. "God, can't you ever leave me alone?"

Then his phone chirped, and that deeper darkness vanished. The voice faded. That stretched feeling seeped out of his head. Micah fell back against the tree and groaned, rubbing his eyes and temples.

Jamie had texted just to check in. The alert had yanked Micah out of that dream state where something huge and indescribably powerful waited, watched, and called to him in a voice that felt like gravity.

Micah got to his feet. He wanted to get the hell out of here before anything else happened. Had anyone else heard the new Team members' codenames? Micah didn't remember for sure. With the way his narcolepsy or whatever it was combined with the voice in his head, he might well have missed it.

As he slipped back to the car, his heart raced; he kept expecting that mountain's voice to return and rip him out of the world. He waited for another ten minutes; he didn't want to be driving if it happened. When he decided to chance it, he made it home without incident and went straight to bed. For once, he didn't dream.

CHAPTER SEVENTEEN

Kenneth had gotten stuck with the Friday evening shift at Larry's. Now, as he turned onto Royal Del Ray Street, he spotted an SUV parked on the road. Groaning, he pulled up beside it. Its window rolled down. Greenwalt motioned for him to lower his own.

"We need to talk," said the fed.

"I got curfew."

"There's still twenty minutes before you're late. Meet me at the park."

"Why can't we talk here?"

"Because I want to meet at the park. Do you really want to take the chance that one of your friends might happen by and see us?"

Kenneth cursed and put the truck back in drive.

At the park, he stopped beside the SUV and killed the engine. Greenwalt was standing just inside the park proper and leaning against a tree. Kenneth got out and joined him.

"Well?" asked Kenneth.

Greenwalt took out a roll of Life Savers and popped one in his mouth. "I need an update on Sterne."

This again. Kenneth's fists clenched. Enough of this bullshit. "I ain't no rat."

Greenwalt's eyebrows rose. "I thought we agreed—"

"You tried to put me in a no-win situation, but I never actually agreed to a damn thing. And even if I had, I can't tell you what I don't know."

Greenwalt stared at Kenneth for a while. Kenneth stared right back. He would not be intimidated by this guy or anybody else. Not anymore. After fighting vampires and shape-shifting gods, after nearly getting cut to pieces by flying alien buzzsaws—Greenwalt was about as scary as your average poodle.

"Okay," said Greenwalt. "I guess there's nothing else to say."

"I guess not."

The fed snapped his fingers. "Oh, right. Did Jamie and Gabby tell you I had a talk with them too?"

Kenneth worked hard to keep from looking surprised, but his stomach seemed to drop somewhere near his ankles. No, neither of them had said a word. Of course, there was no way he was going to tell Greenwalt that. Kenneth might not have been as smart as the other Freaks, but he knew what the fed was trying to do. Frankly, the move seemed clumsy and desperate.

They still should have told me. He mentally counted to ten, took a deep breath, released it. "Hell yeah, they told me. So what?"

"Just making sure you weren't keeping secrets from each other," said Greenwalt. "I suppose they know you're talking to me too. If I asked them about it, they'd be cool, yeah?"

"I reckon you'll have to ask 'em and see." Kenneth concentrated on his breathing. He couldn't take a swing at this guy, no matter how much he wanted to.

Greenwalt's eyes narrowed, as if he could see right through Kenneth, even in the dark. "Your group is losing it, kid. But you? You don't have to lose everything. Think about it." Greenwalt got in his SUV and drove away.

Kenneth watched until the vehicle turned a corner. When it was gone, he turned to the tree Greenwalt had been leaning against, his fists still clenched. "Son of a bitch," he grunted, and he punched the trunk. The bottom half of the tree exploded. The top half fell to the ground nearly intact, missing his truck by maybe three feet. It took down part of the metal cable marking the boundary between the parking area and the grounds. The lower half of the trunk had been reduced to dust, which wafted through the air and covered Kenneth from head to toe.

He looked down at himself. It was like he had worked in the lumberyard all day. Great. Now he would have to sneak in the house and get changed and showered before Mom or Dad saw him.

Maybe I should use my charm on 'em, he thought as he touched it through his shirt and hoodie. But then he'd probably barf all over the place. Not worth it. He'd just sneak in the old-fashioned way.

And, sometime soon, he would have a long talk with Jamie and Gabby.

The next day, Kenneth and Ty went to Elvis Schott's funeral. None of the other Freaks had come. No big surprise. Any of them would have looked and felt out of place after all those years when Marla had ignored or tormented them. Once the service began, Kenneth leafed through a hymnal and waited for it to be over. While he hummed, Ty sang along with the hymns; she had a great voice. His singing sounded like somebody had stepped on a cat's tail.

Afterward, he and Ty and Brayden joined the line to offer condolences. Mrs. Schott, saying little, looked at each mourner with glazed and watery eyes. Marla smiled at everyone and thanked them for coming. She seemed more present than her mom. Would this be one of those situations where the kid had to become the parent? Kenneth hoped not. Marla didn't deserve any of this. Nobody did.

Two old ladies in front of Kenneth and Ty kept putting their heads together and whispering. He had paid them little attention, but now he realized they were gossiping.

"And nobody figured out what was wrong with him?" asked a lady in a floral print dress.

"Nope," said the other, who wore a gray dress. "They say he drank."

"Ha. More like swam in it."

"No! That much?"

"I hear he made three or four liquor runs a week."

"No! Who told you that?"

"Marjorie Meddars. Isn't it awful how people talk in this town?"

Kenneth looked at Ty and rolled his eyes. She turned away, trying not to laugh. Jesus. And people said teenagers weren't self-aware.

As they left the church, Ty took his arm, which drew the usual sideways glances and knitted eyebrows from the usual old people. *That ain't right*, those looks said. *You ought to be ashamed, boy*. Well, screw them. He was damned proud to be with Ty.

Before the procession left for the graveside service, Marla stopped on her way to the town car the funeral home had provided and let Brayden hug her. She looked like she hadn't slept in days, like she had cried herself dry. Then she broke away from Brayden and hugged Ty, who stiffened for a second, probably surprised. The four of them had hung out several times, and though Marla had never been unfriendly, she hadn't exactly tried to make Ty her best friend. After a moment, though, Ty returned the embrace, and they stood there like that, turning from side to side just a bit, while Marla bit back tears. Amazing how a death could close the distance between people, at least if they had any decency at all. The idea that somebody you had seen every day of your life would never come back, never laugh or yell at you or eat their favorite food again, never get another chance to do better or catch up on their reading; that for them everything was just plain *over*—Kenneth could barely get his head around it. He had always known about death, of course. Everybody did. But there was a big difference between knowing about it and really understanding what it meant. He probably still knew very little, despite all the experience he'd packed into the last couple years. But he had a feeling he would learn.

"You're gonna be okay," Ty was whispering to Marla.

"I guess," said Marla. She let Ty go. Brayden put his arm around Marla. She lay her head on his shoulder. "It's so weird."

"What is?" asked Kenneth.

"This whole thing. Dad wouldn't go near the woods for a long time. He drank more than I had ever seen him drink before. Then he quit. A while later, he started again, worse than ever, and he spent every spare minute in the woods. Sometimes he talked about it like he had something to prove. I mean, what was that even about? Nobody thought any less of him for not hunting. Now I'll never be able to ask him."

She burst into tears, turned to Brayden, and pressed her face against his neck. He looked lost, but he patted her on the back and told her it would be all right.

Ty squeezed Marla's arm again. Then she took Kenneth's hand and pulled him away. "Let's give 'em some privacy."

"Okay," he said. "Marla, I'm sorry."

She didn't reply. Brayden waved as they left.

At the truck, Kenneth opened the door for Ty, just a part of the "Southern gentleman" tasks his mother insisted he perform despite how she and Dad felt about Ty. As he started to get in on the driver's side, he glanced up. There was Greenwalt again, leaning against his Suburban parked across the street. He held up his left wrist and tapped it with the first two fingers of his right hand.

"Asshole," Kenneth muttered.

Officer Heck was waiting in his cruiser. When it was time, he would lead everyone to the cemetery, his lights moving traffic aside like a river rock changing the water's direction. Heck spotted Greenwalt and frowned.

Kenneth got in the truck. Ty was watching the fed, her brow furrowed. "You know that dude?"

"He's nobody," Kenneth said as he started the engine.

"One of these days, all y'all gotta tell me about these men who keep showing up everywhere and ruining y'all's days," Ty said, watching Greenwalt until Kenneth drove away.

CHAPTER EIGHTEEN

It was only fourth period, but Monday already felt like it had lasted a month. As she had done for the past three weeks, Ms. Herrera was conjugating a Spanish verb in full-sentence conversational examples and explaining how and why you might use each one. Christian had been furiously taking notes, not just what the teacher wrote on the board but many comments about how to remember everything. At the desk next to hers, Bec doodled, sketching little boats and cat faces. Not fair. Bec spoke fluent Spanish and could write it and read it as well as English. For them, this class might as well have been study hall. They had been tutoring Christian, who simply didn't retain languages well.

She had struggled with other subjects before, but mostly because she lacked real interest. It drove Mom crazy. *Life isn't just about what you enjoy*, she'd said a hundred times. *If you can't learn to put one hundred percent effort into things you don't particularly like, you're gonna have a tough time when you get a job.* Christian knew where Mom was coming from, but that hadn't made spending hours studying every clause in the Constitution any easier. Still, Spanish was different. She wanted to learn it—maybe one day she could gain enough competence to talk with Bec in either language, which would come in handy when they found themselves surrounded by assholes—but she just couldn't get the rules through her head. It felt like advanced math mixed with AP English.

Of course, said assholes would probably tell her and Bec to stop "talking Mexican," but they could go to hell. The world held lots of things worth fearing, but garden-variety bigots didn't make the cut. She was proud of her beliefs. *Anybody* who didn't like it could go to hell.

Today she wore a rainbow pin on her shirt, which had an outline of the United States stamped with *Stolen Property*.

Fighting these everyday battles had preoccupied her, but some things were worth it. That included the Freaks and their latest hunt, which wasn't going well. The dragon had vanished. Jamie had flown over long stretches of woods without finding any sign of it. Christian had run over every inch of ground in three counties. No one's eaves-dropping missions had revealed any Team encounters with it, either. If the feds had made contact, they weren't talking about it, not even inside the farmhouse. And Baltar—well, who knew what Baltar had gotten into? He offered a lot of opinions on Freaks business, but he only seemed to share his own activities and insights when he could make some big, dramatic reveal. Who knew whether that indicated something sinister? Maybe the old man just liked theatrics.

Christian's phone buzzed. She slipped it out of her pocket while keeping her eyes on Ms. Herrera, who was erasing the last sentences and writing some new ones. A text from Bec:

Come over later?
Christian smiled. Bec smiled back. Christian replied:
Sure

Bec sent several emojis, including some hearts. Christian grinned again. When Bec got all squishy or flirtatious, Christian's temperature rose. She always felt a little breathless. It was the closest she came these days to that after-a-workout feeling, where—

"Señorita Allen," Ms. Herrera said, hands on her hips, dry-erase marker clutched in one hand. "¿Te gustaría compartir tu chiste con la clase?" The teacher never spoke English during class.

It made Christian's head hurt. Her smile disappeared. "Um. No, Señora."

"Yo insisto."

Christian tried to remember all the words and forms she would need to respond in Spanish, but with everybody looking, her brain turned to mush. "I don't know a joke," she said.

Ms. Herrera walked down the aisle, glaring and *tsk-tsk*ing. "¿Entonces tal vez encuentras mi lección graciosa?"

"No, Señora." Nothing about this was funny.

"Su teléfono móvil no tiene las respuestas a nuestra próxima prueba." She held out her hand.

Christian sighed and gave the phone over. Then Ms. Herrera held her other hand out to Bec. Once the teacher had both phones, she went back and set them on her desk and resumed the lesson. Christian turned to Bec and rolled her eyes. Bec nodded. At the first of the year, everyone thought Ms. Herrera was cool, and also hot. Now most of the kids looked at her no differently than they did every other teacher. Even the boys who used to talk about her sexy Spanish accent and her cleavage mostly just complained.

The rest of the day crawled by. Christian's love/hate relationship with school had mostly swung in the direction of hate. Before, she had measured herself against Jamie, to whom everything seemed to come easily. Christian could make the grades, but she had always needed to study, at least a little, whereas that kid could pull straight A's without cracking a book. Nothing had changed for him, even with everything the Freaks had to deal with. He was probably on track for a full ride to whatever university he wanted. For Christian, though, every distraction threatened to blow up her future, and these days, distractions were everywhere. The Team, the dragon, her love life, Micah's descent into catatonia—a hundred problems, few solutions. Now she was probably wrecking her Spanish grade too.

When the final bell rang, she walked with Bec to the parking lot. Bec's parents had bought them a used Honda Civic with about a zillion miles on it and rusty patches along the chassis. Over the last few months, all the Villaloboses had worked on the car, buffing out the rough spots and changing the tires, repainting and reupholstering, changing hoses and the carburetor and all the filters. Now it hardly looked like the same car. Bec was hoping for a good sound system sometime soon.

Mr. and Mrs. Villalobos were working, so when Christian and Bec got there, the house was empty, quiet, and warm. Bec's room, like the house, was small but cozy. A twin bed set against one wall under the only window was covered in a plush blue-gray duvet and a pile of pillows. Christian had always imagined Bec sleeping like people did on TV, with their head propped at a ninety-degree angle against that pile. One wall featured a Basquiat print, or so Bec had said; Christian knew very little about art. Around the poster, Bec had hung photographs of varying sizes, all of them featuring the Villalobos family. The other decorations mostly related to bands of various eras: the Beatles and the Doors, the Ramones and the Clash, Black Flag and Bad Brains, Soundgarden and Local H. The first time Christian came in here, she knew she and Bec would never get sick of each other's music. Under the Basquiat and the family photos, Bec's little entertainment center held a 32-inch TV, their game console, and a set of vinyl LPs that Bec hoped would grow into a real collection. One day they might even get a turntable.

The room was too small for a desk, so when Bec needed to charge their laptop, they'd balance it on the console. When they needed to work or goof off online, they sat on the bed. Where would a turntable even go—between the foot of the bed and the closet?

Bec shut the door. Christian raised her eyebrows. They had never closed that door before. From his stern expressions whenever the two of them moved beyond the living room, Mr. Villalobos had probably forbidden it. Pretty standard parent move. But now, alone in the house, on a quiet street where they should have been able to hear any car that drove past or stopped, in this room just comfortable enough for two? What might Bec have in mind?

Christian felt jittery, hot, almost as alert as when she enhanced her senses. Her hands trembled; she clasped them and held tight. Every breath seemed to bring in too much air.

And what did Bec feel? They seemed as chill as ever as they smoothed the wrinkles from the duvet and moved a couple of pillows off the bed. They sat and patted the space next to them.

Christian's heart was playing the drum solo from "Moby Dick." Her clothes felt too tight. Still, she sat next to Bec. When they took her hand, she nearly jumped. Was her deodorant still working? Did she need a breath mint? She and Bec had kissed many times before, had held hands and slung arms around each other, had lain on a bed or couch with one's head in the other's lap while watching a movie or listening to some tunes. Once or twice, a fingertip had dangled just low enough to brush against a breast; during a few of those kisses, there had been some gentle squeezing of a hip or a buttock. But they had never gone further. Not even since Bec got the Civic. Their version of parking had mostly meant sitting in the dark and talking about music.

Now, in Bec's bright bedroom, of all places, anything seemed possible. Every cell in Christian's body seemed to open, even as her breath caught in her chest.

They kissed. The heat doubled and concentrated in the parts of Christian that the world had long resented. Society had always limited what women could dream of and how they could live. They'd been assaulted and worse, had been burned and dismembered, had seen their bodies become the subject of men's legislation, their deepest selves the focus of a hatred older than western society, and so much of that had stemmed from fear of what women might do when they first realized they truly existed, actually held power, could experience pleasure with or without a man. Not so long ago, Christian would have been tortured or killed for whom she loved and how she expressed that love physically. Hell, there were people in Quapaw City who supported that kind of thinking right now, who would look at Christian's hair and her boots and her piercings and her hand in Bec's and believe they knew everything about her, that they had the right to do whatever they wanted to her because she had been born different. And what about Bec? Their looks, their love, even their pronouns—politicians and ministers and conservative citizens had weaponized nonbinary bodies and voices. Even the fact that Christian couldn't bear Bec's touch without intrusive, mood-killing thoughts like these proved how privileged straight people were, how fraught queer lives could be.

She needed to put all that out of her mind and just be present right here, right now. But how?

Bec's hands moved from Christian's shoulders to her back. Their fingers grazed her spine. She shivered. Bec gripped her bra clasp.

And it was suddenly too much. Christian pulled away and stood, breathing hard.

"What's wrong?" asked Bec.

"Nothing," said Christian. "Just—everything, kinda? The world. What it can do to us."

"I'm sorry. I shouldn't have—"

"No, you didn't do anything wrong. I want to do this. Believe me. And I want it to be with you."

Bec stood and put a hand on Christian's cheek. "There's no hurry. Come on. Let's play some *Wizards vs. Romans.*"

Christian got to her feet and embraced Bec. Then she stepped away. "Give me a couple minutes, okay? My head's screwed up. I need some air."

"Air?"

"Yeah." She backed toward the door. "Just for a little while. I've got some garbage in my brain. I need to empty it. If you'll wait, I'll just take a little walk and come right back."

"Okay."

"I mean it. I'll be right back."

"Okay."

Bec walked her to the front door. Christian stepped into the sunshine. The cold air burned her sinuses, but she still felt hot all over. Her hands had not stopped trembling. "I'll just go around the block. And then maybe we can pick up where we left off."

Bec squeezed her upper arm. "Or not. Like I said, we've got plenty of time. When you get back, just come on in. I'll be playing the game."

"Okay."

Christian turned and walked down the road in the direction of town, because in Bec's mind, where else would she go? As soon as she heard the door close, though, she turned into the woods. A walk wouldn't actually clear her head, but a run might.

Enhancing her vision and scanning the landscape for the Team's sensors—without her costume, she couldn't afford to run in front of any cameras, which might be able to capture her image—she zoomed among the trees. Everything smelled fresh and rich. The dry weather had turned every fallen leaf into texture and sound. Her super-speed steps created a noise like static.

Might as well look for the dragon while I'm out here, she thought, though she didn't expect to find it. Mostly, she just wanted a chance to think before she headed back to Bec's and resumed whatever had been about to happen—maybe nothing, maybe everything.

That touch. That heat.

Spotting the Team's hidden surveillance equipment proved harder than it should have been. Her mind kept drifting back to Bec's room, to how the light sparkled in their eyes. Christian had always heard that people driving long distances over familiar roads could fall into their own memories and thoughts; they might cover ten or twenty miles without even paying attention. She had never done that in a car, but she understood. Many times, she had run just because it felt good, and on those occasions, she had gotten lost inside herself too.

To her right and far away, something moved. Scanning the immediate area and sensing no Team devices, she skidded to a halt and focused her vision.

Animals were walking through the woods in a line, mostly deer and squirrels and rabbits, like some elementary-school teacher had come along and organized them. None of them hurried. None got distracted or stopped to nibble greenery. Loud flutterings in the sky—the air had gone dark with birds, all kinds, flying in the same direction the walkers were heading.

Well, that's *unusual.*

She ran forward, parallel to the animals' path, just fast enough to avoid detection. Or so she hoped. Outpacing the lead deer, she kept heading in a straight line, watching the distance for whatever the animals might have been seeking. Really, though, only one thing made sense. She spotted it within a couple of minutes and ran straight for it.

The dragon lay among some trees, its body contorted around the trunks. Leaves and small twigs fluttered as it exhaled. Its scales had taken on a mulberry hue in this light. That weird fringe around its head quivered when it shifted. Its eyes were half-open.

Christian stopped only yards away. It looked at her and exhaled again. The sound suspiciously resembled a sigh. As she stepped closer, it moved its head in her direction. Now those piercing blue eyes bored into her. A low rumble emanated from the dragon's throat, like a dog's warning growl.

"It's cool," said Christian, holding out both hands, palms up. "I'm not gonna hurt you."

The dragon made a staccato sound—*huh-huh-huh*—almost like a chuckle.

Christian moved closer, closer. She couldn't have been more than fifteen feet from the snout. God, this thing was magnificent. "You're okay. I just want—"

Blood spurted from the inside corners of both its eyes, striking Christian like water from a fire hose and knocking her down. The blood was as hot as the inside of the dragon's body must have been. Christian yelped and leaped up and, twirling at super-speed, flung the gore in every direction.

When she stopped spinning, the dragon was gone. Or, rather, it had cloaked itself. The leaves on the forest floor squished and parted as the creature moved away. Christian's clothes were stained deep red, though her motion had dried the blood. Her shirt felt like it was made of flexible wood. Her pants crackled when she bent her knees. While she stood still and tried to slow her thoughts, the conga line of animals caught up. They marched right past, showing no fear, not even looking at her. Overhead, the birds flew in a straight line, the front point of which dipped toward the earth as the leaders reached the dragon.

No way could Christian go straight back to Bec's. She looked like she had murdered someone with an ax. She would have to run home, change clothes, maybe set these on fire or bury them in the backyard, and then sprint back to Johnny Cash Way, all without being seen.

Well, no time like the present. She zipped toward town, still looking and listening for Team devices.

That sound the dragon had made, like a human sigh . . . maybe Christian was thinking magically, assigning human traits and motivations to an animal, but she had gotten the impression that the sight of a human had made the dragon feel tired. *Why won't y'all leave me alone?* it had seemed to think. Was that possible? Dragons were highly intelligent in a lot of stories, but how much stock could you put in fiction writers? It had sure seemed to understand her, though, when she promised not to hurt it. That other sound, like a laugh. Christian doubted it had understood her words—where would it have learned English?—but her mood and tone had probably seemed clear enough. And yes, it had shot hot blood at her—from its freaking *eyes,* like a horned toad—but that had seemed more like a warning, its equivalent of a cat's hiss or a dog's raised hackles. Had it tried to warn Elvis Schott before it fried him? Christian didn't know, but she would have bet it had.

I don't think it's dangerous unless you make it defend itself. That's a good sign, if I can just make Jamie and them see it.

She smiled. The Freaks had spent a lot of time killing things and avenging dead people. Maybe it would feel good to protect something, to save a life.

Christian made it home and managed to shower and change, shove her bloody clothes into a trash bag and stuff it underneath her bed, and run back to Bec's. She traveled at maybe seventy-five percent power, far too fast for the naked eye to follow her, hopefully fast enough that even the best cameras wouldn't show more than a blur. By the time she entered Bec's house, perhaps ten minutes had passed. Christian joined Bec in their room. Together they sat on the floor and gamed for an hour. Neither mentioned what might have been happening earlier—or what might happen next.

CHAPTER NINETEEN

Arsiss the Gentle shrank herself and flew into the tallest tree she could find. Its limbs stretched in all directions and tapered near the top, where she landed. The leaves consisted of one long stem with thin green shoots lining each side, a curiosity, as nothing like them existed in her world. She loved their smell. Now as small as one of the bushy-tailed creatures that ran and lounged here in the treetops, she lay on a bough and closed her eyes, hoping to fall back into the sleep the young biped had interrupted. Arsiss had been dreaming of home. She had not asked to come here. She did not know how to return. The best she could do was to cherish the moments when her dreaming mind carried her to those fields and virgin forests and deep, cold lakes she had once taken for granted. This world was no hellscape, but it was her prison, and she had no idea why she had been sentenced here.

Below, the little ones seeking her protection trooped in and lay under her tree, spreading themselves in formations that, from above, looked like lines of defense. Not that they could stand for long against bipeds like the one she had been forced to kill. Its weapons held little danger for her, but the beings below wore no armored scales. Hidden behind thin layers of skin and flesh, their blood and organs seemed designed to be spilled. She welcomed these creatures but wished their coming hadn't revealed her presence. The bipeds might not know much, but they could follow a living trail.

Not that they were all the same. The shambling, raging one who had tried to kill her had reminded her of rock trolls—huge, wide beings with thick heads and fists the size of boulders. They blundered about, smashing whatever they encountered and eating raw flesh and cracking bones in their teeth. The young one from today, though—she carried no weapons but her own courage and will. Arsiss had sensed great power within her, but the girl's approach, her voice, her gestures, even her expression had differed greatly from the others'. Could some of this world's species *respect* Arsiss's kind? Might they seek her out for reasons other than the usual? Or had the young one simply been more adept at hiding her true intentions?

Arsiss could not know and so had to rely on experience. Sooner or later, such interactions collapsed toward blood, broken bones, fire, ice. A war that served no one and scarred the land. No, better if the young one and her allies stayed far away, which is why she had warned the child with a spray of hot blood. Since landing on the rind of this strange land, she had changed her size many times, had cloaked herself, had flown or trudged ever deeper into these forests. What else could she do? And yet still her enemies found her.

She would defend herself if it came to that. She hoped that it would not.

Arsiss set her back against the trunk and fell asleep. In her dreams, she frolicked by her favorite river under trees whose tops disappeared in the low clouds. Warm, alone, full of her favorite foods and clear, sweet water, she wished she never had to leave.

CHAPTER TWENTY

After the last bell, Gabby met Christian in the hall. Up ahead, Mr. Hoon seemed to be looking for someone. He walked right past Kenneth and Ty, even though Kenneth had one hand in Ty's back pocket, a public display of affection that would normally have resulted in a cold stare and an order for Kenneth to keep his hands to himself. When Hoon passed them without comment, Kenneth smiled and shrugged. Ty grinned and snaked an arm around his waist. Together they continued down the hall, her head on his shoulder. Christian had seen Hoon, too, and she looked as alarmed as Gabby felt, but the principal walked by without even noticing them. Gabby exhaled and laughed a little, feeling silly. Sure, pretty much every authority figure in town had come after the Freaks at some point, not counting parents, but the idea that Mr. Hoon had somehow discovered their secrets and decided to bird-dog them through the hallway? Yeah, right. Christian seemed a bit embarrassed, too, like she had been thinking the same thing and had come to the same realization. Gabby wouldn't have been surprised. All the Freaks seemed on edge lately. Years of dodging federal agents and monsters would do that to a kid.

Then they turned around and nearly bumped into Ms. Herrera.

"Whoa." Christian backed up a step. She goggled for a moment before she caught herself, cleared her throat, and tried to look casual. Gabby didn't blame her. The Spanish teacher, taller than any woman Gabby knew and most of the men, wore a loose green dress that dipped in the neckline, not scandalous but precisely low enough to coincide with an average-height kid's sightline. Her makeup was flawless, each

131

element a perfect complement to the others, the kind of application that Gabby's mom had tried to help her with but that she could never seem to get right. The dress ended just below the knee, revealing unblemished skin and shapely calves. Even her teeth looked like a movie star's.

"Hey, Ms. Herrera," said Gabby.

"Hello," the teacher said, glancing at Gabby but turning back to Christian. "Señorita Allen, may I speak with you a minute?"

"Um, sure?" said Christian. Ms. Herrera turned and headed toward her classroom. Christian looked at Gabby and shrugged.

Gabby leaned against the lockers. "I'll just hang out here." Christian followed the teacher down the hall and into the room as thinning streams of students walked by laughing and joking and hitching backpacks onto their shoulders. Most of them were too caught up in their conversations to notice her, but a few did. Even Steve Whitehead nodded when he passed. No one called her Sister Gabby anymore or said anything so mean she would cry about it later. Maybe they had matured. More likely, though, they had just found something else to focus on. Or, weird as it was to admit, Gabby's regular proximity to Kenneth Del Ray could have bought her some social cachet—not enough to make her cool, but sufficient to take the bulls-eye off her back.

Was it possible that some of these kids might have even been perceptive enough to suspect what was really going on? Could anyone have noticed that she and her three constant companions—Kenneth, too—had never been seen in the same place as the strange figures who had fought inside the school and down at the pond a couple of years back, the same ones still rumored to be skulking around Quapaw City, occasionally doing weird shit and leaving wreckage and evidence of violence in their wake? Maybe some of them looked at Gabby differently because they wondered, even subconsciously, whether she had become someone you did not want to mess with.

Ms. Herrera had shut the door behind her and Christian. Something about the teacher nagged at Gabby. Maybe she just wanted to talk to

Christian about class, but Gabby didn't trust her for some reason. She turned up her hearing and concentrated on the Spanish classroom.

"So. Your grades have slipped," Ms. Herrera was saying.

"Yeah." Christian didn't sound happy.

"That C-minus you got on the last test—that isn't like you. What's going on?"

"Nothing. I've just been busy. And I'm looking for a job so I can get a car."

"That's all fine, but you and I both know you can handle your classes. Even if you don't really like some of them."

Gabby smiled. Ms. Herrera had gotten to know Christian pretty well, at least from a school perspective. Christian was better in some subjects than others, and yes, she had never really applied herself in subjects that didn't excite her, but she was plenty smart. Smarter than she gave herself credit for.

"Yes, ma'am," said Christian.

"I've noticed how you spend most of your time with one group of kids," said Ms. Herrera. "And that Kenneth Del Ray is among them."

"Okay."

"I wonder if they're part of why your grades aren't up to your usual standards."

"Um, what?"

"Look, it's normal for kids to prioritize the wrong things. They put their friends first when they should be looking toward their own futures. And sometimes those friends turn out to be pretty poor influences."

Gabby frowned. No one had ever called her a bad influence before. She wasn't sure if she should be pleased or insulted.

Silence for a bit. Then Christian said, "It ain't like that."

"No?"

"Me and my friends, we . . . well, we've always looked out for each other. Jamie'd be the first one to make me study harder if he thought I was slacking off. Those kids are one of the best parts of my life."

"Even Kenneth?"

Christian laughed. "If you had asked me about him a few years back, I would have said something different. But we're good now."

"Hmm."

"Ma'am, can I go? Me and Gabby had plans—"

"Oh. Well, yes. If you're sure there's nothing we need to address. In class or in your life."

"I'm good."

Now Ms. Herrera fell silent for a bit. Maybe she was looking Christian in the eye and trying to read what was happening inside. "All right," she said. "But I'm here if you need help."

"Yes, ma'am. Thanks. See you later."

As Christian scurried through the door, Gabby turned down her hearing and fell in beside her. They didn't speak until they left the building and were walking toward Gabby's car, now sitting alone in the student lot. "I listened in," said Gabby. "You made a C-minus?"

"Yeah," said Christian. "Between looking for the dragon and worrying about the Team and trying to spend a few minutes a day with Bec, I totally forgot about that test. Stupid."

"Do teachers usually have a talk with somebody after one bad test?"

"I don't know. I'm not used to getting average grades, or worse."

"Me neither." They got into the car. Gabby started it up and turned off the heater. Before the car warmed up, it would just blow cold air. They sat for a minute or two, listening to the engine thrum. "Hey. That new woman's voice out at the farmhouse. You don't think it could be Ms. Herrera?"

Christian turned to her, mouth open. "Oh, shit. You think? I . . . nah. Nah, no way."

"Yeah. Couldn't be."

They sat a bit longer, looking straight ahead, keeping their thoughts to themselves.

At Christian's place, they grabbed a snack and a couple of Cokes, went to Christian's room, and did their homework, or tried to. Gabby kept finding herself staring at her laptop screen, her mind drifting back to Ms. Herrera. Christian paused a lot too. Maybe she was thinking about what to write next, or maybe she, too, was considering the possibility that their Spanish teacher might also be a Team member.

As the afternoon became early evening and the sun went down, Christian finally closed her computer. "You wanna run out to the farmhouse? See what's up?"

"Sure," Gabby said, putting her laptop in her bag. "My eyes hurt anyway."

Christian zipped Gabby out to Grisham's Loop and arrived just as two vehicles turned into the farmhouse's driveway. Tires squealed; gravel crunched; doors slammed, and men shouted to each other. Gabby turned up her hearing as the front door opened and McCreedy stepped out.

Greenwalt: "It got him, sir. Oh, shit, it—"

McCreedy: "Not out here. Civilians use this road. Get inside. Now."

Silence for a few moments, and then the sound of feet on the ground, grass whispering against shoes, men breathing hard, Greenwalt muttering *Oh God* over and over. A door opened and shut. Gabby concentrated, refining her hearing, listening past the intermittent wind and the wildlife sounds and the creaks of floorboards, focusing only on the voices.

Kragthorpe: "What the hell happened out there? Where's Lancer?"

Greenwalt: "Dead. He's dead. Oh, God, it burned him alive."

The men went quiet again. Someone cleared their throat.

Jeffcoat: "Jesus Christ."

McCreedy: "Tell me everything. Canebrake, get him a glass of water. With whiskey."

Greenwalt: "We rode the ATV into the woods, following the sensor's GPS tracker."

The woman called Badger: "Yes, the energy signatures maintained their levels until maybe half an hour before you returned."

Was that Ms. Herrera's voice? Gabby couldn't tell. Christian looked like she was trying to figure that out too.

Greenwalt: "We got to the place. It was dark as hell. Looked like every other patch of woods in this state. We proceeded on foot and used our flashlights. I had the acid rifle. Lancer was carrying his service weapon and the laser scattergun. He took point when we moved out. And then—"

Greenwalt said nothing for a while. It sounded like he was drinking something. When he started talking again, Gabby closed her eyes, too, her mind supplying images for a short film that might have been titled *The Last Moments of Cornelius "Lancer" Vincent*:

The two men march forward slowly. They cover maybe fifty yards before Vincent walks face-first into something. He grunts and falls onto his ass, dropping the scattergun. The air flickers, some shape revealing itself, nothing at all rounding into the contours and angles of a body. Something steps on Lancer's flashlight, crushes it, and the faint beam vanishes like a blown-out match. Vincent cries for help. Greenwalt can barely see him, but he seems to be searching for the gun. Greenwalt sprints forward, and something strikes him in the face. His feet fly out from under him, and he crashes onto his back, somehow managing to keep hold of the acid rifle. Vincent yells for backup again, but the bogey snorts, growls, and roars, drowning him out. The scattergun fires. Bursts of lasers fan out from the barrel and light up the forest. Dazed and possibly concussed, his head pounding, Greenwalt sits up just as the beams strike something big and scaly. The brief glow shows Vincent standing with the gun shouldered, the barrel swiveling. Armored plates sizzle and smoke. Some of the lasers must have penetrated the thinner spots because the bogey roars again. Greenwalt staggers to his feet, sure that Vincent is about to die, but that huge shape turns and moves away.

"Come on! It's retreating!" yells Vincent. His voice shakes with fear or adrenaline. Then he takes off after it.

"Wait!" cries Greenwalt. He picks his way among the trees, having seen what clotheslined him: the stub of a thick and low-hanging limb. The moisture on his face suggests he is bleeding, but he won't know he has lacerated his forehead until he gets back to the Suburban when everything is over.

Vincent doesn't wait for Greenwalt. He fires as he runs, cursing at the fleeing monster, promising it a painful death. More of those sizzling sounds, more roars. "I've got you!" shouts Vincent. "I've got you!"

The bogey turns. White-hot flame belches out of a mouth full of sharp teeth. The fire engulfs Vincent. He screams, a high-pitched sound that reminds Greenwalt of a teakettle. The scattergun explodes, lasers shooting in all directions, setting fire to trees and the forest floor. The blasts cut Vincent into pieces, parts piled on parts, all of it burning. The acrid smell gags Greenwalt. He vomits, falling to his knees, spots before his eyes. His head aches and thuds. When he finally gets up, all the fires are out. He stumbles toward the spot where he believes he last saw Vincent. The trees and forest floor are frozen; he nearly slips. Did the bogey do that too? Put out the fires so the woods would be safe? The monster is gone now, though Greenwalt's flashlight beam reveals a trail in the fallen leaves where it walked away. He sweeps the beam around and finds all that is left of Cornelius Vincent—a frozen pile of ash.

Greenwalt fell silent. Gabby opened her eyes. Christian was looking at her. "Jesus," Christian whispered.

"Right?" said Gabby.

McCreedy: "And did you bring back the cremains?"

Greenwalt: "No. They were frozen to the ground, and I had nothing to carry them in."

Kragthorpe: "I'll go get them when the sun comes up. King, you wanna come?"

King: "Yes. I'll drive. I know those roads pretty well."

Greenwalt: "Watch out for that thing. The heat it generated without even having to build it up—it could wipe us out. Class Three, I think. Maybe Two, depending on how big it can get."

McCreedy: "And you can confirm the bogey is a dragon? There's no chance it was the Sterne boy, somehow made invisible?"

"Oh, for God's sake," said Gabby. Christian laughed without humor.

A pause. Then Greenwalt: "I never saw the whole body, and I only got a brief glimpse of the head. But a dragon's my best guess. It couldn't have been Sterne unless the kid's learned how to shapeshift and change his size."

McCreedy: "Well, this shifts our priorities."

Greenwalt: "We may not be able to find it on foot, given its abilities. Maybe we should stick close to home and use our monitors."

McCreedy: "We can't allow it to roam these woods. We've already lost two operatives in this miserable town."

Greenwalt: "Sir—"

Mossman: "Hell yes. Everyone saddle up. Full weapons complement. When we get out there—"

McCreedy: "No. Stand down."

Mossman: "But sir, you said—"

McCreedy: "I know what I said. But as Prince just told us, this thing's vanished. Besides, barreling out there with our emotions running high sounds like a good way to get killed. You're going to gear up, all right. But we're not about to lose this whole team because we're in pain."

Kragthorpe: "Sir—"

McCreedy: "Tonight, we mourn. Tomorrow you'll do a full inspection of our gear and vehicles while I inform my superiors. They will have many questions, and they will want to inform Lancer's family. On Sunday, we hunt. And we won't come out of those woods until this dragon is dead."

Kragthorpe: "And the kids?"

McCreedy: "They'll keep. Badger, you take the first watch. If you see any sign of the dragon's energy signature, sound off. Does everyone understand?"

Gabby turned down her hearing. Holy shit. Vincent dead, Greenwalt knocked silly, a special weapon destroyed, and the Team shifting their focus. Most of the nights out here yielded little actionable information, but when shit went down, it went down big. "Can you believe all this?" she asked.

Christian looked pale. She shook her head.

Gabby took out her phone and sent the boys a message. They would need to talk about all this in person.

CHAPTER TWENTY-ONE

The next day, Jamie parked his car and made his way to the pavilion—first one there. He took a seat on a picnic table and pulled out his phone. No messages, no notifications. He laid the phone on the tabletop and put his hands in his jacket pockets. The bitter wind made his teeth chatter. The pond was empty and choppy. The weeds and bushes were overgrown; soon, they would obstruct the view entirely. Would the city send a landscaper? Probably not. Should the Freaks cut back the foliage themselves? Being able to see the water seemed important, if for no other reason than to watch what was happening on the other side. When you were being hunted, a good view seemed more like a necessity than a pleasure. No one swam in the pond these days, not even in summer; few fished in it, since the stock seemed to have played out. But everybody liked looking at it. Jamie thought of the night they killed Na'ul. He never would have believed a day would come when that night would seem simple, but now they were facing a *dragon*.

What did Gabby think about all this? Shit had gotten weird between them. Every time he tried to push the Freaks forward, she pushed back. A whole life acting like a mouse, barely able to speak up for herself, and now, of all times, she had found her voice and decided to use it—against him. *Lead us*, they said. *Make the hard decisions. Figure shit out and take our lives in your hands.* He had never wanted that goddam role, had sure as hell never asked for it, but he had accepted it, and now that he was getting the hang of it, they were undermining him. He wished they would make up their minds. As for Gabby, he understood her hesitation, but he couldn't just pretend the dragon was harmless. Surely she would understand that in time. Surely all this bickering would stop and they could go back to being, well, Gabby and Jamie, literal super-couple.

At least until college. He had never really thought much about what would happen to them after graduation. They had both seemed to assume they would keep dating, maybe even go to the same school, but that might have been naïve. Who knew if they would even get into the same places? And if they didn't, or if they chose different ones . . . most people their age couldn't stay together even when they lived in the same town. Lately, Jamie had been leaning toward the University of Arkansas. He probably had the grades and the test scores for the Ivy League, but who could afford those places?

"Hey, man."

Jamie looked up. Kenneth walked with his hands stuck deep in his coat pockets. He wore a Razorbacks beanie that covered his ears, but his nose was red from the cold. No sign of Brayden.

"Hey," said Jamie.

Kenneth joined him on the table, took out his phone, and started typing. No surprise. Except for Freaks business, they still struggled to find things to talk about.

"What's Ty up to today?" Jamie asked, making an effort.

"Shopping with her mom."

Jamie nodded and left it at that. When it came to feelings and relationships, Kenneth was never going to give any more than basic information. Jamie turned his attention back to his own phone.

A few minutes later, Christian and Gabby rounded the bend. Christian had probably caught a ride to the park. She was still the only Freak without wheels, which only posed a problem when she couldn't costume up and run. When they reached the pavilion, Gabby said hello and kissed Jamie on the cheek. He squeezed her upper arm and smiled. She looked troubled. That was also no surprise, given she had called this meeting. Jamie wanted to get started, but they had to wait for Micah. No sense in making Gabby tell the story twice.

"Micah's late again," said Christian.

"Yeah," said Jamie. "We'll give him ten minutes."

But Micah slouched up the walk after only five, no jacket as usual, just a short-sleeved shirt and baggy jeans. Like the rest of them, he had developed a lithe, muscular body, as if their powers had burned through their natural fat stores and pumped all that potential energy into the flesh itself. Kenneth practically hulked these days. Yet Micah also seemed a bit *too* skinny, as if he hadn't eaten enough to maintain that mass in the weeks since his dad had died and now found his body consuming itself.

Baltar ought to be watching him closer than that.

When Micah reached the slab, he stepped up and took a seat on a bench without saying a word. His eyes were red and bleary, as if he had either slept far too long or not nearly long enough.

"'Sup?" said Christian.

"Not much," he said.

"Anyway," said Jamie, "now that we're all here, Gabby can get us started."

She nodded and took a deep breath. "Agent Vincent's dead."

"What?" cried Jamie. The others looked shocked, all except Micah, who seemed bored, and Christian, who already knew. "Why didn't you tell us in your texts?"

"I didn't wanna type the whole story. Besides, we've got some time."

"What do you mean?"

Gabby told them everything. "The Team will be out in those woods as soon as tomorrow."

"Holy *shit*," whispered Jamie. "Then we need to be out there too."

Micah snorted. "What for? If they wanna go get themselves killed, let 'em. Every one down is one less we gotta worry about."

Jamie stared at him. "Bro."

"We can't just sit back and let people die," said Gabby.

Micah scratched his head, miming confusion. "We can't? They'd let *us* die. Hell, they'd kill us themselves. You forget what they did to Christian? Or him?" He indicated Kenneth.

"I'm with Sterne," said Kenneth, rubbing his arm where one of the Team's blades had sliced into his flesh. "Let those son of a bitches go hunting and see how it works out for 'em."

"Man, y'all make shitty superheroes," said Jamie. "I thought we was better than that." He looked at Kenneth. "And it's *sons* of bitches, dumbass."

Kenneth made a dismissive gesture. "Whatever."

Christian hadn't weighed in yet. She was moving some dirt around with the toe of her shoe. Jamie nudged her. "What about you?"

For a few moments, she kept quiet. The others watched her and waited. A jogger trotted past the pavilion, a woman Jamie didn't know, her hair pulled back in a ponytail. She didn't even look their way. Good. Let the world step off. This was Freaks business.

Finally, Christian took a deep breath, exhaled, and said, "We should help 'em. It's like Jamie said. If we're supposed to be the good guys, we shouldn't pick and choose who gets to live."

"Ahhh." Kenneth shook his head in disgust.

Micah shrugged. "Whatever. But don't be surprised when they try to use those stupid guns of theirs."

"Remember," said Jamie, "it's my call. We've gotta deal with the dragon anyway."

Now Gabby bristled. "And by *deal with*, you mean what?"

"I mean whatever it takes."

Christian crossed her arms and laughed bitterly. "Because that's who we are now. We kill stuff that hasn't done anything wrong."

"Excuse me?" Kenneth said, standing up. He loomed over Christian, adopting one of his old bullying stances. "Maybe you forgot it nearly barbecued me and my dad."

Christian didn't seem worried. "You mean when y'all crashed into it and tried to kill it?"

"Look, you mouthy dyke—"

Storm clouds brewed behind Christian's eyes. She started to stand.

Jamie got between them and pushed Kenneth away. "Not cool, man. You wanna start that homophobic shit again, you can deal with the Team and whatever else comes along by your damn self."

Kenneth glared at everyone and sat down, still looking like he wanted to knock Christian's head off her shoulders.

"You back off too," Jamie said to Christian, who made a big show of curtseying before she sat down. "I thought we were past this kind of bullshit. I ain't got time to break up a bunch of schoolyard slap fights."

"I never slapped anybody in my life," muttered Kenneth.

"When all this started, we promised to make up for what we did and protect this town," said Jamie. "The dragon's our responsibility."

Gabby looked as mad as Kenneth. "It's got more in common with us than we've got with the Team. It just wants to live its life, and people keep picking on it."

"*Enough*," said Jamie. "Human lives come first. Hell, *Earth* lives. A dragon could wipe out everything around here."

"And yet humans are the problem," said Christian. "I guess Rabbit didn't teach us shit. This is some xenophobic garbage, man."

"Oh, *God*," groaned Kenneth. "Next you'll start preaching about colonialism again. You know you ain't really an Indian, don't you?"

"Goddammit!" shouted Jamie. He punched the table he had been sitting on. His fist smashed through it, leaving a jagged hole. He yanked his hand out and pointed at each of the Freaks. "Kenneth, grow the hell up. Christian, Gabby, we're gonna handle this dragon with or without you. Period."

Gabby looked shocked. "Are you serious?"

Jamie glared at her. "I've said it before, and I'll say it again. I'm sick of y'all second-guessing every move I make. Me and the boys are going after the dragon. You and Christian can come if you want. If not, stay outta the way."

Gabby stared at him for a bit. Her mouth was a thin, bloodless line. She looked hurt, but she didn't say anything. Instead, she turned away. Jamie hated to think of what this conversation might be doing to their relationship, but lives were at stake, and no matter what they said now, they would always think of whatever happened next as his call. Neither Gabby nor Christian carried that burden. Until they did, they could keep their opinions to themselves.

Micah sat with his elbows on his knees, looking at a spot between his feet. He hadn't moved or even looked up when Jamie struck the other table. Now, as everyone took a breath, he finally stirred and pulled a folded sheet of paper out of his back pocket. "I got something here from Baltar."

"Where is he, anyway?" asked Gabby.

"He had shit to do." Micah unfolded the paper and read. According to Baltar, a full-grown dragon could breathe fire or ice or both and, at full power, could lay waste to a major city. It could blast whole blocks with fire intense enough to melt steel and liquefy stone. Its prehensile tail could crush small buildings and bludgeon crowds like a shoe stepping on insects. If that tail had a barb on the end, it could function like a medieval morningstar. At full size, its wings could generate wind strong enough to tear roofs off houses and send people and even cars sailing down streets. An ice-breather could turn thousands of people into popsicles with just a couple of blasts. It could flatten Quapaw City more efficiently than any human-made weapon short of a MOAB, which, Micah explained, was some kind of huge bomb. "Uncle Baltar says we should 'terminate with extreme prejudice.' But if Christian wants to treat the dragon like a lost puppy, then hey, maybe we should. This town ain't hardly worth saving anyway."

He refolded the paper, stuck it back in his pocket, and fell silent, his arms crossed. For quite a while, no one spoke. Jamie tried to imagine Quapaw City in the aftermath of a full-on dragon attack: his house a pile of smoldering wreckage sitting on a blackened yard, one of his mother's arms poking out like she was calling someone over to help; the high school reduced to so much smashed brick, one wall still standing with a window intact like the dragon had left it on purpose; streets full of cinders that had once been people, the park on fire, thick smoke blocking out the sky. And what if the dragon went on to Crossett or Monticello next? Or Little Rock? Where would it stop if they didn't stop *it*?

Maybe the others were thinking along the same lines. Christian sighed. "All right," she said, sounding as if she hated herself and maybe Jamie too. "But I'm gonna try to keep the dragon away from people without killing it."

Jamie sighed. "Christian—"

"No, dude. That's the best you'll get. If you don't want me along, me and Gabby will go out by ourselves."

He watched her. She didn't look away. "Fine," he said.

Micah laughed. "I'm outta here. Y'all let me know when it's time to go."

"I'll text you," said Jamie. "Meet at the same place as last time."

"Okay."

Micah shuffled off, head bowed, hands in his pockets. Christian got up and followed him without saying another word to Jamie.

Kenneth watched them go for a minute. To Jamie, he said, "You're doing the right thing."

"Jesus, I hope so," said Jamie.

Kenneth walked off, leaving Jamie and Gabby alone. Jamie tried not to look at her, afraid of what he might see—a desire to up the stakes of their fight, or disgust, or, maybe worst of all, pain. He tucked his hands in his jacket pockets and sat on the table, careful not to back his ass into the hole he'd punched. All he needed was a big splinter up his butt. Gabby hovered in his peripheral vision, just a shape that might as well have been a dark cloud over his head.

"What the hell's gotten into you?" she asked.

"I don't know what to tell you," he said.

He waited, but she said nothing else. After a while, she followed the others down the walk and around the bend. Jamie stayed for another half hour, watching the water and wishing for the umpteenth time that they had never opened that goddam trunk in Micah's shed.

CHAPTER TWENTY-TWO

The couch felt much more comfortable than it had ever actually been. The armchairs that had been sitting across from it ever since the first team meeting with Baltar looked like a couple of misshapen lumps in the dark room. A cruddy space with cruddy furniture that had gotten even cruddier since Mom died. *Somebody needs to dust and vacuum,* Micah thought. *But if that somebody is me, we'll be buried in nastiness. It's like somebody stuck a bunch of leeches on my back, but they take energy instead of blood.* The entrance to the hallway could have doubled as a tunnel leading to a deep cave, or hell itself. Curtains drawn, kitchen as dark as every other room, the usual tap leaking drop by drop in its usual rhythm. The whole house was like the inside of somebody's sleeping, dreamless mind, if that person was a freaking slob. And maybe on drugs, too, because those barely visible symbols and runes Baltar had drawn on the walls seemed to glow and pulse. Baltar was standing behind Micah, his deep voice booming as he chanted, which he had been doing ever since night had fallen. Sometimes it seemed more like singing, like some band from another country vocalizing in their native language, accompanied only by the bass-drum thud of whatever made those symbols pulse. Maybe Baltar's heartbeat, or Micah's. In other words, a really shitty concert. Now that Micah thought about it, he felt a weird tingling throughout his body every time that drum pounded.

What the hell's that reject from The Hills Have Eyes *up to?*

Micah held up his hands. The right one glowed red, the left one blue, both pulsing like the runes. *Huh. That's strange. Should I be worried?* To tell the truth, he felt a little more exhausted with every passing

149

moment. And he couldn't remember engaging his powers. "What are you doing to me?" he asked. His voice sounded far away, weak.

The old dude kept chanting, singing, whatever the hell you wanted to call it. Had he even heard? Had Micah spoken aloud, or had he only thought about it?

It could have been ten o'clock, or midnight, or two in the morning. Baltar could sing all night if he wanted to. No school on Sunday, nowhere to be. Every part of Micah's body seemed to sag, to sink farther into the cushions, like the song was sucking out his innards and fusing what was left of him to the couch. Everything else had fallen silent and still, the old man's voice and that stupid drip the only evidence that the world still existed.

What a place to die in. Down among the coffee stains and about five pounds of crumbs.

His eyes were closed again. He forced them open. A weird mist was drifting out of his hands and into—what? He squinted. Something seemed to be—yes, something moved in the air above his head, circled him, the couch, maybe Baltar too. Like dark clouds inside a hurricane. Micah's blood, his breath, his consciousness flowed toward his hands and wafted into that storm.

Baltar's chant had stopped. When had he finally shut the hell up? The symbols no longer pulsed. Micah's hands weren't glowing anymore. Now they looked like two lumps in a darkness too deep for any ordinary room in a common house. Had all that stuff even happened? Maybe he had dreamed it. A crummy dream, but somehow better than the recurring one. At least Mister Sorcerer was human. Maybe.

"You are worried," said Baltar.

"Yeah," Micah muttered, though it wasn't really true. He couldn't summon enough energy to feel worried, or much of anything else beyond a detached sort of curiosity, like everything was happening in a movie he had stumbled on while half-asleep.

"Never fear. You and I are donating some of our energy to the protection spells I have placed on all our houses and vehicles. Your favorite pavilion too. Such magic requires a little sacrifice. I am weary as well."

Yeah, well, you sure don't sound as wiped out as I feel, Micah thought. "Man. Maybe take a little off the others next time."

"Anything is possible." Two hands gripped his shoulders and squeezed. "This will also give me a power reserve I might need when we hunt the dragon. And your own stores will refill while you sleep."

"Cool." Micah's voice sounded like an echo in a deep ravine.

Baltar let go of his shoulders. The old dude might still have been back there, or he might have walked down the hall to his room, the sound of his footsteps muffled in the carpet. Micah slumped farther down, chin on his chest. Even raising his head felt like too much work. Besides, who cared where Baltar went, as long as he left Micah alone? He probably needed to file his teeth or wax his head or some shit.

The time draws nigh.

Micah jerked. That voice—the one from the dreams. He opened his eyes and, using every bit of strength he could muster, looked up.

A figure stood between the armchairs, their arms stretched toward Micah, hands beckoning. It looked human, with two arms and two legs and one head, but those hands had two thumbs, one on either side of the other fingers. Micah could not make out the face or the details of the body. In fact, he could see right through it all the way to the front curtains billowing as the heater cranked up. Was it really there? If he tried to touch it, would it dissipate like smoke?

No, not there yet. But soon. You will come to the water's edge, and my harbinger will rise.

Water? What water? Who did that voice belong to, and why did it keep speaking to him?

"Great," Micah said. "All this Ghostbusters shit, and I ain't even got a proton pack."

Soon you will know true power. And together we will kill. And kill. And kill.

Ugly words. Those ghostly hands reached, reached, reached. Hate wafted off the specter and washed over Micah.

"Piss off, Gozer," he said. "I won't do it. I'll burn your ass alive."

Your fire will strip life from this world, but not my *life. Its heat will serve me.*

"My friends won't let that happen."

Your friends are charred corpses. I have foreseen it. And you will bring it to fruition.

"No. No!"

And in that killing, in all the putrescence and the pain, we will all ascend.

"No."

Micah sat for a long time, repeating that word, but as the night deepened, he found it harder and harder to remember why he should fight.

CHAPTER TWENTY-THREE

Ever since Gabby told them about Agent Vincent, Christian had been thinking about what might happen in the woods. Running into the darkened park to fight Na'ul had been terrifying, but, like her friends, she had also gotten caught up in the rush of her new powers. The Rabbit situation had been different; she had probably thought *too* much, especially given how the trickster had targeted her, and she'd had no choice but to save the person she loved. This dragon, though—it had only fallen through a dimensional hole the Freaks had created. It had tried to live in peace. How could she be party to killing something like that?

And what about Bec? If Christian rode into those woods tomorrow and never came out, would Bec hate her? Or spend weeks, even months, puzzling over why she had gone? Or maybe Bec would just move on, since Christian had clearly been living a double life, had lied, had broken the trust they had only begun to build.

No. Regardless of what else might happen, she wouldn't do that to Bec.

Christian instituted her Going Dark protocol—lights out, blackout curtains drawn, a thick bath towel stuffed under her door. Then, at super-speed, she costumed up, climbed out her window, and sprinted down the street. Seconds later, she arrived on Johnny Cash Way and ducked into the woods across from the Villalobos place. She took off her mask and started to remove her costume, but then she paused. Would the Team have Bec's house under surveillance? She had planned to walk over there and tap on Bec's window. The Team would believe Christian had gone to bed, so she couldn't be seen here.

Focusing on the house, she listened past the night sounds and the rumble of the occasional car on nearby roads, beyond the televisions playing in other homes and the groans and creaks of boards settling. Sure enough, a familiar whine emanated from the Villalobos place. Cameras, bugs, or both? She enhanced her vision. There, at each corner of the roof, angled in all directions and painted the same color as the house: tiny cameras, probably with audio capabilities. Easy to miss if you weren't already looking for them.

Damn. How could she get inside without breaking in at super-speed or disabling the cameras, which would alert the Team? The feds had turned their attention to the dragon, but they wouldn't have left the Freaks unmonitored, at least not until it was time to deploy. And Baltar had refused to whammy Bec's and Ty's houses. Something about "not stretching the magic too thin." Christian had gotten the feeling he just hadn't wanted to bother. That creepy jackass got harder and harder to figure out. Sometimes he seemed like a godsend; at other times, he acted completely indifferent.

In any case, she couldn't do what she had come there to do, so she ran back home, dashed through her window, undressed, and climbed into bed.

Then she texted Bec: need to c u, can u b up by 6
Bec: yeah but why
Christian: tell u later
Christian: trust me
Bec: i do
Christian: pick u up
Christian: night
Bec: k night

Then Christian texted Gabby, who was not happy about having to get up even earlier than they had planned. Her grumpiness clear even though she didn't use any emojis or harsh language, Gabby agreed to drive Christian to Bec's. Christian put her phone on to charge and tried to sleep.

When the alarm sounded at five thirty, Christian sat up, groaned, and rubbed her eyes. Maybe one day she would get a full night's sleep before a major showdown, but somehow she doubted it. After staggering into the bathroom, she brushed her teeth and ran a comb through her hair until it kinda-sorta looked maybe okay. Then she got her go-bag out of the closet, dressed in comfortable clothes that would fit well under the costume, and walked to the kitchen, where she used an entire loaf of bread to make peanut-butter sandwiches. These days, the Freaks didn't need to eat just to keep up their energy, but why take chances?

The sound of an engine, the crackle of tires on leaves—Gabby had arrived. Christian grabbed her bag and headed out the door. Mom wouldn't wake up for at least a couple of hours, probably longer, given that she'd worked the night shift. Christian would have liked to say goodbye, give her one last hug just in case the worst happened, but Mom would sense something, insist on getting up, ask a hundred questions.

The tailpipe of Gabby's car plumed in the cold air. The sky had begun to lighten, though the sun was still hidden behind thick plum-colored clouds. Wind rattled through the trees. Just like the day when the Freaks had ridden off to fight Rabbit, everything looked ordinary. You could live your whole life in a place like this and never see or do one extraordinary thing, and even though weird shit had been happening for a long time, people had stayed here and gone about their lives. Maybe they were brave, possibly just stubborn.

What story would the town tell itself about the Freaks' disappearances or deaths if the fight went badly today? Some parents would probably keep sending their kids out into the night despite Jake Hoeper and Elvis Schott and five more empty seats in Quapaw City High desks. Others might wise up and get the hell out of here before something erased the whole place from the map, which might actually happen today if the Freaks only succeeded in pissing off the dragon. Maybe the

Team and Baltar could stop it, but would they? They had never shown much affection for the town itself.

Christian shook her head, trying to clear away all these thoughts. Gabby gave her a *what are we waiting for* look, so she got in the car and dumped her bag in the back seat.

Gabby pointed to a McDonald's sack wedged beside her on her seat. "Got an extra sausage biscuit in there."

Christian opened the bag and took out the sandwich. "Thanks," she said. She took a few bites, chewed, swallowed. "I'm gonna tell Bec everything."

She expected Gabby to freak out, yell, maybe even turn the car around. Instead, she just nodded. "Just in case, right?"

"Yeah."

"I don't blame you."

Christian finished the sausage biscuit and wiped her mouth with a napkin. "I love them, Gabs."

"I know. Good for y'all."

Christian squeezed Gabby's hand. If she had to be up so early, if she had to participate in a hunt that her heart and conscience had labeled unethical, at least she had a good friend to ride with, to fight beside. And if she died, someone would be there to hold her hand, just like this.

Bec was standing at the edge of their yard, arms crossed, wearing a coat and sweatpants and a Rolling Stones beanie. Christian had given them the beanie and a matching shirt. Despite everything, the sight made her smile.

Gabby drove to the park, pulled into a space, and shut off the engine. "I can walk around a bit. Give y'all some privacy."

"That's okay," said Christian. "It's your car. We'll get out."

"Okay."

Bec had said little so far. Once Christian pulled her bag out of the back seat and shut the door, though, they raised their eyebrows. "Okay, what's up?"

"Let's walk a ways," Christian said, leading Bec into the park. Day had nearly broken, so maybe the cops wouldn't hassle them for being here after hours—or before, whatever you called it when you showed up too early. They angled toward the pond and the sidewalk encircling it. If Christian needed to take this to the pavilion, she wanted a straight shot. So far, the place seemed totally empty. The bulk of Quapaw City's populace would be going to church in a few hours. A couple of joggers might be out here, but that wouldn't be a problem if she saw them coming in time.

Once on the walk, Christian turned right, the shortest route to the pavilion. Bec shivered. "Can we find somewhere to sit?" they asked. "It's cold out here, especially with the wind coming off that water."

Christian glanced around again. Still no one in sight. "Okay."

"I'm all for spending as much time together as possible, babe, but we could have talked in my house."

"No, not at your house. And this isn't something I want to say over the phone." Christian took a moment to steel herself. Then she looked Bec in the eyes. "I have to tell you something. And the reason we can't talk at your house is because the government's watching me."

Bec's eyes widened. Then they laughed.

"No." Christian took one of their hands. "Try to keep an open mind, okay? Because this is gonna sound crazy."

"Crazier than the government spying on you?"

"Yes."

"What's crazier than that?"

"The reason they're doing it." Christian took a deep breath. "I've got superpowers, and so do all my friends. We, uh. We fight monsters."

Bec just looked at her for a moment. Then they burst out laughing again. "Superpowers!" They tried to look serious but dissolved into giggles.

"I'm serious."

After a moment, seeing Christian's expression—probably some combination of indignity and desperation—Bec stopped laughing.

"Okay, straight up, what's this all about? I don't understand what you're trying to do."

"I'm trying to tell you the truth about me."

"And the truth is you've got superpowers. Monsters are real, and you fight them. And oh yeah, the government's after you?"

"I can run at super-speeds and do a bunch of other stuff."

"Look, if you're trying to make me think you're crazy—"

Christian zoomed off, sweeping up Bec in her arms and, a second later, setting them down on the pavilion's concrete slab.

Bec swayed on their feet for a moment. They looked at the picnic tables, the playground equipment, the trees, the pond.

"Say something," said Christian.

Instead, Bec screamed. They turned their head and vomited. Some kind of breakfast cereal hit the slab. Milk and rancid-smelling stomach gunk spattered everywhere.

Christian tried to take Bec's hands, but they yanked away and stumbled until the backs of their knees hit a bench. They sat, hands around their face, and looked at Christian with saucer eyes. Christian's sausage biscuit wanted to climb back up her throat. Tears formed, welled, fell. Bec scooted along the bench, breath tearing in and out.

"Babe—" Christian implored.

"Back up! Get away from me!" Bec dropped to the slab and crawfished backward until they reached the edge. Then they kept going, landing hard on their ass, digging a groove through the dirt. When they stood, they looked around, frantic, as if trying to decide which way to run.

Christian started after them. "Baby, it's still me. I'd never hurt you."

"I said stay away from me, you . . . you—"

Christian's heart dropped into her stomach. "You what? Were you gonna say *freak*?"

Bec jerked as if someone had slapped them. They blinked. "No, I . . . I . . . I don't know."

Christian sat on a tabletop and wiped her eyes. "Well, that's okay. I've been called that for years." Then she broke into deep sobs, the pain and fear tearing loose from her guts and slamming her with every heartbeat, every breath. She put her hands over her face and let it out. Even with all her powers, she couldn't fight heartache and loneliness, two aspects of human experience so common they should have been boring, and yet every time one of them struck you, it felt unique. It wounded you in a way no medicine could touch. You couldn't stop it. You could only try to survive.

For several minutes, neither she nor Bec spoke. Bec stayed where they were, arms crossed, head hanging. Christian tried not to look at them. She held her head in one hand and struck the table with the other—not hard, but the blows still dislodged years of dirt from underneath.

"Christian," Bec said, their voice closer. Christian let her hands fall to her lap. Bec stood four or five feet away, arms still crossed, face pale. "Christian, it's okay."

Christian sniffled. "How? You're afraid of me."

Bec looked away. "I'm afraid of what just happened. I'm scared shitless of what it might mean. But I'm not scared of you." They inched forward, seemed to gather strength, and sat next to her. "It's just . . . a lot, you know?"

Christian laughed. "Oh, man. Do I ever."

"I didn't imagine that, right? You really carried me here in, like, two seconds?"

"You didn't imagine it. And it was more like one and a half."

Bec stared at the concrete for a bit. Then they nodded. "Okay. I'm listening."

Christian told them everything.

When she was done, the two of them sat for a while. The overcast sky muted the gathering sunlight. That cold wind had never stopped blowing. Soon they would have to leave; the Freaks had places to go.

Besides, Bec was shivering. Christian wished she had gotten Micah's temperature powers.

Bec gestured at Christian's bag. "Your costume's in there?"

"Yeah."

"Can I see it?"

Christian removed the uniform. Bec took it, stood, and let it hang from their hands. "This looks and feels about as comfortable as iron underwear."

"Well, I'm getting better at sewing. Maybe I can make some good ones soon."

Bec wiped their eyes. "So Brayden didn't get any powers? I'm not the only ordinary one in the group?"

"He wasn't there when the spell went wrong. He's just Kenneth's best friend. And you know Ty didn't even live here back then, so she's . . . normal too."

"Oh." Bec opened their mouth, closed it, opened it again. "Why'd you tell me all this?"

"Because we're going after the dragon, and I might not make it back. I wanted you to know me—all of me—before that happened. I don't wanna lie to you anymore."

Bec swallowed, nodded. "When do you leave?"

"As soon as we're done here."

"What?"

"We have to. The Team's liable to get themselves killed. Or even worse, they'll just make the dragon mad. God knows what happens after that."

"But you can't be sure they'll even find it. You could go out there and run into it yourself. Get killed while those dudes run around in the woods. Or, hell, maybe they'll find the dragon, and you'll find *them*, and you'll still get killed."

"That's true. But we can't take the chance."

"Why not? If they really wanna kill you, then whatever happens is their problem."

"No. We've gotta be better than them."

Bec stood and paced between the tables, their expression darkening. "Damn it all, you can't just lay this shit on me and bail. What the hell am I supposed to do? Just go home and act like I don't know anything?"

Christian laughed. "Beats the hell outta me. I don't know what to do most of the time."

Bec put their hands on her shoulders. "Don't go. Not today, maybe not ever. Just stay with me."

Christian couldn't meet their eyes. "I can't."

"At least let me get used to the idea."

"I can't."

Bec crossed their arms again. "You mean you won't."

"The dragon—"

"The *dragon*," Bec cried. Christian recoiled. They had never yelled at her before. Their features were distorted with fear and anger. "What if I said I think this dragon's just a bunch of bullshit you made up?"

"What? Why would I do that? I—"

"Because you're scared," said Bec. "You've got something real right here in front of you, so you run in the other direction, even if it gets you killed. You let me fall in love with you, and now you tell me you're gonna go fight a bunch of government assholes armed with alien guns, all for the right to get ripped apart by some fairy-tale monster? Either you don't care what all this does to me, or this is history's craziest excuse not to take a chance on love. Jesus, Christian. What a Sunday morning." Bec backed away, glaring.

Christian met their gaze. No matter what else happened, she wouldn't let Bec believe she was too afraid to look them in the eye. "This is what I do now. Me and the others, we bought and paid for this life when we cast that spell, accidentally or not. Would you even still love me if I could just sit back and let other people die because of me?"

Bec snorted. "I'd rather find out than let you go do . . . whatever you're gonna do."

"I wish I knew how to make this better. To make it make sense. But I don't."

Bec stared at her for several moments. Half a dozen emotions played across their features. More tears fell. Then they held out their hands. "Come here."

"Huh?"

Bec came to her, grabbed her by her shirt, and pulled her up. "I said come here."

Bec kissed her hard enough to hurt her lips. Christian kissed back. The two of them embraced. Christian wasn't cold anymore. She was still crying, but she clung to Bec like letting go would send her floating into space.

Bec fumbled with Christian's shirt, her leggings. For a moment, Christian stood still, letting it happen. Then she took Bec by the shoulders and held them at arms' length. "Wait. What are we doing here?"

Bec's jaw was set. They didn't even blink. "You know what we're doing."

Christian tried to laugh, but she only sounded strangled. "I don't think this is the best time. Jesus, it's freezing, and there's dirt everywhere. I can smell your puke."

"Okay, when would be a good time for you? After you're dead?"

"I'm not gonna die."

"Sure. Right." Bec kissed her again. "Just be with me. Now."

Christian's skin was on fire, her brain swelling inside her skull. Her fingers and toes tingled. She had no idea whether she was ready, but this feeling, just as urgent as when mystical energy surged through her while she ran, this buzzing and burning need, obliterated her conscious thoughts. Only the urgency mattered.

"Come on," she panted, pulling Bec to her. As they kissed, they moved toward the back of the pavilion, off the slab, into the leaves and dead grass that had bunched under an oak tree as if nature had seen this moment coming and prepared a bed. They fell onto it.

When it was over, Christian broke out in goose bumps and shivered. She and Bec gathered themselves, put their layers back on, stood. Christian began to speak several times, but she had no idea what you said in the moments afterward. She had heard that some people talked, joked, just went on with their lives as if nothing momentous had happened, but her body felt sluggish, her brain like mush. She wanted nothing more than to find a blanket and curl up somewhere and sleep for twelve hours.

Bec put their hands in their pockets and kicked at the leaves with the toe of their boot. Christian could not interpret their expression. Sadness? Resignation? They pulled out their phone and looked at the screen. "We've been gone a long time. Gabby's probably wondering if we drowned."

Christian had forgotten all about Gabby. "So what now?"

Bec turned away. "Now I guess we go back."

"Don't you think we should talk about what just happened?"

"No. We can talk after you come out of the woods." Bec was already walking away.

Christian grabbed their shoulder. "But I might not get back. I told you that."

Bec turned on her. "Well, you damn well better. You hear me? You goddam well better make it."

"But—"

"Take me home."

"Babe—"

"Just fucking take me home!"

Christian's heart cracked again. How long before it crumbled?

She scooped up Bec and ran back to Gabby's car. Bec opened the door and climbed in the back. They refused to look at Christian.

Another crack. The base of Christian's throat burned. Was this anything close to how military personnel felt when their significant others left for deployment? And if it was, how did they survive? She climbed into the back and shut the door. Frowning, Gabby glanced at her but said nothing. Good. Christian totally did not feel like talking about it.

Gabby angled her rearview mirror at Bec. "You good?"

"Yeah," Bec said. "Sure."

Gabby watched a moment. Then she readjusted the mirror. "Okay, then." She turned on the car and backed onto the street.

When they reached Bec's place, Gabby parked. "See you later," she said.

Bec got out. Then they leaned down and looked at Christian. "Come back to me. You hear?" But they walked away before Christian could reply.

Christian got out and took the passenger seat, leaving her go-bag in the back, where it had sat beside Bec.

Gabby drove toward Jamie's place. "How about you? Are *you* good?"

"Freaking peachy," said Christian. She had cried perhaps twice in her entire life before today. Now she burst into tears again.

CHAPTER TWENTY-FOUR

Arsiss's bones ached in the cold. She nestled deeper into the heaping bed of leaves and grass she had gathered. Nowhere near the worst temperatures she had ever experienced, yet the weather seemed to sap more energy than those awful winters spent hibernating in her favorite cave while raging winds covered the entrance with snow. Or the rare and miserable years when she had flown for days until she reached the temperate lands and the wide, flat rocks spat out of the planet's belly long ago, stones that soaked up heat all day long. They were perfect for long naps, yet even during those bitter days, the bipeds followed her wherever she went. Hard to sleep with pests' sharp blades prodding you. They charged her on the backs of their beasts, coming in their dozens and hundreds. Maybe those times had contributed to what she felt now: a heavy weariness that rendered even the smallest movement a chore.

Or perhaps Arsiss the Gentle had simply grown too old. In truth, the greatest lethargy lay in her mind. Just living in this alien land, far from her kin and her favorite meadows, sapped her energy as effectively as a days-long battle. New bipeds hunted her. More denizens of the woods sought her protection. Everything different and yet all of it familiar. She still moved from bed to bed and den to den just to find a moment's peace. Her kind had a word for this feeling: a short grunt followed by two clicks of the tongue and one low bark. Any dragon hearing that sound would rush to the sufferer's side and nuzzle, caress, embrace. In this way the family gave their time and their warmth and their love to lift a distraught spirit. Arsiss had seen and taken part in these moments, two dragons or dozens sharing each other's pain and kindness. Here, though, she was alone, hated, hunted, and even in her extremis none would usher her through whatever gate opened when her time came to leave this world.

Now the hunters were coming again. She could sense them the same way she knew when a violent storm brewed beyond her range of vision and hearing, a knowledge that originated in the heart and the gut rather than the brain. The brothers of the one she had burned would come with their weapons and their white-hot hatred, yet they concerned her less than the children. She had met the young ones in the forest and had sensed their tremendous energies, their fury. What would it feel like when those forces were truly unleashed? And their emotions—some had emanated affection and a species of awe, but the others' hatred and fear matched the worst that any hunter had ever brought. Youth, power, and terror: a combination that could save a people, a civilization, a planet. Or doom them all.

Why did so many interactions between different species reduce to violence and death? Every being spent life filling itself to bursting with experience, knowledge, and perspective. Yet their most common feature seemed to be a desire to kill. Such a waste.

Now it would happen again. Arsiss did not speak their language. They did not understand hers. She had turned her tail and run several times, and yet they sought her out again, and again, and again. It would not end until she had passed beyond the horizon and into the lands of eternal light—or when all of them were dead.

If only they would leave her alone. Why did they believe she had any investment in them and their societies, that she would descend on them unprovoked? Better by far to gather a mound of meat you could roast or freeze until you hungered. Better to craft a bed, as she had done here. Better to find a clear stream for drinking, or a nice cave where you could dream in peace. Those on this planet did not even seem to want her body's so-called magical properties, the things the bipeds of her world had believed in and spoken about when they invaded dragons' lairs—a ground-up dragon's tooth to cure diseases, a daily drop of dragon's blood to slow aging, a mouthful of dragon's brain to expand perceptions, a raw dragon's heart for virility and strength. All nonsense, but better to stand between a dragon and her meal than to suggest a biped's beliefs might be wrong.

No, they had always misunderstood her kind. Dragons on her world had learned the bipeds' language over the course of long centuries, though their tongues could not form the words. Here, she lacked even the advantage of understanding what her enemies said and believed; she could only try to interpret their actions. Such could lead to grave misunderstandings, even more violence. The knowledge lay on her soul and weighed it down like a desperate need for sleep upon the eyelids. How many friends had she lost? How many kin? If she could have added up all the time she had spent trying to avoid beings who sought her out because they feared the very encounter their actions ensured, how many years would she total?

Some of them walked the forest even now. Others would come. She could cloak herself and make herself small; she could grow as large as one of these hills or hide in the tallest treetop, and yet sooner or later, someone would find her, would raise their arms against her. Hiding only delayed the confrontation. She would have to fight, to kill them or die. The same story playing out the same ways, only two outcomes possible.

Arsiss the Gentle felt like weeping. By all the gods of all the forests in all the worlds, she was tired.

Yes. She had lived too long.

CHAPTER TWENTY-FIVE

When Jamie got into the car, he said hello to Christian and kissed Gabby on the cheek. Gabby smiled and squeezed his hand. *Maybe it'll be okay*, she thought. *There's a good chance we won't even find the dragon. And if we do, Jamie will always be Jamie. Right?* Those hopeful thoughts lasted as they drove through town and onto the back roads, asphalt eventually giving way to gravel. As soon as they rounded the last curve and reached their staging area, though, tension filled the car like smoke. Gabby could barely breathe through it. Jamie leaned forward, straining against the seatbelt, frowning. Christian unbuckled and leaned forward, too, one hand on each of the front seats.

Two dark SUVs had parked in the ditch. Empty flatbed trailers were attached to both.

"Damn," said Jamie. "Stop and back up. Let's park around the curve."

"They're probably out there getting lost," said Gabby. "Or killed."

After reversing until they could no longer see the Team's vehicles, she pulled off the road and killed the engine. The three of them got out. Jamie walked through the ditch and fifteen or twenty feet into the woods, where he stood with his hands on hips. Gabby looked at Christian, who shrugged. The two of them leaned against the car. Gabby took out her phone. No new messages from Micah or Kenneth. Probably on their way, though you could never tell, especially with Micah. He had carried a lot of the weight when they fought Na'ul, and though his grief and anger had made him dangerous even to the other Freaks, they had known he was on their side. Against Rabbit, he had started off well, but some kind of fit had caused him to miss the second half of the fight.

Now, given how he had been acting, could they trust him at all? The kid might just curl up under a tree and fall asleep.

One of these days, Gabby thought, *he'll be a straight-up liability. I just hope it ain't today.*

"This *sucks*," Jamie said as he stepped back over the ditch. "I wish Kenneth and them would hurry up."

"Chill," said Christian. "The Team can handle themselves. And if they can't, well, they shouldn't have gone out there."

"You could say the same thing about us," said Jamie. "When we suit up, let's do it a ways into the trees. Somebody might drive by." He stuck his hands in his pockets and looked at the ground.

Gabby forced herself to smile. "Look at it this way. If the dragon eats the Team, they'll give it a bellyache so bad it won't want to fight us."

Neither Jamie nor Christian even looked at her, much less laughed. Gabby had to admit it wasn't much of a joke.

The three of them stood around for ten more minutes before the sound of another engine grew closer. Hopefully one of their friends and not some rando who might remember their faces if whatever happened today spilled back to town. Should they have costumed up already? No, because then the same passersby would see three costumed Freaks and Gabby's car in the same place. Not that a lot of cars used this road—Gabby could remember seeing maybe two in all the times she had been here. But with the Freaks' luck, somebody would march a whole damn parade past this spot.

It turned out to be three cars, not one. Baltar's Lexus led the way. Kenneth's and Brayden's trucks followed. Brayden and his dad had spent a couple of weekends fixing the minor damage taken when his ATV had rammed Rabbit. What would Mr. Sears say if Brayden brought it back in worse shape than last time? Or in pieces? Or burned to slag?

Aw, screw the damn four-wheeler. Any one of us could die today.

If that happened, some people might figure out the identities of the masked weirdos who had been spotted around Quapaw City, adding the Freaks' sudden absence to the names of the dead and calculating a possibility they had never considered before: that even kids like her had secrets and rich lives. Other people might conclude the masked Freaks had murdered the local teens before bailing. Everything that had happened would pass into a legend that would leave people going, *Huh, that was weird.* And for a whole lot of townsfolk, her death, her friends' disappearances, would mean nothing at all. *Who?* they would say, looking confused. *Did they live around here? Who were they kin to?* Before long, this group would mostly forget about the dead, recalling them only in distorted tales told around hunting campfires and on drunken late nights.

We shouldn't even be out here. This is like killing a bear that mauled some jackass who tracked it down and shot it in the ass.

Jamie was frowning, his brow wrinkled. As the others parked and got out, he stomped over. "What the hell took y'all so damn long? The Team's got God knows how much of a head start, and I've been standing here scratching my ass."

Kenneth's expression hardened. "We came as soon as we could. Get outta our faces."

Brayden just smiled that dopey smile of his, the one he used when he felt uncomfortable and wasn't sure who was right. It was his camouflage, like a chameleon changing colors.

Gabby stepped between the boys. "Um, how's Ty? She good?"

"Yeah," said Kenneth, glaring at Jamie. "She's got church."

"Me too," said Gabby. "Mom's gonna kill me when she finds me gone." She turned to Jamie. "Yours won't be happy either."

"I guess not," he said, and turned away.

Boys. Give 'em thirty seconds, and they'll find some reason to punch each other.

Baltar and Micah got out of the Lexus. Micah wandered over with his bag on his shoulder. Creepy-ass Baltar followed, daylight shining on his shaved head. As always, he had dressed in all black: a turtleneck, jeans, hiking boots, and a light jacket. Maybe the cold didn't bother him much, either. They stopped beside Gabby and Christian. The old man sniffed the air and looked at the sky. Thick clouds were blowing in, most of them dark. Before she had left that morning, Gabby had heard some guy on TV talking about the weather. Thunderstorms expected by mid-morning at the latest and lasting the rest of the day. She was looking at the leading edge of that system. On top of everything else, the Freaks would be getting wet if this hunt took much time at all.

Baltar seemed to read her mind. "The rain will be here sooner than expected," he said. "And approximately three miles that way, the forest is burning."

"What?" said Jamie. He paused, tilted his head back, sniffed. "He's right. Everybody move out. Once the road's out of sight, get dressed and saddle up. Christian, don't wait for us. Go find 'em. Then come back and lead us in." He turned to Baltar. "You rolling with us this time?"

"No," said the old dude. "As before, I will fight this battle on a separate front."

Jamie shrugged. "Whatever."

Brayden and Kenneth unloaded the ATVs. Everyone got their bags and headed into the woods. They stopped maybe fifty yards deep. A blur and a whoosh, and Christian stood before them in full costume. "Be back in a minute." Then she was gone.

The rest of them began to suit up. Kenneth got his legs tangled in his costume and nearly fell over. Brayden caught him. They really needed to get Brayden an outfit, even though he had no powers. This was only the second time he had come with them on a mission, unless you counted how he had accompanied Kenneth on surveillance a few times, but it would be pretty hard to deny who was under the Freaks' costumes if people saw Brayden Sears hanging out with them like some kind of half-assed Robin. Hell, he could have given everything away when he torpedoed Rabbit with his ATV. The Team had been concussed and too far away to see him do it, thank God.

"You absolutely, positively can't get involved this time," Gabby said to him. "In fact, you're gonna have to let us off before we get to wherever we're going. The Team's already there this time."

"She's right," said Jamie, struggling to pull his costume over his shoulders. "In fact—"

Before he could continue, Christian appeared beside him. Jamie's costume billowed out. He cursed and tried to smooth it back into shape. "Gotta hustle," said Christian. "The Team's getting its ass kicked."

Jamie turned to Kenneth. "You and Brayden take Baltar and get there as fast as you can." He turned to the old man. "Unless you got a flying spell, we ain't got time to wait."

Baltar scowled as he looked over the ATVs, probably calculating how many times he was likely to bruise his tailbone or fall off. "I am not sure this is a good idea."

"Ah, c'mon." Brayden slapped him on the back. "You're in Arkansas. You're, like, legally supposed to ride four-wheelers in the woods."

"That law's only for rednecks," said Micah.

"Dude, really?" Brayden looked hurt.

Baltar frowned and pulled away from Brayden but said nothing else.

"Stop screwing around," Jamie said, looking at Micah and Brayden with only a little more warmth than the old guy had. Then he turned to Kenneth. "Use your senses to home in on us. Me and Christian gotta get Gabby and Micah out yonder now."

"Maybe I should just stay here," said Brayden. "Kenneth can carry Uncle Baltar."

The old man's lip curled, either from the prospect of riding with Kenneth or because Brayden had called him "uncle."

"Nah," said Jamie. "We might need you to haul somebody out."

"Or if we get in trouble, we could throw him at the dragon," said Micah.

Brayden scratched his head. "Man, did I sleepwalk over to your house and piss in your Corn Flakes this morning?"

"*Enough*," said Jamie. "Move out."

Kenneth got onto his ATV. Brayden let Baltar climb on first; then he took his seat and started the engine.

Gabby got onto Jamie's back. Christian walked over to Micah and picked him up. He used to hate it when she did that, but now he looked as tranquil as ever, one arm thrown over her shoulders. As Gabby and Jamie rose over the treetops, she traced Christian's passage through the woods, which led them in the same direction Baltar had pointed earlier. Gabby hadn't known the old man had enhanced senses, too, but he had smelled that fire. He had even known how far away it was. Had the others noticed that?

Once she and Jamie cleared the canopy, smoke was visible some distance away. It was too far to see or hear what was happening without turning up her senses. She didn't bother. They were going there anyway, and at a pretty good clip.

This is gonna go bad. I just know it.

Now they were angling down. Jamie landed, skittering a few steps, and set her down on her feet. Christian and Micah stood a few yards away. When they were all suited up like this, Gabby usually felt a charge of adrenaline, a kind of giddiness, like what she imagined football players experienced just before they ran onto the field. Now, though, her stomach turned over, and her teeth kept chattering. The cold weather explained part of it, as did the usual fear for herself and her friends' lives. She chalked the rest up to her recriminations. Going over it yet again would do no good, though. She and Christian could only back their friends' play or abandon them, and she could not bring herself to walk away. Still, her conscience would talk to her long after all this had ended, assuming she survived. For perhaps the first time, she felt some admiration for the Team—not their methods or their goals, but their sheer guts, to walk into something like this without powers.

She stood beside the others as they took in the scene.

The dragon stood maybe twenty-five feet tall, about twelve feet wide at the chest. It slithered between the trees, roaring and hissing at the men spread around it, all of them hiding behind the thickest foliage in the area, popping out long enough to shoot before taking cover again. Mossman carried a long, cylindrical weapon that looked bazooka-ish, though it must have been light and balanced enough for him to hold it one-handed. He propped it on his crooked left arm and fired. A round laser beam the size of a soccer ball sizzled toward the dragon and struck it on its flank. When the dragon moved, the laser burned a dark streak across those scales. Mossman cut several trees in half once the creature glided out of his line of fire. The trunks crashed to the ground, all of them on fire.

The dragon moved away, its back to the Team. When Mossman shouted for the others to engage, the creature picked up three of those flaming trees in its tail and flung them like spears. Everyone scattered or hugged the ground. One of the flaming projectiles struck a hickory and rattled it. Leaves and nuts rained down. The other two trunks carried on until their momentum faded. They struck the ground and dug deep furrows in the soil. No one was hit.

Greenwalt, Jeffcoat, and Kragthorpe converged on Mossman. Each carried a special weapon. "I got this," Kragthorpe said, stepping forward and fitting the sonic cannon to his shoulder. He fired. Even with the distance, the sound made Gabby's teeth ache and sent sharp, stabbing pains into her head. She covered her ears. The dragon fell, roared, turned, and sent a long tongue of blue fire straight at the Team. They saw it coming. Kragthorpe broke left. The other three went right. The fire went out as the dragon turned away.

"Let's get in this shit before those fools get murked," Jamie said, taking to the sky.

"Get some," said Micah. "And if you accidentally knock a fed into the next county, don't waste time crying." Tough talk, but he still sounded dreamy, half-asleep. At least he was moving. He walked forward, his left hand glowing blue as he waved it around. A block of ice swallowed the dragon, freezing it in mid-step.

Gabby followed Micah, the energy starting to cycle up inside her. She had recently watched a TV show in which a character got an echocardiogram, his heartbeat going *whoosh-chuck*, *whoosh-chuck*. It had been precisely the sound she had always imagined her energy would make when she prepared to use her force beams. Her hands began to glow white.

The Team was turning toward Gabby, Micah, and Christian. Mossman hadn't given another order yet, but he, Kragthorpe, and Jeffcoat started to raise their weapons again. Only Greenwalt hesitated.

"Light them up," said Mossman. He fired.

Micah met his blast with ice. His beam was so cold it cancelled out the laser. "Quit it," he said, sounding disgusted. He waved his red right hand. A tower of fire appeared between the Team and the Freaks. It was taller than the trees, maybe twenty feet wide, and it hovered an inch above the ground and all those dead leaves. None of them caught fire. Neither did the woods, even though that wall came close to touching lots of branches.

I didn't know he could do that.

From the sound of it, neither had the Team. They were speaking to each other, the words fast and fevered. Something cracked out there, like a giant had stepped on a full-grown oak and snapped it like a twig. Micah tilted his head, looking exactly like a curious dog. Then he gestured at his fire wall. It disappeared.

The dragon stood amid big chunks of ice. It shook itself, flinging water and little shards everywhere. Then it turned back their way. A sound emanated from it. To Gabby, it sounded exactly like a sigh, as if this being straight out of legends had grown tired of the whole scene. Opening its mouth wide, wider, the dragon roared, the sound even louder than Kragthorpe's rifle, overwhelming, almost like a solid force. Everyone covered their ears. Some fell to their knees.

The already oversized lizard began to grow. And grow. And grow.

Gabby's bladder clenched. Her heart hammered. Na'ul had been big. Rabbit had made himself even bigger. She had always been grateful they hadn't found out how much he could grow. Now it looked like the dragon would show them precisely what it could do. Its body expanded, bulging into the pines around it, bending them, snapping the trunks. And still it grew.

CHAPTER TWENTY-SIX

At first, Kenneth navigated by hearing alone. Too many trees and hills to depend on line of sight. Hoping Brayden and Baltar could keep up, he pushed the ATV as fast as he could without risking a crash. Panicked voices faded in. Then loud cracking sounds nearly burst his eardrums. Wincing, he turned down his hearing. As he crested a little hill and swung around a thick copse, the source of the noise revealed itself: the purple dragon was growing, expanding, its head pushing past the treetops, its body splintering trunks. Kenneth forgot to breathe for a second or two. His bowels wanted to let go. He clenched his teeth and willed himself to calm down. *Don't you dare freaking panic. You wanna see Ty again? Keep your head.* He parked several dozen yards from ground zero and flagged down Brayden, whose eyes seemed ready to pop out of his head. At least Kenneth probably wouldn't have to worry about whether Brayden would try to join the fight again; he looked scared enough to drop a load in his britches. As for Baltar, he was gripping the sides of Brayden's coveralls with his long, bony fingers, his face set in concentration. When the ATV stopped, the old fart climbed off as fast as he could and backed away several steps, like he was afraid the machine would turn on its own and run him down.

"I gotta get up there," said Kenneth. "Brayden, get gone."

Brayden wiped his leaking nose with the back of his hand, his bulging eyes locked on the dragon. "What about your ride?"

"I hope it won't get damaged this far back, but better it than you. Remember not to get involved this time. If you drove into that thing, it'd probably just step on you."

"Yeah," said Brayden. "Okay."

Kenneth put a hand on his shoulder. "Look, if this goes bad, tell Ty . . . tell her—"

"Don't worry. I'll figure something out."

"Okay." The thought of never seeing Ty again nearly knocked Kenneth on his ass. But he had to do this.

Baltar had been studying the scene. "Go. I will help when I can."

"Uh-huh," Kenneth said, and then he ran, heading straight for the dragon. *This is crazy this is crazy this is crazy,* he thought, forcing himself forward when every instinct told him he was running the wrong way. Funny how people used to believe he was a dumbass, and now that some of them were realizing he had more than two brain cells, he kept finding himself doing shit like this. *You should have texted Ty this morning. If the last thing you ever said to her turns out to be* Bye, see you later, *you're gonna feel really stupid.*

The ground between him and the others had mostly leveled out, providing him a good view. Mossman stepped from behind a tree and aimed his special weapon. A thick laser shot out and struck the dragon along its belly, sending up thin, dark smoke. When Mossman stopped firing, the scales looked blackened but intact. Mossman let loose a string of curses that probably made Gabby blush, though Kenneth could barely hear over the sounds of his own breathing and his feet crunching through fallen leaves. As Mossman took shelter again, Kragthorpe tried to take his shot—the sound cannon—but the dragon belched fire, driving the fed back to cover. Greenwalt blasted away with the acid gun. Most of the goop hit the foliage and reduced it to smoking heaps, but one glob struck the dragon's foot. The lizard shook its leg, flinging green junk everywhere. The foot itself seemed mostly unharmed. Jeffcoat must have dropped his big weapon somewhere, because he was peppering the dragon's upper chest with one of those Han Solo blasters. Surely he knew that little thing wouldn't do shit if the cannons hadn't worked. Maybe he was buying his friends some time to regroup.

Kenneth reached the other Freaks, who were huddled up and arguing. He bulled his way into the ring.

"Dammit to hell," Jamie was saying. "We're not talking about this
again."

"The hell we ain't," cried Gabby. "We can just drive it off! *We don't
have to kill it!*"

"In case you didn't notice, it's the size of a damn building," Jamie
yelled. "You think we can make it go where we want?"

"We could *try*."

"How? Throw a big-ass leash over its head?"

"You haven't even tried to think of a way." Gabby was pissed.

"All I know is we can't let it threaten human life again."

"Human life chased it down." Christian sounded much calmer than
the other two. "Human life shot it. Are you one of them people that
think we should, like, kill a coyote that wanders into a neighborhood
somebody built on its old territory?"

Jamie's eyes narrowed. "This ain't no coyote. You ever seen one that
could breathe fire?"

"Y'all are crazy," Kenneth said, panting. "I'm going after the giant
monster that's over there trying to barbecue people. It ain't gonna burn
my family to death or freeze Ty like an ice cube if I can help it."

"Yeah, the hell with this," said Jamie. "Micah, Kenneth, let's do this
shit. Hit your stealth charms."

Jamie said the magic word. The usual puff of air, or whatever it was,
cascaded over him. He took off without waiting for anyone else. Micah
just wandered away like a drunk.

This again, thought Kenneth. He didn't look forward to what was
about to happen. Still, he saw the wisdom in it. Putting his hand over
the charm embedded in his chest, he said the word. His legs collapsed
beneath him. This time he actually barfed, and some of it stuck to his
mask. It steamed in the cold air. Every muscle felt like rubber. His bones

creaked and throbbed. The top of his skull pounded like his brain had engaged an ejector seat. "Oh, man, that *sucks*."

"You're breaking my heart," said Christian. She and Gabby moved off, not engaging their charms. Were they so damn stubborn, so determined to save the monster, that they'd stay visible just to give Jamie the finger? Apparently so.

As Kenneth struggled to his feet, a little strength returning already, Jamie flew up, circled the dragon a couple of times, and then shot down straight at its head, striking it with both fists. He bounced off, careened through the air, and righted himself, hovering just over the trees. The purple lizard staggered, shook its head, and raised its snout. It blasted ice into the sky. Jamie maneuvered away from the stream.

Kenneth tried to flank the dragon. If he could get behind it, he might be able to do some damage without taking any himself. "If you give a shit about us, you'll get off the sidelines," he yelled to the girls.

Christian cursed darkly, but she ran right at the dragon, up its belly, and onto its head, where she did her tap-dance move. Godzilla Lite roared and swung its head back and forth, but somehow Christian kept her perch. Gabby got in the game, blasting the dragon's legs and chest, her white beams sizzling. She used short bursts, plus some of those floating spheres that lazed their way to the target and burst, sending tongues of sheer force up and down the monster's torso. It roared, staggered, but did not fall. Then she created a whole series of spheres, a spiraled column that surrounded the dragon from feet to neck, that rotated faster and faster and condensed until they seemed to bind its body like chains. When they touched the scales, they pulsed. Gabby was clenching and unclenching her fists, the bubble strands mimicking her grip. Her energy flashed and pulsed, faster and faster until the spheres crackled like electric wires. The dragon bellowed as Christian struggled to stay on its head.

Where had the Team gone? Except for Jeffcoat, who seemed to be shooting at both the dragon and Christian, they had disappeared.

Knowing those jackholes, they were probably regrouping or planning a sneak attack on the Freaks.

"Quit that," yelled Gabby, throwing a weak burst at Jeffcoat, striking him in the left arm, and spinning him around. He fell and landed hard on his right side, where he lay groaning.

"Bitch," someone shouted, and then that big laser beam nearly cut Gabby's head off. It clipped her and knocked her down. Mossman again. The bubble strands vanished. Jamie dive-bombed Mossman, but Kenneth had no time to watch the fun. The other fights had been like this too: so much going on you couldn't keep up with it all, too many threats, and you had to take it easy on the Team even though you wanted to put your fist through their heads. *Engage your charms, dumbasses.* But Gabby and Christian apparently planned to get themselves killed. Kenneth yanked a sapling out of the ground and fastballed it in Mossman's direction just to give him something else to think about. It struck the ground in front of the fed, who jerked away, the barrel of his weapon pointed at the sky. He spotted Kenneth, leveled the cannon, and fired. The laser beam struck Kenneth full in the chest. He barely had time to flex his muscles and engage his aura, and though the laser did not penetrate that magic barrier, the force drove him through the trunks of another two saplings. He landed on his back, his upper torso a few degrees warmer than the rest of him. He lay there for a few seconds, letting his pulse slow. *Should have charmed myself against them, too,* Kenneth thought. *You'd think they'd work with us this time, since we came here to save them. Bunch of dipshits.*

Raised voices cried for backup. More trees fell. The dragon bellowed.

Get back in the game. Gavin's voice was in Kenneth's head again. Maybe it would never leave him alone. For the rest of his life, every time he took even a split second to let others fight, Gavin would come back and remind him that inactions had consequences too.

"You're the only dude I know who got killed and turned into an even bigger asshole." Kenneth rolled over and got to his feet. Gabby and Mossman were blasting each other as Jamie and Kragthorpe played tug-of-war over the sonic gun, Jamie hovering just over the fed's head, Kragthorpe's heels dug into the ground. Jeffcoat raised the laser pistol and aimed at Jamie, but the gun started melting. He screamed and dropped it, favoring his clawed hand. Sterne must have heated the gun, but the kid was nowhere in sight. Hiding, or had he cloaked himself from Kenneth just to be a dick? Greenwalt was shooting acid at the dragon, which ignored him as it tried to knock Christian off its head. She was still stomping away. Kragthorpe yanked downward with one hand and slugged Jamie in the jaw. If it bothered Entmann, he didn't show it.

You're still just watchin', said Gavin.

"Yeah, well, *you're* still just a half-assed ghost." Kenneth tried to circle behind the dragon, which was now using its tail to swipe at Christian. Its ass and hind legs were only twenty feet away from two white oaks. Both trees looked at least forty feet tall and as big around as a garbage can. It would have been nice if some of those California redwoods grew in Southeast Arkansas, but these would have to do. The tail whipped from side to side, like a jump rope, as Christian leaped over it and ducked under it. The dragon's huge body blocked everyone else from Kenneth's view, but whoever had won the tug-of-war must have shot the dragon with the sound gun, because pure noise nearly ripped Kenneth's ears apart. He covered them and screamed. When the sound cut out, he opened his eyes. The dragon, lurching backward, was about to step on him. He dove behind the two trees, but the monster caught itself before it crashed into them and blasted fire, a wave of flame so wide Kenneth could see it even with the dragon in the way. It could have killed all the Freaks and the Team too.

Christian was no longer on top of the dragon's head. Maybe she had gone to check on the others.

People were yelling, so at least some of them had lived. Gabby's bacon-in-a-frying-pan sounds filled the air, then the electronic sizzle of lasers.

The dragon reared up on its hind legs. Its tail thrust straight back, probably for balance.

"Now!" cried Kenneth.

He grabbed the tail at a point maybe five feet from the tip, planted his feet, and yanked. The dragon stumbled backward, pinwheeling its front legs, roaring in surprise. Kenneth retreated several steps, grabbed the tail again, and yanked. Same result. The lizard dropped to all fours and tried to turn, but Kenneth had dragged the tail between those trees. Now he placed his feet against their trunks, wrapped his arms around the tail, and clasped his hands. When the dragon tried to run, Kenneth held it in place, braced against the groaning and shaking trees. Acorns rained onto his head. Sweat dripped down his face. Old Godzilla Lite growled, set all four of its feet, and leaned forward, taking one halting step at a time, trying to drag Kenneth back through the gap in the trees. When the dragon stopped driving ahead long enough to gather its strength, Kenneth yanked the tail backward again and braced himself.

Godzilla Lite craned its neck around and looked at him. Those blue eyes seemed both tired and fierce, but Kenneth pulled the monster backward until its ass rested against the oaks. Using its front feet, it began to drag itself sideways and back, curling around the trees, jaws snapping. Those giant teeth came nearer to Kenneth every second.

"Somebody freaking do something!" he yelled.

Gabby's beams struck the dragon, as did Mossman's laser and Greenwalt's acid. It snorted and growled but kept pursuing Kenneth. Jamie dove out of the sky and smashed into the lizard's jaw, knocking it sideways. It looked everywhere, trying to find Entmann. Gabby increased her intensity. The air filled with crackling and sizzling.

Kenneth choked up on the tail and yanked again. Old Godzilla Lite sighed. Its blue eyes turned to Kenneth again. He tensed.

The tail detached at the point where it joined the torso.

Kenneth stumbled backward and fell on his ass, the tail on top of him. After a moment, he stood up and brushed himself off. "Well, shit."

Godzilla Lite stepped toward the others, crunching downed trees under its feet. It opened its mouth and breathed fire, panning its head from side to side. Everyone retreated. Then it closed its eyes and clenched its teeth and grunted.

What's it doing now? Taking a dump?

A sharp, barbed protrusion poked out of the dragon's body where its tail had been. The monster flexed again. More tail squeezed out. It really was like watching an animal poop. The new protrusion was scaled, like the rest of the dragon's body, with ridges along the top. More and more revealed itself.

Kenneth ran forward and tried to grab this new one as the others broke their own paralysis and resumed firing. The dragon took two steps to the side. When Kenneth touched the new tail, it whipped, sending him flying. He glanced off one of the oaks and cartwheeled through the air. By the time he dragged himself to his feet, the new tail had completely grown in. Blasts of ice had driven back the other Freaks and the Team. The ground between them and the monster sparkled in the muted light. Hunks of ice the size of refrigerators dotted the land.

The dragon unfurled and flapped its wings, stirring up the forest crud and the smoke. Kenneth squinted, his eyes watering. By the time he had rubbed all the gunk out of them, the monster was in the sky.

CHAPTER TWENTY-SEVEN

O nce Kenneth had rendered the dragon stationary, Jamie had hurled himself against it over and over, striking its snout while Christian tap-danced on top of the skull like she had done to Rabbit. Gabby had blasted its torso and front legs. Even the Team had helped. Greenwalt had done the most damage with the sonic cannon, probably because it was the only weapon that didn't need to penetrate those armored scales. That last time Jamie struck the dragon, though, it seemed to lose patience. It had set its feet, thrusting its head forward. Jamie had flown down and yelled for everyone to fall back. Before most of them could cover much distance, the dragon had opened its mouth and unleashed what felt like the power of an arctic storm, a wall of ice that dwarfed Micah's fire wall.

None of that ice had touched them. It struck some invisible barrier and shot straight up and out to both sides, but it came no closer. Even the cold hadn't penetrated.

Jamie had turned and focused his vision, looking for whatever had shielded everyone. Nothing. It must have been Baltar. The old man had probably used an invisibility charm and then conjured the barrier. Every time Jamie started to think Micah's great-uncle needed a good ass-kicking as much as any monster did, the wizard proved himself all over again.

That was when the dragon had taken to the air. Now it was soaring high. At first, Jamie thought it was changing sizes, growing smaller, but soon enough he realized it was booking. He flew after it.

Now I know how dogs feel when they chase eighteen-wheelers.

Lasers and pure sound ripped the sky around him. That godawful noise almost knocked him out of the air. He wavered and lost some altitude, but then the sound faded. The lasers stopped. His friends had probably distracted the Team—that, or the feds had decided maybe they shouldn't kill the super-powered help quite yet.

Jamie poured on the speed. Those huge, leathery wings kept flapping. What would the dragon look like from the ground? Just another bird? Strong winds jostled Jamie off course. He adjusted his angle and tried to go faster. The dragon seemed to grow larger and larger as he closed in. It was still gaining altitude, like it knew height might equal safety, but surely they had climbed above the radar threshold. If the military scrambled fighters, would the pilots fire on the dragon alone, or would they strafe Jamie too? Maybe lob a few missiles at the others?

He needed to get this thing back to the ground.

Jamie caught the tip of the dragon's tail, the barb driving into his stomach as he grabbed at the scales. He held on to whatever he could find, still flying forward and pulling himself along hand over hand. The dragon must have felt him. The tail flicked, nearly slinging him away, but he recalibrated his angle and stayed on course. Straining to pour on more speed, he skimmed over the surface of the dragon's back, its neck. Just a little more.

Now flying just between its ears, Jamie took off one of his gloves and put a hand on the dragon's head. Then he called up every calming image he could think of—a dog lying in the sun beside a slow-flowing river, a swaddled infant, the wind blowing through a field of flowers, a dozen others. The dragon grunted and barked, twisting under Jamie's hand. He held steady, projecting a sense of ease. The dragon made a *zzzrrrrddd* sound. Then it began to lose altitude. Jamie pulled himself down onto the skull and wrapped his arms around one of the ears, gripping the edges. They circled in the sky, riding the currents, drifting down. The frozen ground, the chunks of ice, the splintered trees and broken logs, the Freaks and the Team as small as ants—Jamie closed his eyes and projected this image, as bright and clear as he could make it. The dragon kept dropping.

Then, as Jamie took a deep breath and let his concentration lapse for just a moment, images smashed into his brain like a bullet. He gripped the ear as hard as he could, locked his legs around it, and lost himself.

He was curled in a tight ball, surrounded by some kind of warm liquid and smooth white walls. The world was made of peace and diffused light. He moved, just the shifting of a limb, the flexing of digits. The wall scraped under his nails and cracked. Brighter light shone through the aperture. Air poured in, bearing scents he'd never dreamed of. His mouth watered. For the first time, he truly realized the shape of his body, the length of his limbs. When he stretched, the enclosure fell apart. Standing for the first time, crunching the shell under his feet, he found himself in a capacious nest made from tree branches and mud and moss. More eggs had been piled everywhere. He unfurled his wings, shook the liquid away, and, for the first time, tried to roar. It sounded more like a chirp.

When Jamie blinked, the world shifted. Now he was walking along a forest floor, following the lumbering body of a much bigger dragon. *Mother.* Deep green with black markings like woodgrain, she led him through trees on a path he had never traveled. Sometimes she looked back and called to him in her deep, throaty language. He answered. Soon they came to a valley that seemed to glow, bright yellow and many shades of green, daylight kissing its surfaces. Hundreds of dragons flew, walked, or ran, as plenteous as trees. A river flowed through the center of the valley, its banks covered in rocks. On the flatter ones, tens of thousands of dragons dozed, his kin, most of them shrunk to their smallest size. Everything before him whispered love and harmony. He understood that he would come here many times over his long, long life. Where these others would go after the great gathering he couldn't have said, but he hoped he would meet them again on the world's twisting paths.

Blink—Now an adolescent that had not yet learned to use all his talents, he stood over his first solo kill, a three-legged creature with two horns and a body made for running at high speeds, all muscle and sleek design. He had burned it to death in mid-leap, and now its carcass smoldered, acrid smoke rising on a breeze that smelled like sweet grass. The cooked meat brought thick drool and a kind of crazed need to feel flesh between his teeth. Yet before he could eat, his mother—Nessas, the Grand Huntress—drove him away from the body. As he watched, she kneeled before it, bowing, her chin and neck on the ground even as her back legs locked. Then she rose, ripped off a piece of meat, and flung it away, high and through the trees. *A sacrifice to the forest that sustains us.* She turned and watched him until he came forward and repeated her actions. Only then could he partake. *Never savor a death*, said Nessas. *Never indulge base desires or gluttony. Never take more than you need, so that all might have enough.* She trumpeted a specific call, six high-pitched barks, and other meat-eaters came forth from the woods and waited. She allowed Jamie to eat first, a privilege reserved for the one who bore the weight of a life ended before its time. Spitting juices ran down his throat. When he was done, those others ate until only bones remained. Other creatures appeared and cracked the bones with their teeth and claws, drinking the precious marrow. Nothing was wasted. *Honor the fallen that give you life*, said Nessas, *for in the multiverse's great chain, each link is attached to every other.*

Blink—Full-grown, he stood over Nessas's dead body, she who had lived long and long, who had finally died of old age in a field of high green grasses tasting of hot spice. As she had taken her last breath, she had looked deep into his eyes. *Beloved daughter*, she had said, and his heart had nearly burst. The forest's inhabitants had come to see her cross the last great valley and climb the mountain where all good creatures someday went. Ripped open by sadness and loneliness, he bowed as she had shown him long ago and stayed that way for three days. When he finally stood and left her, his heart lay heavy inside him like a stone. The forest would use Nessas's body as it used all the others. Life giving way to more life. He partook of the grasses, eating his fill, enough to sustain him through many turns of the day. She had taught him everything. He had learned her lessons so well that every kill brought him to tears. As he left that place, the other beings who had come to see the great Nessas one last time whispered his name, the one he would carry through two worlds: *Arsiss the Gentle.*

Blink—Another memory began, but before a complete picture could coalesce, an ear-splitting whine jolted Jamie out of the dragon's mind and jostled him off its head. He fell, the earth still hundreds of feet below but far too close. The sonic cannon blasted the dragon again. She cried out in pain.

Gabby and Christian were right, and Baltar was full of shit. It doesn't wanna wipe out Quapaw City. What have I done?

And yet he had no choice. The dragon had killed at least two people, and whatever else Baltar might have been wrong about, he had nailed his assessment of its power level. Anything that could grow so big and spit so much fire, anything with almost impenetrable armor, posed an existential threat to Quapaw City and beyond.

All those images, though, those scenes, those emotions—Jamie's head swam. His mental connection to Arsiss had gutted him and replaced his innards with truth.

If we kill it, we're no better than the Team and what they've done to us. But look at what's happening right now. Folks ain't gonna leave the dragon alone. Can I really sit back and take a chance that it'll roast Mom and Dad? Or the Davisons? Or Ms. Frey?

No, he couldn't. He just hoped he could live with himself after he'd done what he had to do.

Something struck Jamie hard enough to rattle his brains all over again. He wavered off course and began to fall. The air smelled burned. Mossman must have blasted him with that laser cannon, and now he was tumbling, the sky and the ground changing places every second, the trees growing closer. If his aura hadn't been engaged, that shot would have cut him in half. Slapping himself, hoping to clear the fog from his mind, he shot forward, swooping over the treetops and gaining altitude again. Below, Greenwalt and Mossman were struggling over the cannon. Good. At least one of those fools had some sense.

Jamie spotted Gabby and flew down to her. She was preoccupied with chasing Kragthorpe around while the fed tried to find a good place to stand and return fire. Jamie landed and ducked into the space between four hickories, their branches close enough to intertwine. He called Gabby's name and waved her over. She sent one last force beam Kragthorpe's way and ran to him.

"Help me disarm the Team," he said.

She was breathing hard, but fire practically shot from her eyes. "I thought you and Kenneth and Micah could do it by yourselves."

Jamie's costume felt too tight, his mask too constricting. He wanted to rip them off and yell at her face to face, but as usual he had to hold back, be the cool one. "Look. We may not agree about the dragon, but—"

A sonic blast struck them. Jamie's head seemed to swell as he fell to the ground. Someone had shoved spikes into his eardrums. His brain was splitting down the middle. Gabby kneeled next to him, hands over her ears, her mouth open in a scream. Even the trees shook.

When the sound ceased, Jamie took off, heading straight for Kragthorpe. The noises of battle had dimmed; they might have been coming from miles away. Kragthorpe's eyes widened. Jamie slugged him in the jaw, then landed and picked up the sonic cannon and hurled it as far as he could. It sailed end over end, bounced off several trees, and disappeared in the distance. Kragthorpe lay senseless at Jamie's feet.

"Now you're on mute," said Jamie.

Kragthorpe groaned.

A strong wind kicked up. Christian stood beside Jamie holding the rest of the Team's weapons. One by one she chucked them in the same direction Jamie had thrown the sonic cannon. Maybe twenty yards away, Mossman tried to pull his service weapon, but a block of ice formed around it, and he dropped it, yelping. Christian took off again.

In a moment, all the feds stood in front of Jamie, their coats pulled down around their arms, the sleeves tied together behind their backs.

"Son of a bitch." Jeffcoat tried to yank free. Christian's makeshift handcuffs held for the moment. He let loose a string of curses that might have embarrassed a Quentin Tarantino character. Kenneth walked over, keeping one eye on the dragon as it righted itself and circled overhead. All the long-range weapons and flight combat had pretty much left him with nothing to do. His hunched shoulders and clenched fists suggested he might take out his frustration on the feds. Micah shuffled toward them, having spent most of the fight just standing around. Sometimes Jamie wanted to slap that kid upside his increasingly thick head.

On the other hand, Micah had lost both his parents. His legal guardian—where the hell *was* Baltar, anyway?—hardly seemed like a model of stability and comfort. More like the guy who might buy a teenager beer and then spike it with laxative. He had proven himself as a teammate, but Jamie still had a hard time trusting him as a human being. As for Micah, you couldn't predict what grief would do to anybody, much less a hormonal teenager who had always struggled with his temper. No one could call a time-out from depression. If Jamie had to deal with Micah's contributions to the Freaks, or lack thereof, he couldn't forget that.

"Let us go, you little shits." Mossman's voice was tinged with fury, his face deep red. "That thing killed one of us. It's ours."

"Yeah, right," said Kenneth. "Your weapons barely tickle it. All you're gonna do is get yourselves killed. I'd be okay with that, but for some reason, some of us wanna save you."

Jamie scowled, though with the masks the effect was probably diluted. Then he turned back to the Team. "He ain't wrong, y'all. You might as well be shooting them old cap guns like you probably played with when you were kids."

Kragthorpe laughed. "What makes you think that's all we've got?"

"And what makes you think we're that *old*?" asked Greenwalt, indignant.

Jamie ignored them. "If y'all quit shooting at us, we'll kill the dragon."

Christian stepped between him and the Team. "Um, who's 'we'?"

Gabby punched his shoulder. "When did you get so hard-headed? We've got other options. Are you *ever* gonna listen to us?"

Jamie looked at them one at a time, and when he spoke, the coldness of his voice surprised even him. "I don't need to listen to you. I made the call. You can follow the order, or you can get the hell off my team."

Gabby cocked her head. "*Your* team?"

"You damn right."

Christian crossed her arms. "You ain't no dictator, dude. I never said I wouldn't ask questions. None of us did. If you can't deal with that, maybe you ain't fit to lead."

"Fine!" shouted Jamie. "After this is over, I'm done. See how you get along without me."

Christian opened her mouth to reply, but at the same time, the dragon roared. Jamie looked up.

It was diving straight at them. It opened its mouth and spewed white-hot fire.

Before even Christian could move, that invisible barrier stopped the flames. They ran up and along it, an almost perfect rectangle of heat and light. Jamie squinted and held a hand before his eyes. The others were backing away, including the Team, who shuffled in tandem, yelling at each other to hurry up.

Micah stood there with his arms crossed, watching Arsiss as she poured on the fire. When she took a breath and the flame dispersed, he laughed. "That all you got?"

"Christian—" Jamie began, but she was already gone. Mossman disappeared at the same instant the coat-cuffs fell around the other feds' knees. Then Greenwalt vanished. Jeffcoat and Kragthorpe reached for their service weapons, which had been secured in shoulder holsters.

Jamie flew forward and slugged Jeffcoat, who started to fall, but Christian whooshed him away before he could hit the ground.

The dragon flew higher.

Kragthorpe bent and rifled through the coats. When he stood, he was holding a grenade.

"Oh, *shit!*" cried Jamie. He flew as fast as he could, grabbing Kenneth and Gabby by the wrists and dragging them along, Kenneth making a *woop woop woop* noise as he tried to keep his balance. It would have been funny in some other situation. Jamie looked over his shoulder. Micah was backpedaling away, his hands glowing, just as Christian arrived and put her hands on Kragthorpe.

The grenade exploded.

A wave of greenish energy battered everyone. Jamie lost his grip on Kenneth and spun through the air, still clinging to Gabby, who yelled something he couldn't understand. They hit the ground and crashed against a tree. Pinecones fell onto their heads. Micah had been knocked onto his ass; he lay propped on his elbows. Christian and Kragthorpe were tangled together on the ground near the far edge of the grenade's blast radius. Even with her speed, she hadn't been able to make it far. The forest floor had been swept clean in a circular pattern maybe forty feet in diameter.

"Oh my God," Gabby said as she sat up. "Christian. Is she—?"

"I don't know," said Jamie. "That was an energy grenade, not the kind that makes shrapnel. Look. It's on the ground where Kragthorpe dropped it, and it looks intact."

"We gotta go see about her." Gabby got to her knees and tried to stand.

Jamie got up too. They leaned on each other. His legs had turned to rubber. The healing factor would fix him up if Arsiss left them alone long enough, but for the moment, he could barely walk.

Good thing Gabby can't read my mind. She'd give me all kinds of shit about irony.

Across the way, Kenneth had managed to stand. He shook his head and dusted himself off. Then he glanced up, did a double take, and yelped like somebody had jammed a safety pin in his ass. He sprinted across the forest floor as a huge shadow fell over him, and then a burst of flame engulfed him.

"NO!" cried Jamie.

Gabby's breath stopped. She put a hand over her mouth.

The dragon's armored belly struck the treetops and broke them. Limbs and trunk fragments rained down. When the fire and smoke cleared, Kenneth was still running in the same direction as before. His aura must have protected him.

"Oh, thank God," said Gabby.

"Don't just stand there, you assholes!" Kenneth called over his shoulder. "*Do* something!"

The shadow fell on him again. Arsiss was coming back for another shot. How, when she couldn't see him? Maybe she was tracking his movements in the leaves or following him by scent.

As the Freak that fire couldn't hurt, Micah could have stood between Kenneth and the dragon, but he was dragging along even more slowly than usual. The shadow over Kenneth grew and grew and grew.

I can't tell Gabby what I know about Arsiss. I can't tell any of 'em until this is over. Jamie put a hand on her shoulder. "Blast that thing."

She looked at him like she could barely remember who he was. Then she blinked and shook her head. "I don't want to."

He pointed to the sky. "Look! It's gonna strafe Kenneth again! Who knows how hot it can get?"

"But—"

"Micah's out of it. You're the only one who can do this! Do you wanna tell his parents you didn't try to save him? Do you wanna tell *Ty*?"

"I don't wanna hurt it! It just wants—"

"*I don't give a goddam what it wants!*" cried Jamie, his nose almost touching hers, spittle flying. "We ain't got time to talk philosophy! Just do it. Do it *now!*"

She glared at him. Her eyes were clear now. Oh, yes. And they seemed to carry a message meant just for him—that she would not forget this moment, how he had talked to her, what he was making her do.

"Get your hand off me," she said, her voice cold and dead. Jamie let go of her. Then she set her feet and raised both hands. The first fat raindrops fell, soaking into her costume and mask.

Arsiss was diving through the treetops, zeroing in on Kenneth, who was high-stepping as fast as he could go.

CHAPTER TWENTY-EIGHT

Sounds faded in: cracks and thuds, someone's footsteps in the leaves, raised voices that seemed scared and furious. Christian opened her eyes. It was raining drops the size of quarters. Thunder crashed. The ground seemed to shake with it. Lightning arced across the sky, leaving afterimages on her field of vision. Groaning, she sat up. One of the Freaks was running like hell—Kenneth? Then came a familiar sizzling sound, and a white glow lit up the woods. Gabby was blasting the dragon. It flew low, knocking trunks and branches aside like bowling pins. Gabby shot it in the belly, and though the beams didn't penetrate the dragon's scales, the creature roared and headed higher into the sky. Gabby was running around and trying to stay under the breaks in the canopy as she fed the dragon a steady diet of beams. Jamie walked behind her, yelling encouragement. If Gabby was listening, she gave no sign, but she kept pouring it on. Every time part of a tree met her beams, it simply disintegrated. Had she ever let loose like that? No. If she had used that much power on Na'ul, he would have splattered like a bug on a windshield. She was getting stronger.

A chill ran down Christian's spine as she remembered Rabbit's warning about the Freaks' powers and what would happen if they grew strong enough to threaten the world. Trapped between defending themselves and letting loose the full scope of their abilities, how would they get through this?

She also couldn't forget that the Freaks and the Team had somehow become co-conspirators. After nearly three years of conflict and low-level espionage, *this* was why they had joined forces? To antagonize, harass, and abuse a poor animal? It already felt like things had gone too far, like they had crossed the Rubicon.

Micah, Jamie, Kenneth—I'll never forget this. Never.

Christian waited until the dragon swooped low again, preparing to strafe Micah, who just stood there and watched. Then Christian took off. The rain fell hard, limiting visibility. Up ahead, a tall tree had fallen against the intertwined branches of two others. The dragon seemed to be heading for the area right above them. Christian ran up the leaning trunk, slaloming around some branches and stepping over others, building speed with every step. When she reached the truncated top, she ran straight into the air as the dragon passed over. She grabbed hold of a wing and flipped herself onto its back, clutching one of its spines. Then she vibrated her hands as hard as she could, hoping to stun the dragon or at least keep it occupied.

The dragon pulled up, raised its head, and let out a surprisingly high-pitched roar. A bunch of scales shook loose and fell to the ground. The bare spots looked tough and leathery and wrinkled—exposed skin. Would the armor regenerate? If so, how long would it take?

If it stays this size, those missing scales present a pretty big target, Christian thought. *Gabby or Micah could hurt it. The Team's weapons might too. Damn it to hell, what did I just do?*

But she knew the answer: She might have made the dragon vulnerable enough for the others to kill. If the boys saw that chance, they would take it. She still didn't want to be part of that. The Rabbit affair had taught her that supernatural didn't have to mean evil. The trickster hadn't threatened Quapaw City; he had only wanted to protect the world from what he perceived as a threat. In doing so, he had served as the spark that ignited her fire to learn, to embrace the parts of her heritage she had never known about. Why hadn't the boys learned a similar lesson? *People* had made this mess, like they almost always did. They had invented murder and slavery and genocide, colonialism and the ruination of the whole damn planet. Maybe the world would be better off without them, the same way a field would be better off without a plague of grasshoppers.

The dragon bucked, yanked its head from side to side, and shook like a dog after a bath. Christian held on with all her enhanced strength. "Come on," she said through clenched teeth. "Don't make me hurt you. Please." As if in answer, it started to dive-bomb Kenneth again. Cursing, Christian vibrated. The dragon roared. More scales fell off. Blood dripped from its ear. Tears welled in Christian's eyes. The longer this fight went on, the more likely she would do something unforgiveable. Maybe she already had.

As they neared the treetops, she jumped off and into a pine, adjusting at super-speed so she landed on her feet, a thick branch breaking her fall. Before it had fully bent under her weight, she was racing down the trunk and onto the ground.

The dragon was circling just above the trees and shaking its head. Kenneth rushed over to its severed tail, picked it up, swung it round and round, and let go, hurling it skyward. It struck the dragon under the chin and snapped its head back. The creature sagged and plummeted, wings furling. When it struck the ground with a tremendous thud, more branches fell from the beaten-to-shit trees. It lay there a moment and then scrambled to its feet, growling low. Kenneth charged. Its tongue flicked out, almost as long as the dragon itself, and wrapped around him, squeezing him like a python and yanking him back. His arms trapped, feet off the ground, Kenneth could only bellow in outrage and fear as he flew toward the open mouth and all those teeth. His voice grew muffled as the dragon took him in and bit down. He screamed. All this happened in the space of a second.

Christian was running before she even realized it, striking the dragon's mouth with her shoulder. Three teeth shattered. Kenneth fell out and barely had time to hit the ground before Christian scooped him up and carried him a hundred yards away, laying him down behind a pine tree. The needles smelled sharp and fresh. Christian was covered in sap; everyone was. Bits of leaves and pine straw and dirt clung to them all. The wind had carried most of the smoke in other directions, though even here the air was tinged with it.

Dragon slobber dripped from Kenneth's costume and mask. His right leg was drenched in blood, his costume torn, the wound on his outer thigh like something from a grenade. White bone peeked out from churned flesh. The skin around his eyes looked ashy.

"Get me back over there," he groaned. "I'm gonna rip that thing's head off." He was clenching and unclenching his fists, his usual way of engaging his aura and jumpstarting his healing power.

"Dude, you can't even stand up," said Christian.

"I can fight," he grunted.

"Kenneth—"

"Just do it," he said, the last word a little high-pitched. "It tried to kill my dad. You get that?"

She shook her head and picked him up. A moment later, she set him down next to Jamie.

"You okay?" asked Jamie.

"A goddam dragon nearly bit my leg off." Kenneth grimaced as he tried to put weight on the wounded limb. The blood had already clotted; the flesh was regenerating while they watched. "So, yeah. Just another Sunday since I joined y'all."

Our healing powers keep leveling up. Maybe one day we'll be immortal. Christian didn't know whether that would be good or bad.

"Well," said Jamie, "I—look out!"

Roaring like the thunder, the dragon blew ice at them. Christian zipped away on instinct. "Y'all okay?" she asked, turning back around.

Jamie and Kenneth had been frozen in a block of ice. The dragon was rushing forward. Christian had no idea what the creature might have in mind, but it couldn't be anything good.

She sprinted over and slammed her shoulder into the block. It had frozen to the ground, but she managed to tear it free and shove it across the uneven forest floor before the dragon could reach her friends. She peered over her shoulder; the dragon had skidded to a stop and was looking around in confusion. Agent Greenwalt had made his way back to the battle site and now watched with his mouth hanging open, his goop gun pointing at the ground. To his right, Micah leaned against a tree as if nothing was happening. Roughly halfway between them, Gabby stood with one hand over her mouth.

"Help me!" yelled Christian as the dragon spotted her and the Jamie/Kenneth block. "Keep it off us!"

Gabby braced herself and fired. White force beams struck the dragon in the side. It turned toward Gabby. Micah didn't move.

Greenwalt must have been wearing an earpiece. "If Hannibal's ready, get it up here now!" he yelled.

Hannibal? Christian thought. *How many new Team members are there?*

But she had no time to worry about it. While Gabby threw beams at the dragon, Christian put both hands on the ice block and vibrated. Concussing Jamie and Kenneth was better than letting them suffocate or freeze to death. Tiny cracks appeared in the block. They grew, became crevasses, and split wide open until the whole thing fell around Kenneth's and Jamie's feet. The boys dropped, gasping for air and shivering.

Jamie wheezed as he tried to crawl away. "That sucked."

Kenneth lay where he had fallen and began clenching his fists again.

Greenwalt's gun burped three times. The globs of acid struck the dragon along its torso. It emitted a high-pitched cry and thrashed, rubbing itself on the ground.

That shit's burning it where I knocked off the scales, Christian thought. *I did that.*

"Where's Hannibal, goddammit?" Greenwalt cried.

The dragon grunted and snorted, acrid smoke billowing off its body. It shook itself like a wet dog again. Acid and blood flew everywhere. The Freaks ducked and covered, everyone yelling. That blood was hot enough to burn.

Another noise, beginning as a steady, low rumble, barely discernable, and growing gradually into a roar broken by the shotgun cracks of saplings crunching under heavy weight—a powerful engine. Something new was coming, and it was knocking down even more of the woods.

"For Christ's sake, *now* what?" asked Kenneth.

A dark-red beam crackled out of the woods, shooting over everyone's heads and striking the dragon, which had just gotten to its feet. The force blasted it backward. It smashed through splintered pine trunks, creating a path thirty feet wide. Christian ran forward and peered down this new, uneven corridor. The dragon had come to rest a quarter mile away. It lay on its side, unmoving.

Christian turned back to where the blast had originated. That engine had grown closer. The ground shook. Then the thing making all the noise finally came into view.

I guess you're *Hannibal.*

It was a tank, or something like one: an oval chassis made of some metal Christian had never seen, smooth and sleek and black, maybe fifteen feet tall at its highest and thirty feet long; around forty treads, twenty per side, that seemed to operate individually and in any direction, like each had its own gyroscope; minute seams along the frame, only one of which was open right now; and, extending through that opening, a five-foot-long horizontal cylinder. It had to be the barrel of whatever weapon had just fired. The vehicle rumbled onto the contested grounds.

"Yeah," said Jamie. "Yeah, now might be a good time for y'all's charms."

More thunder pealed across the dark sky. The rain fell harder, visibility now at around twenty feet, maybe less.

Over with Micah, who seemed uninterested, Gabby shifted from foot to foot, probably trying to decide whether she should shoot the tank or join the rest of the group or dig a hole and try to hide.

Like her friends, Christian had worn her charm under her costume. Now she pressed it against her chest and opened her mouth to say the magic word, but the tank's treads shifted and turned so fast that she forgot what she was doing and just watched. How could something that big and bulky move so fast, so smoothly?

"Scatter!" shouted Jamie.

Christian didn't wait to see why. She just zoomed, dragging along Kenneth on his injured leg as he yelled *ow ow ow ow.*

Aw, quit it, you big baby.

Another of those blasts roared by, taking down more trees in the distance. If the Freaks had stood still, even their auras might not have saved them.

Oh, you sons of bitches. She let Kenneth go. More blasts followed her as she circled the tank over and over. Somehow it could turn almost as fast as she could move. Its sensors had to have come from some other world. No human tech could do that. She tightened her circle on every revolution, getting a little closer, a little closer. The tank evaded in a seemingly random pattern, graceful as any deer. Every time it changed direction, she had to adjust, which made her slow down a fraction. A few times the blasts nearly deafened her, but she managed to stay ahead of them, circling, circling, until she was finally able to run onto the vehicle itself.

She stood on top of it and raised her hands in triumph. "Gotcha!" she said, half a second before some of those barely visible seams shot open and another barrel protruded, this one sticking straight up. It fired a similar but smaller blast and nearly blew her face off. "Jesus!" she yelled, staggering backward. She caught herself, leaped at the barrel, and wrapped her arms and legs around it. "Somebody help!"

The rest of the Freaks had hit the ground and flattened themselves out, all except Micah, who was still just watching. Christian was going to murder that shithead when this was over. Now Kenneth was bear-crawling to the tank, staying under the horizontal barrel's blasts. When he reached the vehicle, he performed a flat-footed jump from the ground to the top. "Move!" he cried, drawing back his fist. Christian let go and fell back just before he punched the vertical barrel and broke it off at the hilt. An electric charge buzzed around the opening. The broken end skittered end over end and vanished into the forest. The stub dropped back into the chassis, and the seam closed.

"How'd you do that with your leg torn up?" asked Christian, rubbing her tailbone where she had fallen.

Kenneth grimaced and pulled his tattered costume aside. The wound looked angry and raw, but the massive hole had filled in. "It got better," he said. "But it still hurts like a sumbitch. Something else I gotta hide from Ty."

She stood. "Let's open this can."

As if the drivers could hear them, the tank shot forward. Christian tumbled off, ass over elbows, and landed on her back. The breath shot out of her. She rolled around, gasping and wheezing.

Kenneth had hung on, his fingertips buried in the weird metal. The tank's smooth passage over the uneven ground worked against it, since nothing was jostling Kenneth. He raised his fists and pounded the roof, one shot at a time. The whole frame shuddered with each punch.

Gabby ran forward and started blasting the shit out of the tank, hammering it just under the horizontal barrel. Jamie flew over and grabbed a tread, which ground to a halt in his hands. He tried to fly upward and rip it off.

"You kids cut that out!" yelled Greenwalt.

Get off my lawn, Christian thought, and then she laughed. What was he going to do, ground them? At least he hadn't shot at anybody, but his buddies would probably be back any second now, and they would. Christian had caught her breath, so she ran back to the top of the tank. Kenneth had gotten his fingertips into one of those seams and was trying to tear it open. There was just enough space for her own fingers to fit. "Don't let go, or I'm gonna have to type my final papers with my nose," she said, straining and grunting. The metal creaked, groaned, and finally parted. Once he had more room to work, Kenneth yanked the panel open.

A ladder led down into the guts. Christian jumped through the opening, not bothering with the steps, and found herself in a cockpit, every wall covered in control panels with levers and switches and buttons and blinking lights and computer screens. Sitting in cushioned chairs that moved around the interior on multidirectional tracks, a man and a woman were working separate sets of controls—this had to be Badger and King. Concentrating on trying to keep Kenneth from taking their ride apart, neither had turned, but the man casually tossed something over his shoulder, a cylindrical metal object that banged and thumped toward Christian. She circled away from it at super-speed. It exploded without a sound, filling the cockpit with light that slowly faded, leaving spots before her eyes. *Just a flash*, she thought. The man hadn't been willing to set off a fragmentation grenade inside, or one of those energy doohickeys Kragthorpe had used. Good. Christian zipped up as fast as she could in the close quarters and unstrapped the drivers. She grabbed the backs of their shirts and ran up the ladder, dragging them behind her. Once on top of the tank, which was still moving forward but slowing, she tossed the drivers over the side. They landed face-down in the churned earth, one big man and one average-sized woman.

Kenneth jumped off as Gabby and Jamie joined them. The four of them circled the Team members they had heard but never seen. After a moment, the feds rolled over, hate in their eyes, their mouths pulled down in twin snarls.

Christian's legs turned to jelly. Gabby gasped.

"What the hell?" whispered Jamie.

Vin and Patricia Villalobos got to their knees. Vin had gotten hold of himself and now stared straight ahead, expressionless. Patricia's gaze bored into them, as hot and destructive as their cannon.

"Get away from them, or I'll be forced to shoot!" Greenwalt yelled from a million miles away.

Vin spat near Christian's feet. "If you're going to kill us, do it," he said. "But don't make us breathe the same air as you mutants."

"They don't have the stomach," Patricia said, sneering. "They're cowards."

"Hey, bitch, maybe you ain't noticed what's been happening, but we're fighting a dragon," said Kenneth.

Patricia ignored him. "Which one of you is Christian Allen?" She looked at each of them. Then she fixed her gaze on Christian, despite the mask. "You."

"Don't talk to her," said Jamie. "I'm in charge here."

He might as well have been talking to a brick wall. "Do you know what it's been like to let you near our child?" asked Patricia.

"What?" said Christian.

"Like watching them date a pig," said Vin.

Kenneth stepped forward. "You want me to punch their noses through the back of their heads?"

"No more, you monster," said Patricia. "You freak."

Thunder rumbled. The rain's intensity increased. Christian's costume had soaked through, but she barely registered the weight.

"I—I don't—" Christian couldn't think straight, couldn't make the words come. It was like she had run out of Hannibal and into some other world where everyone looked like the people she knew but nothing made sense.

"I mean it," yelled Greenwalt from somewhere behind them. "Step away!" He might as well have been speaking Greek. Christian couldn't understand anything. Jamie, Kenneth, and Gabby looked at each other, as lost as she was.

Patricia Villalobos reached inside her jacket and drew a gun. Not a special weapon, just a plain old .38 revolver. And then she shot Christian in the chest.

Christian staggered backward, stumbled to one knee, and sat down. There was no real pain yet, but she had lost her breath again. Like someone the size of a pro wrestler had front-kicked her. Broken trees jutted above her like rotten teeth. Her friends were shouting, bending over her, cradling her head. She let it loll, looking beyond the Freaks and down the blast corridor.

Lightning struck a tall tree in the distance, briefly lighting up the forest and setting the tree afire.

The dragon was rising. It shook debris from its back and stretched its neck. Then it charged, heading straight for them, its wings folded over its back.

Christian lifted a hand that seemed to weigh a hundred pounds and pointed. The others turned.

Micah must have seen the dragon coming. He walked out to meet it.

CHAPTER TWENTY-NINE

Micah hadn't put much thought into anything he had done since they'd come out here. A kind of heatless fire raged in his every cell. He could feel them all moving and pulsing with a stronger, purer energy than he had ever experienced. A single word had been seared into his brain: *KILL*. The voice speaking that word sounded deep and felt immensely powerful, the mental equivalent of putting your hand on the metal covering of a jet engine that had been throttled as high as it would go. Some kind of barrier separated Micah's psyche from full contact with the owner of the voice. With a little pushing, that malleable wall would come down, and everything on the other side would spill through. Filling Micah. Erasing him. And maybe that would be a relief. After so many months of semiconsciousness, of waking moments filled with pain, of sleep bursting with nightmares, giving up sounded fine, even right. Nonexistence, no wind, not even the sensation of floating in a void. Just an endless darkness of which he would not even be aware. He had barely moved or thought because, once the battle started, he had been trying to ignore that voice and what it wanted him to do. If he divided his attention, who knew what might happen to him or what he would do to everyone else?

Even the arrival of the alien tank and the booming of its pulse cannon hadn't distracted him from what was happening inside him. Somehow, though, this last ordinary gunshot had broken through, had quieted that bellicose voice. Micah looked up in time to see Christian fall. The woman on the ground held a pistol.

Well, if anybody needs killing, Micah thought, *that woman does.* He raised his right hand.

Behind him, the dragon screeched. Micah glanced over his shoulder. Through the curtain of rain, a shape grew bigger and bigger. The monster was running toward them.

Okay then. You first.

Micah had never given much of a damn about Quapaw City or the troglodytes who lived there, but he hated monsters even more. Beings that weren't supposed to exist, mother-killing animals. And here came the latest, all scales and claws and wings and teeth, a fire-and-ice breather, a giant lizard with powers like his own.

Only one of them could live through today. Still, that gunshot, that thud as Christian hit the forest floor, the gasps of his friends—surely that was even more important. Wasn't it?

KILL KILL KILL

Yeah, but what about Christian? Maybe I can help.

KILL KILL KILL

But my friend. My friend.

KILL KILL KILL

Fine, yeah, but what about—

KILL KILL KILL

GET OUTTA MY HEAD!

Micah screamed, head tilted back, chest thrust toward the sky, and then he fired a flame burst at the dragon, which skidded to a stop and turned its face away. When the fire struck it, it bellowed in pain. Micah's head cleared a little. Jamie, Kenneth, and Gabby had huddled around Christian, Jamie cradling her across his lap with her head in the crook of his arm. Blood trickled from her mouth, but she was moving, even . . . vibrating? Shot in the chest, she had nevertheless managed to keep her cool and jumpstart her powers. She would heal.

Good. One less thing to worry about.

Greenwalt stood some distance away, looking from the dragon to the Freaks, his gun held with the barrel straight up. He didn't seem to know what to do. Bec's parents—wait, *Bec's parents?*—were standing up and brushing dirt from their clothes. Mrs. Villalobos had shot Christian. She was smiling.

Smiling.

She lowered her pistol, pointing it at the back of Gabby's head. The other Freaks didn't even notice, all their attention on Christian.

Micah raised his left hand and fired a series of ice shards, the ends as sharp as any knife. Mr. Villalobos saw them coming. He yanked his wife aside. She tumbled to the ground and skidded through the mud, the gun firing into the air. An ice shard struck Vin in the side of the head, the others passing over him as he fell, and cut off half his ear. He fell in a mud puddle, blood pouring down that side of his face. Mrs. Villalobos sat up, still holding the gun, as Vin tried to push himself to his knees. At the second shot, the other Freaks had nearly jumped out of their costumes. Jamie must have realized what Micah had done; he gave a thumbs-up.

Glad you approve, boss man, thought Micah, but he couldn't muster much sarcasm. It felt like a lot of work.

A roar from behind Micah. He turned. The dragon was charging again, its head low to the ground, its jaws opening.

Micah backpedaled out of the way. At the same time, Jamie took off from his sitting position and carried Christian in his arms as he soared above the trees. Gabby and Kenneth scattered. The dragon steamrolled by, so close it nearly knocked Micah down, and headed straight for the Villaloboses.

Greenwalt shot five or six acid rounds that struck the monster and dripped down its sides, crackling and smoking, but it didn't stop. It opened its jaws wide. Mrs. Villalobos emptied her gun into that mouth, but if the shots bothered the dragon, it gave no sign. Instead, it dug its feet in and skidded through the leaves and soil, throwing up clods as it raised its head like a snake about to strike.

Mrs. Villalobos grabbed her husband's arm and yanked. "Get up!" she screamed. "You have to get up!"

Vin got to his knees. He swayed, still out of it, half his torso covered in blood that continued to drip from his jawline.

A blur, and Mrs. Villalobos disappeared. A moment later she was sitting on the ground dozens of feet away, her gun gone. Christian was on her knees nearby, hands pressed to her chest. Blood trickled between her fingers and hung in ropes from her mouth. Shot in the chest, and she had saved the woman who did it. How had she even gotten back on the ground? Where was Jamie?

Before Micah could figure it out, the dragon belched white fire that whooshed across the ground and struck Vin Villalobos. He vanished in the glow.

The fire also engulfed the tank. The dragon poured it on, white flame beginning to fade into blue, but before it could get any hotter, the tank exploded. Fragments flew everywhere. The Freaks and Greenwalt ducked and covered, except for Christian, who disappeared. Smoke issued from wide fissures and the open hatch. The one extruding barrel was bent down at a forty-five-degree angle.

The dragon took off and soared through the trees. It flew in a jagged pattern, clearly wounded. Micah let it be. Maybe it would just go away, leave all this for another day. He wanted to check on Christian.

Patricia Villalobos stood and stumbled away from her. Christian stayed down, vibrating her hands. Even in his own addled state, Micah could barely believe she had dragged a grown woman around while wounded so badly. Mrs. Villalobos stopped in the burned zone a few yards from the smoldering tank and looked around, a wild expression on her face, one hand pressed against her chest like she was the one who had been shot.

"Vin?" she called. "Vin!"

Greenwalt approached, his gun in one hand, the other reaching toward her. "Badger," he said. "Come on. Something else in there might blow up." He put his outstretched hand on her shoulder.

She shoved him away. "Where's Vin?" she screamed. "Where's my husband?"

Greenwalt looked stricken. "I—"

Realization dawned. Her wide eyes filled with tears. They fell down her dirt-and-soot-covered face. "What did it? The dragon, or that brat over there?" She pointed at Micah.

Greenwalt laid his gun down and eased toward her, both hands held up like he was surrendering. "It was the dragon," he said. He had turned pale. "I think it was going for Hannibal."

She glared at him. "I don't give a damn what it was going for. I want that thing dead. You hear me? *Dead!*" She picked up the acid rifle and shot at the creature circling overhead, but the goop fell short of the target.

"Stop it," said Greenwalt. He reached for the gun. She tried to yank it away, but he kept hold of it. "That won't help. You're just wasting the charge." They struggled over the weapon for a long moment. Then Patricia seemed to shrink. She let go and just stood there, sobbing. Greenwalt took her by the elbow and led her away, the Freaks apparently forgotten.

The five of them walked toward each other, Christian still wheezing as her body knitted itself back together. If her condition concerned Jamie, he didn't show it. "Who's got a line on the rest of the Team?"

Gabby pointed past Greenwalt. "I'd guess they're maybe a hundred and fifty yards thataway and closing."

"That's . . . about . . . where I dropped them," said Christian. Wincing, she forced herself to straighten up.

Jamie nodded. "Then we've got maybe thirty seconds to engage before they butt in. We need a plan."

Kenneth's eyes grew wide. "I don't think we're gonna have to hunt it down," he said as the foliage stirred around them.

The dragon was hovering just above the trees, its enormous wings flapping. Micah squinted against the gunk in the air. Lightning strobed in the clouds. Thunder pealed again and again.

The dragon opened its mouth wide and breathed fire right at them. The rain steamed off it as the tongues of flame rushed toward the Freaks.

Micah stepped in front of his friends and shot ice out of his blue left hand, meeting the fire halfway. The two streams sizzled and hissed at the point of impact, more steam rising, condensation falling from Micah's ice even as the rain slacked off. The dragon poured on flame. Micah strained a little harder, sending colder, thicker ice to meet it. The energy inside him, mostly dormant for months, awakened and stretched. It was like an electric charge in his blood, his breath. It seemed to expand, to hollow him out and fill him up with itself. The air around him crackled. And then came a weird sensation like invisible hands on his shoulders, invisible fingers digging into his skin. He grunted, gritted his teeth, braced himself against whatever this was, not pain but something like it. A new energy flowed through those unseen hands, dark energy, a kind he had seen and felt before but could not name.

Kill, said that voice, whispering now. *Kill. Kill. Kill.*

He increased his power, shooting more and more ice until it began to surround the fire, extinguish its oxygen, creep up the line leading back to the dragon's mouth. With each renewed effort, that new, dark energy supercharged his own. They melded, expanded. He had to keep expelling it, or it might consume him.

Kill. Kill. Kill.

The raised voices of Mossman, Jeffcoat, Kragthorpe, Jamie, and Kenneth sounded far away. From what Micah could make out, the Freaks were trying to convince the feds to help, rather than shooting him in the back. Not that those popguns would do much against his aura. *If you gotta shoot, shoot the dragon*, Jamie was yelling, and Del Ray was spouting some macho halfwit bullshit. Maybe those voices helped, because laser beams and pure sound shot past Micah and hit the dragon. It shrieked. Micah had only heard its like once before, when Dad had taken him to see the horse races in Hot Springs and one of the animals had stepped badly, broken its leg, and screamed, a horrid sound no living thing should be able to make. The dragon's fire cut out. Micah's ice filled the space it had occupied, striking the dragon in the chest and lower throat. The monster fell and bounced off a fractured tree trunk before slamming to the ground.

Gabby cried out miserably. Christian came over and grabbed Micah's shoulder, shook him, told him to *Stop it now, just quit, it's down*, but he pulled away and walked toward the dragon, which had pushed itself to its feet. It was trying to shake off the ice, the deadly cold that might stop its heart or sap its will.

Kill. Kill. Kill.

Jamie and Kenneth were in a shouting match with Gabby and Christian. Gabby shot a force beam at the dragon. It shattered the ice, allowing the overgrown gecko to regain its feet. Had Gabby done that on purpose, or was she trying to keep the dragon on the defensive? Now Jamie was yelling at her, more furious than Micah had ever heard. Micah kept moving toward the dragon, leaving the Freaks behind. He could not be concerned with their demands and their fears. Gabby must have pushed past Jamie and Kenneth because she grabbed Micah's arm and pleaded, begged, *Take it alive, we can help it and still protect the town, don't do this.* Micah didn't look at her. The Team's weapons fired again. Some of the shots hit the dragon. The rest seemed to churn the forest floor where the Freaks stood arguing. Maybe the feds wanted Micah to take care of the monster that had killed their friend, or maybe they had decided to take the opportunity to kill the preoccupied Freaks. None of it seemed to matter. Whatever the Team might do, however the Freaks responded, none of it could touch this feeling that the hands of some minor god had imparted him with its own power, raising him above human concerns and human weakness. Only the power remained, and the ways he could use it.

Kill. Kill. KILL.

Thought, emotion, and conscience faded. The world shrank to the distance between him and the dragon. Another vicious, parent-killing monster.

KILL. KILL. KILL.

Christian ran into Micah's path, broke toward him, and dodged a laser blast. Jamie swooped in and tackled her and carried her out of the way. Kragthorpe's sonic gun fired again and knocked the dragon onto its side. Gabby backpedaled in front of Micah, stepped aside, and fired a force beam that traveled over his head. Del Ray bumped Micah as he ran past and chased Gabby away.

KILL. KILL. KILL.

Now, despite the feeling of those hands on Micah's shoulders, something walked beside him—that dark figure, the smaller one that had lingered in his house like a ghost. It seemed less human than it had before: taller than Baltar and just as thin, arms that hung to its knees, those weird double-thumbed hands, two legs like a goat's, an overlarge head, no hair, a face hidden in darkness. Again, Micah knew the voice in his head didn't belong to this figure. It felt more like the specter was an amplifier tuned into some unimaginable frequency. Micah would have sworn those hands gripping him were real; four thumbs dug into his shoulders, even though the being walked beside him.

Hard to think. Hard to know what was true. The voice thudded between his ears, behind his eyes. It threatened to split his skull apart. It demanded and demanded, and it would not be denied.

KILL. KILL. KILL.

The dragon managed to stand, its head hanging, its breathing ragged. It bled from a dozen places where its scales had fallen off. Some of the wounds were deep. Now it looked Micah in the face. Its deep blue eyes bore into his. They looked tired, sad, lonely. He had seen those looks in his own mirror often enough to recognize them. It coughed and spat out blood.

Micah hesitated.

KILL. KILL. KILL.

Tears fell from the dragon's exhausted blue eyes. They splattered the ground and soaked into the soil without leaving a trace.

Micah, no! Gabby was screaming. The feds and the rest of the Freaks kept yelling. Those fancy guns fired again and again.

KILL. KILL. KILL.

The dragon trumpeted like a wounded elephant. When it tried to walk forward, its front legs collapsed.

It looks like a deer somebody shot. Some stupid, thoughtless asshole like Del Ray's piece-of-shit father. Like drunk-ass Elvis Schott. Not like Na'ul at all.

NONE OF THAT MATTERS, BOY. KILL. SHOW THEM WHO YOU REALLY ARE.

But—

KILL.

Look at it. It's—

Those hands on Micah's shoulders squeezed. Pain ripped through him, driving him to his knees.

KILL.

Every other thought was blasted out of Micah's head. He raised his left hand.

With one mighty effort, the dragon flapped its wings and rose. Hovering over the splintered remains of dozens of trees, it opened its mouth and breathed fire.

Micah met it with ice again. The hands on his shoulders squeezed. Energy poured into him. Ice encased his left hand and ran down his arm and along his torso in all directions. Soon it covered him, but he could still move, still see. Like Iceman. The ground and the trees began to freeze. Frost formed everywhere, then a thin coat of ice that thickened with every passing second. Micah must have been generating extreme temperatures, might have even been headed toward absolute zero.

The dragon shut its mouth and tried to fly away. Micah froze its wings. It fell to the ground. The wings shattered, and the monster bellowed, a sound like nothing he had ever heard, as if all the pain and misery in the world had found a voice.

STOP IT, MICAH! someone yelled.

POUR IT ON! shouted someone else.

KILL, said the unearthly voice in his head.

Something struck Micah in the back, knocking him forward and shutting off his ice. He landed on his side. Several yards away, Gabby was pointing her hands toward him. She had blasted him when he wasn't looking, and now she was going to do it again. Jamie landed between them. Christian tried to rush him, but Del Ray intercepted her. The feds were fanning out and pointing their guns at the dragon.

Micah turned back to it. The monster stood, its legs shaking. Those blue eyes still looked worn out beyond the telling, mournful.

It whimpered.

Something in Micah's heart twitched. Again, he hesitated.

The specter leaped in front of him and opened its mouth, a cavernous maw like Na'ul's, the smell like rotten seaweed.

KILLKILLKILL.

It came closer.

MICAH DON'T DO IT, someone was screaming. *KENNETH GET THE FUCK OFF ME! JAMIE, NO, NO, NO!*

KILL.

The voices were ripping Micah apart from the inside. The specter's open mouth was like a chasm. Micah fell into it.

His left hand raised. He looked at it curiously. He didn't seem to be making it move. Ice colder than anything he had ever generated shot from that hand and covered the dragon's entire body, from feet to just below the head. It screamed again. More tears fell and froze.

From overhead, Jamie shot like a missile, his right fist held out in a Superman punch. He plunged through one of those weeping, miserable eyes and deep into the skull. The body vibrated with the impact. Ice chunks fell everywhere.

Very good, said the voice in Micah's head. Then those hands let go of his shoulders. His head cleared. The feds had lowered their weapons. Christian and Kenneth lay on the ground, arms wrapped around each other, as if they had been wrestling. Gabby had fallen to her knees. All of them were staring at the dragon. Its head lolled. Its mouth hung open, the remaining eye already going glassy. Jamie fought his way out of the empty socket. He was covered in white goo. Once he freed himself, he floated to the ground and joined Micah, who gestured. The ice cracked, and the dragon's body collapsed, steam rising off it. Thunder boomed. Lightning strobed behind the clouds. A long tongue of it struck something hundreds of yards away, the sound like a car crash.

The others joined Micah and Jamie. They fanned out in a semicircle around the body.

"Jesus," whispered Kenneth.

Gabby wept. Christian said nothing, but behind her mask, her eyes were cold and furious.

Jamie turned to Gabby. "It had to be done," he said. "I—

Gabby slugged him.

Jamie fell flat onto his back. He propped himself on his elbows for a moment. Then he sat up, holding his jaw.

"Don't talk to me," said Gabby. "Just don't."

"Jesus!" Kenneth said again. "What the hell's wrong with—"

"Oh, shut up," said Christian. "All three of you make me sick. Didn't you see its face? Didn't you *hear* it? Y'all didn't have to do that, but you did. You *did*."

"It was a monster," said Micah. Now that he could think, he was realizing that two of his oldest friends might just hate him. He knew he should care, but he had never been so tired.

"Go to hell," said Christian. Her chest hitched. She wiped her eyes. "I hope you three assholes are happy together. Me, I'm leaving, and you can lose my number. Come on, Gabby."

The girls marched off together, not looking back. Jamie stood up, still holding his jaw. "Gabby—" he began.

Without looking back at him, Gabby raised her middle finger. She kept walking.

Kenneth put his hands on his hips. "They're crazy. They act like we killed a sack of kittens."

Jamie said nothing. Micah kept quiet too. He no longer felt that old surge of anger whenever Kenneth spoke, no longer had to stop himself from freezing the kid's nuts off or turning him into a cinder. In fact, he didn't feel anything at all. His emotions were like background noise. And while he knew intellectually that this very lack of investment should disturb him, it didn't. For a few moments, he had felt sorry for the dragon, but now the carnage all around him barely registered. Over the last three years, the Freaks and their battles had done more to deforest Southeast Arkansas than any timber operation. Surely someone would notice. So what, though? What could anybody do about it? Micah didn't give a damn about their opinions or their outrage. He only wanted to forget about this shitty day, one in a long series.

And yet, for a few seconds there, he *had* cared. What did that mean?

Kragthorpe, Mossman, and Jeffcoat had rejoined Greenwalt. How long had they stood there, watching Micah do the dirty work? Maybe he should have been mad about that, but he couldn't even be bothered to shrug.

Mossman studied the dragon's body. "You did it," he said. "You killed a dragon without any special weapons."

Jamie crossed his arms. "No thanks to y'all. All this time, and you still don't know your real enemy."

Kragthorpe laughed. "We know exactly who we're fighting, kid."

Mossman held up a hand. Kragthorpe looked at him for a moment, then shrugged and stepped back. "That goddam lizard killed one of us," said Mossman, "and you took it out. That buys you a reprieve. For now, you can go."

Kenneth puffed his chest out. "We don't need your permission. We go where we want."

Jeffcoat cocked his weapon. Mossman glared at him. Jeffcoat lowered the gun, muttering something about taking no chances. Mossman moved a little closer to Jamie. "Go ahead and act tough. But sooner or later, we'll finish this."

Jamie said nothing. The fed turned and shouldered his way through his colleagues, who followed him, all but Greenwalt. The special agent's red hair was matted and sweaty, his face covered in soot. He looked almost apologetic. "For the record," he said, lowering his voice so his teammates wouldn't hear, "I know what you did for the world today. Looking at it in light of the last few years, I no longer believe you're a threat to this nation. I'm only one voice, but if I can do anything to move us off your case, I will."

"As long as one of us turns in another, you mean," said Kenneth. He sounded bitter. Jamie exchanged a glance with him, like they had a secret.

"No," said Greenwalt. "That's over. Besides, after this, I doubt it would matter. You're too strong. Either the federal government will find a way to live with that, or the Team will come after you. There's no third choice anymore."

The three Freaks stood shoulder to shoulder, silent, arms crossed. Greenwalt turned and followed his teammates. When he was gone, Jamie put a hand on Kenneth's shoulder. "You and Brayden get Micah outta the woods, okay? I've got some thinking to do."

"Yeah, okay," said Kenneth. "Come on, Sterne. I wanna get home and get cleaned up and see my girl."

Jamie flew away. Micah followed Kenneth, knowing that, with Kenneth's back turned, one high-velocity ice dagger to the base of the skull could end their long feud. Micah could tell the others anything he wanted—self-defense, a sneak attack from the Team, even a new monster popping up out of nowhere. Even as he thought about it, though, he knew he wouldn't do it. He didn't even want to.

From behind them, someone grunted with effort as they kicked through fallen leaves. Micah looked over his shoulder. Baltar was gathering something from the dragon's corpse, from the ground surrounding it, and putting whatever it was into a satchel. No matter how much he stuffed in there, it never seemed to get full. He pressed the monster's wounds, catching the oozing blood in little glass vials. He put those in the satchel too.

What are you up to, old man?

But Micah wasn't very interested in that either.

CHAPTER THIRTY

The following Saturday, after Bec and their mother had taken some time to process and grieve, the coffin of Vin Villalobos was interred at Saint Gabriel Cemetery, located on a back road two miles outside of town. Everyone parked near the fence surrounding the place and made their way to the gravesite.

Christian had barely spoken to Bec since Sunday. What had Patricia told them about their father's death? Surely not the truth. Christian didn't know what to say, either. How did you tell the person you loved that their father had tried to kill you, that you had fought to defend his killer? Could you explain the moral gray areas, the dilemmas you had wrestled with? Christian's own father had been a bigoted piece of shit who abandoned his wife and daughter, but Bec had loved Vin, whatever he had done in secret. Would it be better to lay it all out so Bec could deal with it, or would that information prove too much, the final straw that broke both Bec and their relationship?

It seemed weird that Mrs. Villalobos had insisted on buying the sleek black coffin, on burying it empty. Maybe the government had paid for it. Maybe it would serve as physical proof that Vin had existed, that his life had mattered to someone.

After the burial concluded, Christian's mom leaned in close. "I'm heading back to the car. Take your time."

"Okay."

Mom wove through the crowd, speaking to several folks, giving and accepting hugs, shaking some hands. Soon she was gone.

Bec was busy speaking with well-wishers, people from church they probably didn't even know well yet. Unsure how long it would be before she could get a word with Bec, Christian strolled around the grounds looking for recognizable names on tombstones.

Mrs. Villalobos stepped in front of her. The woman's hair looked flawless, her makeup perfect, her black dress without so much as a stray hair or speck of dust. She had been wearing sunglasses through the whole service. Now she took them off. The whites of her eyes were bloodshot, the deep brown irises almost black. "Hello, Christian," she said.

"Um," said Christian. "Hi." What did you say to the person who had shot you?

"I like your blouse," Patricia said, dusting a stray hair off Christian's shoulder. Then she slid her hand down and jammed her thumb onto the exact spot where the bullet had passed through. Christian's eyes widened. She stopped herself from pulling away. "Hmm. I guess the theory is true. You have some kind of healing power."

"I don't know what you're talking about," Christian said, looking around.

"We turned this town inside out after that trickster kidnapped Bec," Patricia said, as if Christian hadn't spoken. "That's why we weren't in the woods that day. If we had known—if, for instance, you had told us you knew where Bec was—we would have been there."

Christian moved closer, still glancing around, hoping no one was listening. Lots of people were looking their way, their expressions sympathetic, but no one tried to intrude. "Mrs. Villalobos—" she began, keeping her voice down.

Now those beautiful eyes hardened, staring into Christian's heart. "I wonder. Will you tell Bec what really happened in those woods? It would be a shame if they blamed you and your mutant friends for their father's death. On the other hand, if they found out another way—if, for instance, *I* told them—well, then they might realize what a liar you are. What a sneaky, miserable little weakling. What a *monster*."

Christian smiled, nodded, and wrapped her arms around Patricia, who stiffened. "I don't know what you're talking about," Christian whispered. "But if I did, I might wonder how they'd react if they found out just how much *you've* lied."

Patricia pulled away, held Christian at arm's length, and stroked her hair as if sharing great affection. "I'm confident my relationship with my child can survive my professional secrets. Do you feel the same way about yours?"

Christian forced herself to keep smiling. "I'm sorry about Mr. Villalobos. I really am."

"Oh, child." Patricia put her glasses back on. "You have no idea how sorry you can be. But you'll find out."

She walked away. Christian trembled, her pulse racing.

Bec spotted Christian, smiled, and waved her over. A moment later, they were hugging, Bec hanging on as if Christian was a life preserver in the open ocean. Christian held them tightly too. If either of them let go, the world might open and swallow them. Christian had never been in love before, had never felt so safe and true to herself, yet what had happened in the woods could shatter all that. Or maybe love was always that way. Maybe it could survive wars and poverty and illness, and then some simple fact would kill it like frost kills a flower. What would happen if she told Bec the whole truth? What would happen if she didn't?

"I can't believe he's gone," Bec said, their voice shaking.

"I'm so sorry," said Christian.

"When I was texting you that day, I didn't even know——" Bec pulled away, squeezing Christian's hands a little too hard. Bec searched Christian's face, their expression veering toward desperate. "Wait. That's the same day you got hurt."

Christian still didn't know precisely when Bec had learned about Vin's death, but given the conversation at the pavilion, she hadn't thought it prudent to lie when Bec came to her window late that night, wondering why she hadn't texted back. Christian had shown Bec the gunshot wound, already healed enough that it might have been any kind of injury. When Bec pushed for details, Christian had kept things vague.

You had all this time to think of an explanation, and you wasted it. What the hell do you do now?

"That's weird, right?" asked Bec, their eyes searching Christian like she might offer some bit of wisdom that would put the world back together. "That you both got . . . hurt . . . that day?"

"Yeah," said Christian. "Weird. Hey, I think Mr. Hoon wants to say something."

Bec stared at her for several moments, eyes narrowed. "What aren't you telling me?"

"I—"

Then Mr. Hoon stepped up, giving Bec an expression that said *I'm sad and I'm sympathetic.* "I'm so, so sorry," he said, offering his hand.

Bec shook it. "Thanks. Mom and I really appreciate it."

"Of course." He hesitated a moment. Then he patted Bec's shoulder, barely making contact, as if they might break. "If you need anything, just let us know. The school will do whatever we can."

"I will," said Bec. As Mr. Hoon walked away, they turned to Christian and started to say something. Then Ms. Herrera stepped in, and Mr. Singh. Christian stood off to the side and played with her phone, just to give her hands something to do. Bec smiled and shook hands and gave side-hugs, seemed to say all the right things, looked people in the eye and presented an image of being absolutely present. Yet they kept glancing at Christian, their brow furrowed for half a second each time.

Please don't push this. Please.

The two of them didn't get another chance to speak privately. Too many interruptions. After a while, Christian told Bec that her mom was waiting.

"We're gonna finish this talk soon," said Bec. "Yeah?"

"Okay," said Christian.

She made her way to the parking area and got in the car. "You okay?" asked Mom.

"I'm good."

Mom started the engine. As they drove home, Christian leaned her forehead against the window and watched the town pass.

CHAPTER THIRTY-ONE

On Monday, the projector cast a United States map onto the screen. Each of Sal Paradise's and Dean Moriarty's trips had been plotted out in different colors. Mr. Griffin was comparing and contrasting part one of *On the Road* with part two. Jamie had taken notes through the first twenty minutes or so, but now his mind kept drifting. Hopefully, Mr. Griffin would post the map online. Maybe the lecture notes, too, especially all that stuff about the evolution of the American journey narrative. Otherwise, Jamie would have to skip lunch or stay after school some afternoon before the test. Right now, he just wasn't feeling the lesson.

He had barely slept all week. The dragon's dying screams echoed in his brain whenever he closed his eyes. Images from his mind-meld ambushed him at odd times: in the shower, the moment before a video played on his phone, the whole length of a game's load screens. Arsiss hadn't been evil. She had only wanted to live in peace.

But what else could he have done? *She killed two people. Plus, Baltar and the Team said she could have destroyed a major city.*

He could go crazy thinking about this, but he kept concluding that, no matter how he tried to justify his actions, he had gone too far. Half your friends didn't diss you for a minor fuck-up. In the wake of Gabby's punch, of Christian's harsh words, striking first seemed just as stupid as waiting around for some monster to rip off your head. Every single action needed context. Every plan required awareness of what had made the plan necessary. Flying headfirst into any fight just seemed like a good way to concuss yourself.

Being a superhero sucks.

At least the Team had left them alone. Had even Mossman finally gotten it through his thick head that the Freaks weren't evil mutants? Not likely, but you could always hope. Maybe McCreedy had given them some down time. They had lost two more colleagues, after all. Not even covert government operatives could take so much loss with no effects. Could they?

Mr. Griffin had moved on to talking about Jack Kerouac and Neal Cassady. Jamie had missed the segue. He sat up straight and tried to focus.

Gabby still wouldn't talk to him. During lunch, he had sat with Kenneth and Micah at their usual picnic table. Sometimes Brayden and Marla joined them, but Christian and Gabby hadn't even come outside. Or maybe they were going to the parking lot and eating in Gabby's car. In classrooms and hallways, the girls wouldn't look at Jamie, sure as shit wouldn't talk to him. As for Ty, Kenneth had told her the girls were mad at the guys over some gaming trash-talk that had gone too far. It had been the best idea he could think of at the time, even though it sounded trivial. He had texted the girls, who had backed up his story. Ty thought they were all being silly and spent most of her lunch hours with one group or the other, trying to talk them out of their petty bullshit.

Unable to stop himself from dwelling on all this, Jamie slouched through the rest of the day. He bombed a math test because he couldn't concentrate. Swimming deep in the dark waters of his psyche, he missed two bells. The teachers had to call his name three or four times before he grabbed all his shit and scurried into the hall, face burning.

After school, he walked to his Bug alone. Kenneth and Brayden were climbing into their trucks as Jamie stored his backpack. He waved. They waved back. A couple of aisles over, Micah ducked into his Escort and drove away without looking at any of them. The kid was drifting away. Not just from the Freaks, but from life. Nothing anyone tried had brought him back.

Some hero. Some human being. I don't know what to do.

He drove to Gabby's house. She was shutting her car door when she spotted him. Her shoulders sagged. Not good. He parked and stepped into her yard, standing several feet away with his hands in his pockets.

"Hey," he said.

She crossed her arms. "Yeah?"

"Look. I'm sorry. About everything."

"Okay."

They looked at each other for a while before he realized she wasn't going to say anything else. "You gonna keep punishing me forever?"

She laughed. "First, it's only been a week. Second, I'm not punishing you. I'm accepting how I feel about the situation, and I'm acting accordingly."

Jamie hung his head and kicked at a bare spot in the grass. He and Gabby had never fought before, not really, had never gone so long without speaking. Gabby was his first girlfriend. He hadn't imagined them married with kids; they were seventeen, for God's sake. But he hadn't really considered that they might break up, either. He had taken her for granted. Just another terrible decision in a long string of them.

"I need to tell you something," he said.

She stared at him for a while. Then she walked over, put down her backpack, and sat against the house. Jamie joined her.

"Well?" she asked.

"I mind-melded with the dragon," he said. "I knew her name."

Gabby's jaw tightened. "And?"

"They called her Arsiss the Gentle." He told her about the images he had seen, the scenes he had experienced, the emotions he had felt.

When he was done, Gabby stared at him again. "Why are you telling me this shit? Are you trying to make me feel even worse?"

He blinked. "No, baby. I wanna be honest. So we can deal with this and move on."

She laughed. "Move on. How are we supposed to do that?"

"I—"

"Jesus, Jamie. You really think this is gonna make things *better* between us?"

"But I—"

"No. Stop it. It's worse than I thought. You knew what she was, and you killed her anyway. Even after I asked you not to. *Begged* you."

"Yes, goddammit!" he cried, dropping a hammer-fist on the ground. "I knew, and I killed her. You think that was easy for me? Or fun?"

Gabby's eyes narrowed. "I'm sorry it was all so hard for *you*."

"Well, it was. I saw her memories! I was there when her world's people hunted her family! I felt her heart breaking a hundred times. I felt her sadness, how tired she got, how sick of the stupid chest-thumping games people play. That *I* was playing. And there at the end, when Micah was killing her, she was so scared. Exhausted, yeah, but she didn't want to die, and if she had to, she didn't want it to hurt so damn bad. If she could have said anything to us, she would have screamed one word: 'Why?' Or maybe 'please.' I felt all that. I saw it. I heard her voice just as clear as I hear y'all's. And *you're* mad at me? My God, don't you know I hate myself right now?"

When he had finished, he stared at the ground between his feet for a long time. In his chest, a ball of pure hurt grew a little more, rose a little higher. Soon it would spill out of him. He hoped to be home before that happened. He hated crying in front of people, and if he needed to punch something else or scream, he didn't want to dump that on Gabby, too. But he had started this conversation, so he would stay until it was finished.

"All that," she said, "and you shot into her brain like a missile?"

She might as well have stabbed him. "All I could think about was what she could do if we let her go. All the guilt and the shame I've carried around since monsters we let into the world started killing people—I couldn't get past it. I tried, but I just couldn't."

Gabby nodded. "I get that. I really do. But all the good intentions in the world can't bring her back to life."

He winced. "I know. I've barely thought about anything else." He tried to take her hand.

She pulled away. "Let's just . . . not, okay?"

Another knife between his ribs. "Oh. It's still like that."

She sat up straighter and lay her hands in her lap. "I believe you feel bad, and I'm not trying to hurt you more. Honestly. But I can't just forget what happened, either."

"Baby—"

"It's not even so much what you did." A tear fell down her cheek.

"Then what?"

"You didn't listen to me, Jamie. You treated me like everybody else always has. Like I don't matter at all."

Now the knives were piercing his heart. "Gab, I can't even tell you how sorry I am. I'd never make you feel like that on purpose. I just . . . everything got to be too much. I didn't handle it right."

She took his hand and squeezed it. Then she let it go. "I don't know where to go from here. I need time."

"For what?"

She stood. "To think. To figure out how I feel about us."

"*Is* there an us?"

Another tear fell. "Maybe someday. But now? No. I don't think there is."

"Baby—"

"I gotta go," she said, and went inside.

Jamie kept his seat for a moment, hoping she would come back. When she didn't, he walked back to his Bug. An old car with a two-tone paint job puttered down the street belching exhaust. Somebody's cat lay on their driveway in a patch of sunlight, its whiskers twitching as it dreamed its feline dreams. The world moved on, even as it shattered all around him. He got into his car and managed to start it before he burst into tears. Then he drove away, hoping no one had seen him cry.

He stopped by Micah's. Baltar answered the door, tall and unsmiling, and let Jamie in without a word. Jamie went to Micah's room and tried to tell him what had happened, but Micah kept nodding off. *Hell with it*, he thought as he walked down the hall. *This is a waste of time.*

Baltar was waiting at the door, holding a package to his chest. Wrapped in plain brown paper and tied with twine, it was about as big as his torso. He smiled as Jamie entered the room. Then he held out the package.

"For you," he said. "It will serve you well in your battle with the supernatural."

Jamie's eyes narrowed. He took the package, which felt as light as a feather pillow, even though whatever it contained seemed solid. "What's this?"

"Open it."

Still looking Baltar in the eye, Jamie untied the twine and pulled the paper away. He whistled long and low. Then he took the object to the nearest burning lamp and examined it, running his fingers over the surface, watching it catch the light. It was a shield made of Arsiss's scales, teardrop-shaped like the individual components. They had been fused together so that they formed an uneven but unbroken surface. On the backside, the old man had fixed two padded metal handles. Jamie fitted his left arm through them and held the shield up. It took no effort at all.

"Wow," he said, despite himself.

"Yes," said Baltar. "Given the material, it is lightweight but practically indestructible. It seemed to me that you would benefit from it the most."

Jamie had no idea what to say. Even with his aura, a shield like this would come in handy. It was the kind of thing he had in mind when he had agreed to let Baltar into the group. "How'd you get the scales to stick together?"

"Magic can accomplish what science cannot."

Jamie ran his fingers along the edges again. "Thanks," he said. "Really." The old guy's gesture was oddly touching.

"It was my pleasure. Use it well."

"Yeah. Okay."

Jamie went out to his car and put the shield in the back seat. Gabby and Christian would hate it, of course. But hell, they weren't talking to him anyway, and it wasn't like they'd turn down a prize like this. Yes, he would keep it. The shield didn't lift the weight from Jamie's heart, but it made him feel a little easier about Baltar's intentions.

Still sick to his stomach and lonely as hell, Jamie headed home. Halfway there, his phone buzzed. He pulled over and read the text. Brayden and Kenneth were going to Pizza of Mind.

Jamie stared at the message. The tears had stopped for now, though the nauseated feeling remained. Could he eat? Could he be around people without falling apart?

"Screw it," he muttered and texted Brayden back. Then he drove to Pizza of Mind and waited for them to show up. A few slices wouldn't solve his problems. A little companionship wouldn't unbreak his heart. But when had pizza with friends ever made anything worse?

CHAPTER THIRTY-TWO

That evening, Gabby reached the Surveillance Tree around seven p.m. and leaned against its familiar trunk. Estranged from the boys and with Christian having promised her mom a quiet night of TV and popcorn, Gabby had nothing else to do. She had already finished her homework, dodged a text from Jamie, and eaten supper. Mom had taken her phone for a week because she had missed Mass to fight the dragon. It had been inconvenient, but she had gotten off easy. Now even that light punishment was over. It felt like she and her friends should have paid a much higher price. Gabby kept seeing Bec's ashen face, their wide and bloodshot eyes, their stunned expression that had reminded her of Micah's at his mother's service. How in the world could Micah or Bec or Marla Schott even get up in the morning? For Marla and Bec, the pain had just begun.

Gabby was sweating despite the cold. She took off her jacket and draped it over her shoulder. Another overcast night, the moon and stars hidden behind a thick layer of clouds. It had rained on and off all week, and now the temperatures were rising. Southeast Arkansas, where if you didn't like the weather, you just had to wait a couple of hours. Yesterday had been windy and cold. Today the temperature was hovering in the forties. The clouds threatened rain, though none had fallen. Tomorrow would top out somewhere in the high fifties. Soon enough the hot months would arrive. What would she do all summer without her friends?

The cameras and microphones in her house and car still hummed and whined, though from what she could hear now, no one on the Team seemed to be monitoring them. Or if they were, they weren't talking

239

about what they saw and heard. Instead, the conversation involved their dead colleagues—the condition of Floyd Parker's family, Cornelius Vincent's many accomplishments, and whose turn it was to ride over during school hours and check on Patricia Villalobos. The Team must have gone out for food, at least, but Gabby hadn't caught any of them leaving or coming back.

For that matter, she had no idea whether the others had kept to the spy schedule. Christian had, but the boys? She supposed she would have to talk to one of them long enough to find out.

She closed her eyes, still the best way to concentrate on her hearing.

Mossman: "—can't believe it."

McCreedy: "Your skepticism is noted. But in light of these two deaths, we've been greenlit."

Greenwalt: "What's the catch, sir?"

McCreedy: "The same as usual. If the operation goes south, nobody in Washington knows anything about us."

Jeffcoat: "Goddam politicians."

Kragthorpe: "We all knew the risks when we signed on."

Greenwalt: "True. But that doesn't mean we should just barrel straight ahead. Especially given everything that's happened."

Mossman: "Not this shit again."

Greenwalt: "They haven't hurt anyone since Sterne attacked the football team. And look how many they've helped save."

Mossman: "Yeah. And while we're looking, take a gander at how their powers keep growing. If even one of them breaks bad, we may not be able to stop them."

Kragthorpe: "Mutant-lovers on the Team. How do I get transferred out of this chickenshit outfit?"

Greenwalt: "You can both kiss my ass."

Chairs scraped along the floor. Men grunted and cursed.

McCreedy: "Stop it! All of you belay this nonsense right now!" The sounds of struggle ceased. Kragthorpe and Greenwalt muttered apologies to McCreedy. "Now. I've made my decision, and each of you *will* get on board. Do you understand me?"

Everyone: "Yes, sir."

McCreedy: "Good. We should take out the Sterne boy first. Frankly, his powers scare me more than the others'. I want three plans for luring him to an isolated location and eliminating him."

Oh my God. They're really gonna do it.

Mossman: "It'll be easier than it would have been even a few weeks back. They're already fractured."

McCreedy: "Yes. But once we begin, we'll have to move quickly. When they realize what's happening, they'll almost certainly put their differences aside for the duration."

Jeffcoat: "I'll get to work on the special weapons. Make sure everything's good to go."

McCreedy: "You've got a week to get those plans on my desk. I—"

Something smashed into the back of Gabby's head, burrowed inside it, filled her skull with heat and lightning. Her teeth ground as she groaned and fell on her face, smushing into the wet leaves and soil. She closed her eyes, but instead of the usual darkness, everything glowed, like a blank movie screen. Her brain seemed to pulse, to roll like a wave. That pulse repeated once, twice, three times, four, five. Gabby rolled onto her back, screaming behind her clenched teeth, hands thrust against her eyes even though the glow seemed to be coming from inside her.

Then everything stopped. She lay with her nose pressed against the ground, wet gunk on her face, her mind throbbing. The pulses were tapering off; soon the sensations stopped altogether. She opened her eyes and saw spots.

"What the hell was *that*?" she asked, sitting up. Forcing herself to her feet, Gabby leaned against the tree and focused on the farmhouse again. She needed to hear anything else the Team might say. Then she would alert the others. The Team was right about this much: the Freaks would put aside their differences for self-preservation.

The voices coalesced. McCreedy: "—and so I've decided not to move forward just now. We need more information on this evolving situation. Too much is at stake."

Greenwalt: "I agree, sir."

Mossman: "I don't. But I respect the call."

Kragthorpe: "Ah, the mutants aren't even that bad. I'm kind of rooting for Entmann and Davison. Those crazy kids."

McCreedy: "The more I consider it, the more I think we might as well go back to Washington and await our next assignment. The dragon's dead, and the children haven't hurt anyone since that out-of-hand prank two years back. I'll make my recommendations to my superiors in the morning."

Jeffcoat: "What do you guys want for dinner tomorrow? Pizza?"

Mossman: "Not again. If I have to go in that stupid place and look at one more Iron Maiden poster, I'm liable to pull my service weapon. I hate Iron Maiden."

Kragthorpe: "What? That's un-American."

Mossman: "They're British."

Kragthorpe: "So?"

Gabby turned down her hearing and scratched her head. What the hell had just happened? McCreedy had been about to squeeze the trigger. Except for Greenwalt, the others had been ready for him to fire. Now he had just . . . changed his mind? And everybody sounded *okay* with it? Kragthorpe was rooting for her and Jamie? It was like Gabby had fallen asleep and woken up in a completely different conversation.

She held her head, even though the pain had stopped. When something gave you a whopping migraine, you expected it to last. What or who had the power to get inside her mind like that, though? She enhanced all her senses and let herself experience the totality of the woods at night. Innumerable sounds and scents grew clearer, more immediate—nocturnal claws scraping wood, animal grunts, nightbird calls, decaying vegetation, damp grass. Every vein in every leaf had been painted in vivid colors that stood out even in the dark. And yet she sensed no trace of any supernatural being or attack. If the pain she had experienced and the Team's weird change of heart had originated with some enemy, Gabby couldn't detect it.

Did Christian and them feel it?

Feel what, though? She had lost her train of thought. Something about the Team's plan, somehow related to Micah. She had gotten scared, had been ready to call the Freaks and sound an alarm . . . but for what?

She would text Christian and compare notes. Maybe between now and then, Gabby could remember what she had been thinking, what she had been about to do. She wouldn't contact the boys, though, not until she had no choice.

She snuffled. Tears welled in her eyes.

No, she thought, wiping them away. *You're not gonna cry over Jamie again.*

Holding her head high, she walked back toward her car. She had had enough of the woods for a long time.

CHAPTER THIRTY-THREE

On Tuesday after school, Kenneth sat on one of the benches near the pond. The water looked brown and stagnant. According to his phone, the wind had topped out at around three miles per hour, and the overcast sky would darken and drop an inch of rain on Quapaw City before the sun rose tomorrow, which would be warmer. It felt like the day itself was waiting for some sort of indication on how to proceed.

Last night, at Pizza of Mind, he and Brayden and Jamie had spent an hour and a half stuffing their faces from the buffet and drinking, like, a gallon of Coke apiece. Jamie had seemed preoccupied and sad, probably over Gabby, but Brayden had talked his head off. If he even noticed Jamie's mood, he had ignored it and done his thing. Then, today at school, the three of them had eaten lunch with Ty. No sign of Christian or Gabby, no texts or DMs, not a whole lot on either one's social media. A few years back, this kind of ugly breakup among the nerds would have tickled Kenneth. Now he was surprised to find he actually felt bad for them.

He checked his phone. 4:38. He'd give Greenwalt another ten minutes, and then he was out of here. Ty expected him to come around no later than six for a study session. He wouldn't make her wait because of some dumbass fed, even though he dreaded seeing Mr. Webb. The man could barely stand to be in the same room with Kenneth.

Footsteps on concrete. Kenneth stayed seated but looked over his shoulder. Greenwalt was walking this way, hands in his jacket pockets, a scarf around his neck. Kenneth turned back to the water. This bench, located roughly halfway between the parking area and the Freaks' pavilion, sat well within the area where families generally brought their kids, but the threat of rain seemed to have kept them away. He had only seen a few joggers and power-walkers, and most of them hadn't even looked at him. This wasn't exactly a remote location, but it was better than meeting for a snack at the City Café.

Greenwalt veered off the walk and sat on the other end of the bench. He wore his federal-agent sunglasses, so Kenneth couldn't see his eyes, but he looked paler than usual. Two pink blotches stood out on his cheeks. His red hair hadn't been combed. The two of them watched the still water for a while.

"Let's get to it," said Kenneth. "I got places to be."

Greenwalt rubbed his temple, like his head hurt. Maybe it did. The guy definitely gave off hangover vibes.

"I don't even remember why I wanted to meet," said Greenwalt. His expression stayed neutral, but Kenneth detected a tremble in his voice. Was the fed . . . scared?

"Well, don't ask me," said Kenneth. "I don't know what goes on in your head."

Greenwalt removed his glasses and rubbed his eyes. "I've lost three colleagues on this detail. Three." He put his glasses back on. "I try to rein the others in, but honestly, I don't know why the Engineer hasn't sent us after you with everything we've got."

"Maybe he knows you'd get your asses kicked."

The fed laughed. "Don't be so sure. We're tougher than we look. But you don't have to worry anymore. We're pulling out."

"What?"

Greenwalt shrugged. "I guess I'm more persuasive than I thought. Or what you did to that dragon finally made the Engineer open his eyes. Either way, we're breaking down our equipment. We'll be gone by next week at the latest."

Kenneth had no idea what to say. He felt like somebody had struck him, maybe with a wrecking ball. After everything, all these months, the feds were just . . . leaving?

"Damn," he muttered. "And just when Micah's lost whatever was left of his mind."

Greenwalt jumped a little and started to say something. Another jogger trotted by, earbuds in, their eyes glued to the walk. When the man had passed out of view, Greenwalt turned to Kenneth. "What do you mean?"

You dumbass. Now you got him interested again. Why can't you keep your big mouth shut? Kenneth's face burned. Talking behind the others' backs made him feel slimy, and now, because he was just as dumb as people said he was, he had to do it again. And just when he and Micah had finally accepted each other well enough to coexist.

Kenneth sighed. "Nothing. The kid ain't been around lately, is all, and even when he's there, he ain't there. You know what I mean?"

"He's not exactly stable."

"I didn't say that. He's just . . . quiet. Sleepy."

Greenwalt raised an eyebrow. "And this has what to do with my job in this town?"

Baltar. The old man's done something to him. The bastard looks at us like my dad looks at a ribeye on the grill. He's shady. "Nothing," Kenneth said aloud. "It's just weird." Without thinking about it, he touched his chest where the stealth charm had fused to his skin. He couldn't show Greenwalt the charm any more than he could detail how the old fart had whammied the Team's devices. *Baltar's careful. He told us he wanted to help us get through a tough time—Gavin, the Sternes, Jake Hoeper—but he mostly just . . . what's the word? Lurks. He lurks around, watching and listening, and when he actually does something, we almost never know it's coming.*

Greenwalt frowned. "Don't bullshit me, kid. I know you like to keep up appearances, but don't talk to me like I just got here."

Kenneth sneered. "What, you never met a messed-up teenager before? Let me break the news to you. We're all fucked up. Micah's just sadder than most."

Greenwalt's eyes narrowed. "So Micah's not a super-powered

mutant, and there's nothing here for me. You're still sticking to that ridiculous story."

"Yep."

Greenwalt watched the water for a while. He seemed to be deep in thought. Then he turned back to Kenneth. "I think you're full of it, but it doesn't really matter anymore. The bogeys we've fought, the attacks on the high school and the football field, my colleagues' deaths—I'm sick of your town, kid. I want out."

Kenneth shrugged. "So go."

"You do realize that if something else happens around here, we'll probably come back."

Kenneth groaned and threw his hands in the air. "Jesus, mister. What do you want me to do, predict the future? I don't know what's gonna happen tomorrow, or next year. Sometimes I think I don't know shit about anything."

Greenwalt stood and tucked his hands back in his jacket pockets. "The whole reason I came to you is that I didn't have time or opportunity to play detective on the side. My team would have noticed."

Kenneth scoffed. "You didn't seem to care much about whether my team noticed me hunting around for some kind of half-assed clue."

Greenwalt turned up his collar and ran a hand through his wild hair. "We've all got problems. I'm tired of you. And I hope I never see you again."

He walked away. Kenneth watched him go and waited another fifteen minutes. Then he got up and made his own way out of the park.

He got to Ty's on time. Mrs. Webb answered the door. "Hey, Kenneth," she said. "Come on in."

"Thanks," he said, stepping inside.

The house smelled like smoked meat. He didn't ask Mrs. Webb what it was. She didn't volunteer any information. Ty met him in the living room. Mr. Webb was sitting in a brown leather chair and reading on his phone. A ball game played on TV, though nobody was watching it.

Kenneth said hello to Mr. Webb, who grunted and made a gesture that a really generous person might have called a wave. Ty took Kenneth's hand and led him back to her room. Kenneth sat in her desk chair. She chose the bed. They sat and listened to music for a while.

Finally, Ty turned down the volume and took Kenneth's hand. "So. When are you planning to tell me what's going on with Gabby and Jamie? Or why Gabby and Christian won't hang with the rest of us?"

Kenneth shook his head. "Jamie and Gabby have just got different ideas about what they want outta life. Anything beyond that, you'd need to ask them. I don't know how to tell you without talking shit behind their backs."

"Uh-huh. So what about the bigger problem, whatever's keeping both of them away from *all* y'all?"

"Me and Sterne took Jamie's side. Christian took Gabby's."

Ty watched him a moment. Then she sighed. "Man, it sucks when your friends split up."

"Yeah. I reckon they wouldn't have stayed together forever, though. Most high school couples don't."

She narrowed her eyes. "*We're* a high school couple. You planning to get rid of me, K?"

He laughed. "*Hell*, naw."

"Good."

She fiddled with her phone. Kenneth wanted to pull her to him, kiss her, tell her everything. These lies and half-truths felt like chains around his wrists. He had had enough of them. Still, talking about the future filled him with dread. What was the point?

If monsters still live in this town after graduation, none of the Freaks will leave. Or if they do, they'll just come running back. Hard to keep up your grades when you're fighting, I dunno, an intergalactic werewolf. But he couldn't say that to Ty. It was no longer even a question of whether the others would get mad at him. The truth was that he feared she would dump him if she knew the truth.

And yet he couldn't keep lying to her. He just couldn't.

"What are you thinking about?" she was asking.

"Um," Kenneth said. "The future. School, jobs, how we'll make it on our own."

"And . . . ?"

"Well, Entmann could probably go wherever he wanted, as far as grades go. Christian and Gabby could get into most state schools."

"What about Micah? Brayden? You?"

He laughed. "Micah's sleepwalking through high school. He'll be lucky if he even graduates. Brayden's going to work. I think his dad's got some friends that can get him on in the chicken-processing plant over in New Everton."

Ty cranked up some R&B song Kenneth didn't know. He had always hated soft-ass music, but Ty had turned him on to some good stuff. "I'm glad Brayden's got options, but I figured he'd at least give college a shot. It's not like he's dumb."

"We're talking about the same kid, right? I love Brayden, but he ain't no rocket scientist."

"And what about you, K? You still too dumb for college?"

He looked at her a moment, then turned away. God, did she always have to do that? Look right into his heart and zero in on precisely what he assumed? He had scraped through elementary school, middle school, junior high. In high school, the administration had steered him toward basic math, lots of gym and study hall, wood shop and metal shop. Like they had examined his brain while he slept and discovered a good blue-collar job represented the upper limit of his potential. Not a bad choice, but his *only* choice.

He shrugged. "What are *you* gonna do?"

She wagged her finger. "Uh-uh. We're talking about you."

"I just wanna know."

"College. I don't know where yet. Now stop trying to change the subject. Do you think you're too dumb?"

He sighed. "That's what everybody's always said. I figured I'd look for a job. Go to a technical college somewhere nearby, maybe that one in Crossett. Try to get on at the police department or Walmart. Something like that."

She got up and held his face in her hands. Then she ran her fingers through his hair. "You gotta quit that shit, K."

He looked up at her. "Quit what?"

"Letting people who don't really know you tell you who you are. After you and me started going out, I bet three or four dozen kids told me you was just a piece-of-shit bigot. Seemed like you thought so too."

"Maybe I'm exactly who people think I am. Maybe all this trying to be somebody else is just wasting my time. And yours."

She kissed his forehead. "The only real question is whether *you* believe that. Nobody else matters. Not even me. If you do believe it, then you'll have the kind of life all those people see when they look at you."

"And what *do* you believe?"

"I'm with you, K. That ought to answer all your questions. I felt something when we met. I wanted to know the person, not the reputation. And I'm still here."

Kenneth rubbed his temples. Thinking about heavy shit like this gave him a headache. "I used to know who I was. Maybe I was a dick, but I didn't have all these damn questions."

She squeezed his shoulder. The light from her overhead fixture sparkled in her brown eyes. "Look. Being with me don't necessarily prove them folks wrong, and working instead of going to school don't necessarily mean they're right. It's your life. What's gonna make *you* happy? If that's a job where you get your hands dirty, fine. If it's something else, well, only you can decide to go for it."

The song ended. As the next one began, Ty's mother called her to supper. Kenneth walked her to the living room. "I'll holler at you later," he said.

Mrs. Webb was taking two big bowls out of the fridge. Mr. Webb stood at the kitchen counter, carving racks of ribs into twos and threes. Kenneth's mouth watered.

Without looking up, Mr. Webb said, "You gonna get in on this, Kenneth?"

Kenneth nearly fell over. He looked at Ty, who smiled. "Yeah, K. You gonna?"

"We got potato salad and slaw," said Mrs. Webb.

"Is this how your dad's gonna kill me?" Kenneth whispered. "Rat poison on my ribs? Glass in my slaw?"

Ty laughed. "No, but his dry rub's liable to burn a hole in your stomach. I hope you like it spicy."

He smiled. "Just watch me."

She took his hand again. Together they walked into the kitchen.

Kenneth ate a dozen ribs and a pile of potato salad. During the meal, he mostly kept his mouth shut and listened. He learned Ty had once had a little sister who had died in her cradle, only a month old. Mrs. Webb wiped away tears as they talked about how cute the baby had been, how her eyes seemed old and wise. Mr. Webb mostly grunted. Ty reached across the table and squeezed his hand. He nodded and ate another rib.

Later, over an excellent peach cobbler, he asked Kenneth what he thought of the Razorbacks' latest football recruiting class and whether the coaches knew their asses from a hole in the ground. Kenneth seemed to win favor by saying the staff had done a much better job than anybody had really expected, even though the team still had a way to go before they caught up with the conference's major powers.

After dinner, Kenneth and Ty put away the leftovers and loaded the dishwasher. Mr. Webb headed out back, where he apparently had a small woodworking shop. Mrs. Webb sat on the couch and began to browse Netflix.

"I guess I better go home," said Kenneth. "I still gotta do some research for that English paper."

"I'll walk you out," said Ty.

In the driveway, where Kenneth's truck was parked behind the Webbs' cars, he leaned against his passenger door. Ty put her arms around his neck. "That was nice," said Kenneth.

"Yeah," she said. Then she looked at the moon. "I like this light. Selfie?"

"Sure."

She pulled her phone out of her pocket. They smiled, but as Ty adjusted her angle, the phone slipped out of her hand. She tried to catch it, but it hit the driveway and bounced under the truck. On her hands and knees, she looked around. "Damn. It's right in the middle. I'm gonna have to crawl under."

"Hang on," said Kenneth. She looked up at him and waited for him to continue, maybe volunteer to get the phone for her. Instead, he hesitated. At first, he wasn't even sure why, but an idea was forming: *I don't want to lie to her anymore.* He didn't want to live a second life that didn't include her. Telling Ty about the Freaks, about him, might drive her away, and that would break his heart. At the same time, she deserved to know everything about him. About what might happen to her if she stayed with him. Even if she dumped him, she deserved the truth.

"What is it?" she asked. The moonlight shone in her dark eyes.

Kenneth looked around. No one was on the street or in their yards. Hopefully, they weren't looking out their windows. "You're gonna scrape yourself up. Let me help."

He went to the rear end, flattened one palm against the undercarriage, and lifted until the rear bumper rose as high as his rib cage. Still holding up the vehicle, he squatted and picked up her phone with his free hand.

"Jesus and Mary!" yelled Ty, her eyes widening. She jumped to her feet and staggered backward until she stood in the middle of the yard.

"Ty—"

"Mmm-mmm. Mmm-mmm. Mmm-mmm," she said, shaking her head, one hand over her mouth.

Kenneth put the truck down and took a few steps toward her. She didn't run, but she held up one hand. He stopped.

"Look," he said. "I need to—"

"Did you just pick up that truck with one hand?"

He shrugged. "Yeah."

She looked around, like she was hoping somebody would jump out from behind a tree and tell her it had been a prank. When no one did, she turned back to him. If her eyes got any wider, they might pop right out of her skull. "What the *hell*, K?"

He tried approaching her again. This time she let him, though she was still clearly about one careless word away from running until she hit an ocean. When he reached her, moving as slowly as he could, he took her hand and placed her phone in it, never taking his eyes off hers. He moved closer and brushed a bit of leaf out of her hair.

"Let me tell you about me and my friends," he said.

"What do your friends have to do with how you just *lifted a damn truck*?"

"It's a long story," he said. "But if you're gonna be with me, you need to hear it."

She stared at him for a long time. Several times, she began to speak before closing her mouth again. Kenneth let it play out. Rushing her would only make things worse. Finally, she took a deep breath and let it out again. When she spoke, her voice trembled. "Okay. Tell me."

Together they walked back over to his truck and got in.

EPILOGUE

Micah swayed on his feet like a strong wind was about to knock him over, though the occasional breeze barely ruffled his hair. The night seemed even darker than most. He stood on the banks of the Quapaw River, the water stretching maybe thirty yards to the far shore. It had risen high on its banks. Strong currents swirled under the dark, overcast sky. The woods' night sounds had risen everywhere, the world reduced to sets of shapes in varying shades of black. How had he even gotten here? He had been at home, lying on his bed with his hands laced behind his head, listening to music without really hearing it. He had closed his eyes. When he opened them again, he was here.

Baltar appeared at his side, arms loaded with supplies: several jars, a mortar and pestle, one of the old books from his trunk.

"What are we doing here?" asked Micah. The breeze on his bare skin registered as gentle pressure, but it felt remote, like after your pain meds kicked in and the dentist asked if you could feel anything sharp here, here, here.

"Moving to the next stage," said Baltar.

"Okay," said Micah. What had happened in the first stage? He couldn't remember.

Baltar kneeled in a bare patch and took a long, sharp knife out of a scabbard attached to his belt. He used the blade to carve in the dirt: a wide circle containing a pentagram. In the spaces beside each point, he drew pictographs related to the four elements, plus others Micah didn't recognize. Then Baltar opened the various jars and poured some of the contents into the bowl, a pinch here, a handful there. Holding one jar, he said, "This is dragon's blood. I have been awaiting such an

ingredient. I should thank you and your friends for providing it." He
ground the elements together for a long time. Micah drifted. Maybe he
even slept on his feet until the old man grabbed his wrist and turned
his hand over, palm up. "This may sting," Baltar said, and then he drew
the blade along Micah's open hand. Much like the breeze, the sensation
registered with Micah, but he attached no importance to it. It seemed
to be happening to someone else. Next, Baltar squeezed Micah's hand
into a fist as he held it over the bowl. Blood pattered onto the mixed
junk in there.

"What's up?" asked Micah.

"Now I read from the book," said Baltar. "One of those I left in
your shed for you to find. To read. To use. And as always, you did not
disappoint."

Baltar opened the book, flipped through it, and marked his place.
Then he took a box of matches and lit one. When he dropped it into the
bowl, the contents flared like a firework. Baltar put the burning bowl in
the center of the pentagram. Then he opened the book again and began
to chant. The sound faded in and out. One moment, Baltar's clear voice
thundered right next to Micah's ear and spoke some language he didn't
recognize. The next, darkness swallowed the world, and Micah floated
in it, bodiless, almost mindless, the universe reduced to two sensations,
the soft, cloudy nothingness that carried him along and the sound of
that too-familiar voice, urgent and demanding.

Rest now in the world between worlds, said that voice. *I am coming. You
will prepare my way with glorious slaughter.*

Who are you? cried Micah, though only in his mind.

My harbinger will reveal my name.

I won't kill for you. I won't.

You will.

No.

Kill. Kill. Kill.

NO.

KILL. KILL. KILL.

NO!

KILLKILLKILLKILL.

Micah fought with every ounce of his strength just to open his eyes. Baltar was still chanting, his back to Micah as he stood between the symbol and the river, arms raised, the book in one hand and the dagger in the other.

"The language is Enochian," Micah muttered. He didn't know how he knew that.

Now Baltar lowered his arms. He smiled, those sharp teeth like a wolf's. "The endgame has begun."

Micah skirted the circle and stood beside the old man. Together they watched the fast-moving currents. After a moment, something crackled down there, orange flames bursting forth *under* the water, flaring up, erupting through the surface and shooting skyward. The currents in the middle of the river veered, twisted, swirled. A vortex formed, a whirlpool. The flame condensed into that vortex, illuminating every bubble. The earth trembled. Micah stumbled and almost fell into the circle where the bowl still burned. Baltar caught him, held him up.

"Whoa," whispered Micah.

"Indeed," Baltar said, laughing. "Indeed."

Something was rising out of the river, that whirlpool, that fire. Just a shadow at first, a shape, but as it rose, a clearer form revealed itself. And even in his addled state, Micah recognized it. His knees buckled, and he hit the ground hard, a mostly buried rock cutting into him. The pain barely registered. And now the form was rising above the river, floating as all that orange flame danced around it.

"What the hell is that?" whispered Micah.

"Now comes the Harbinger," said Baltar. "We have prepared the way for him. And he will prepare the way for our master."

The figure floated across the water and touched down in front of Micah: fishbelly-white skin, overlong arms that ended in two-thumbed hands, legs like a goat's, cloven hooves for feet. It wore a cloak with a hood that concealed its face. It rose to its full height. Though it had come from the river bottom, it bore no trace of mud or damp.

"I don't wanna be here," said Micah. Was he whimpering? Crying? He couldn't tell.

The figure's arms rose. Micah wanted to recoil, but he couldn't seem to move. Those hands—looking at them made Micah feel crazy—dropped onto his shoulders. Searing pain where they touched. The fingers dug into his flesh. He wanted to scream but couldn't open his mouth. He could barely breathe.

Then the pain faded, and so did his conscious thoughts. That sensation of floating returned, but the darkness didn't. Under the figure's hood, there was no face. Nothing at all, just smooth skin. Micah stared into that blankness, and though an alarm seemed to ring deep within him, it grew fainter and fainter. Soon the world calmed. His fear disappeared.

This mouthless entity spoke with his mind, the words crawling through Micah's brain like stinging insects, the syllables gurgled as if Micah had been dragged underwater. The words came through in English. Magic? Or had this thing learned the language after all that time inside Micah's head? Maybe Baltar had helped it.

In the name of dread Ctothl'dhrish the Devourer, youngest and most inexorable of the Ageless Ones, I accept your tribute and your servitude. When our lord arrives, he will keep his word and raise you on high.

"Fire," Micah whispered. He had to be dreaming again, so his words didn't matter. Nothing mattered. Not the pain, not that ever-fainter alarm, not his life, not his friends.

Yes, they do, he thought, trying to fight, to swim against the rip current that pushed him deeper and deeper into himself. *They matter. I matter. Whatever this is, it's wrong. I have to stop it.*

The hands gripped him harder, and from their touch he was flooded with energy, the darkness itself. Hatred surged in his heart. Friends?

Yeah, right. They had long ago chosen Kenneth Del Ray over him. They had lectured him, patronized him. They had abandoned him when his parents died, when all this weird shit happened. No friends. No family but Baltar. Nothing mattered but Ctothl'dhrish, whoever that was, and this being who had gifted Micah the emptiness, darkness, power. Yes, power. It surged through him, locked onto whatever generated his fire and ice and healing and stoked those energies until he felt like he could outburn the sun itself.

My name is Astonath, gurgled the entity. *Called the Harbinger. Together we will open a path from the Ageless Dimension. Together we will manifest our lord in this reality. Together we will stand at his right hand as he rules.*

No, screamed Micah, the real Micah, trapped somewhere in the farthest recesses of his own mind.

Yes, said Astonath.

"No," whimpered Micah.

Yes, said Astonath.

"Yes," said Baltar.

The Harbinger squeezed Micah's shoulders again. Pain flared, then faded and vanished. And all the voices inside Micah ceased except the one that said *Kill.*

"We have a place for you," Baltar said to Astonath.

Take me. Our preparations will require time and privacy. Best to get started.

Micah said nothing. This was a dream. Only the hatred and rage felt real.

Baltar took him by the hand and led him away. Astonath floated beside them, his goat hooves six inches above the ground. Thunder boomed. Rain pattered the ground. When lightning streaked down and struck a tree, setting it afire, Micah did not flinch. The world was already burning. Soon the flame would spread.

ACKNOWLEDGMENTS

All writers work in solitude until they don't. Though I spent hundreds of hours locked away in my office, this book would not exist without the kindness and support of others. I would like to thank Maya Myers, the editor of this series, for her insight and her bedside manner. She makes these books better (and often shorter) than they would have been otherwise. She couches her advice in terms and connotations that provide strong artistic advice without shredding the ego. Thanks, Maya. I'm grateful for you.

Likewise, this book would not be possible without Mark Sedenquist, Megan Edwards, and the rest of the great people at Imbrifex Books. Thanks to everyone for believing in these stories.

The College of Southern Nevada not only employs me as a professor of English, but they also approved the sabbatical during which this book's early draft was written. Thanks to everyone on the sabbatical committee. Thanks as well to my colleagues who have bought, helped publicize, and generally supported my work. I would like to single out my department chair, Professor Levia Hayes, for her letter in support of my sabbatical and for everything she does to spread the word about my writing.

Nilla the dog, Tink the young pup, Cookie the cat (how we miss you), and Tora the tiger-in-cat's-clothing provided me entertainment, love, and balm for the weary soul. Thanks, y'all.

My family continues to support me, even when I'm not very easy to live with. Thanks to my wife, my best friend, my first reader, and my partner in all things, Kalene Westmoreland. I didn't know what happiness was until I met you. Shauna Songer, John Songer, Brendan

Riley, and Maya Riley, the best kids anybody could ask for—thanks for sticking with me on this journey. To Nova and Luna Songer, I hope you'll be proud of Pops when you're old enough to read this.

Thanks to God, without whom I am nothing.

And much appreciation to you, Reader. Whoever you are, wherever you live, we're in this car together. Let's turn up the music, roll down the windows, and floor it.

ABOUT THE AUTHOR

Brett Riley is a professor of English at the College of Southern Nevada. He grew up in southeastern Arkansas and earned his Ph.D. in contemporary American fiction and film at Louisiana State University. His short fiction has appeared in numerous publications including *Folio, The Wisconsin Review,* and *The Baltimore Review.* He has also won numerous awards for screenwriting. Riley's debut novel, *Comanche,* was released in September 2020. *Lord of Order,* a dystopian novel set in New Orleans, was published in April 2021. *Freaks,* a superhero thriller featuring dangerous aliens and badass high school kids, was published in March 2022. The second novel in the Freaks series, *Travelers,* was published in August 2022. Riley lives in Henderson, Nevada.

Connect with the author online:

🌐 OfficialBrettRiley.com

🐦 @brettwrites

📘 @BrettRileyAuthor